Alan, born in London at the start of the Battle of Britain, was brought up and educated in Scotland. He is a Reiki and magnatherapist healer. Retired and living in the beautiful Cotswolds, Alan took up writing about fifteen years ago, mainly in the spiritual and body energy vein. Married to Jennie, his youngest granddaughter keeps him on his toes.

Firstly, I would like to dedicate this book to 'Aurora', the spirit being and main character in the book, as without her input this book simply would never exist. I also know that a couple of parts caused her pain as she related the story, her story, to me.

Alan D. H. Moyes

AURORA'S STORY

A MAGICAL TRIP
THROUGH HEAVEN

A CIP catalogue record for this title is available from the British Library.

ISBN 9781786126443 (Paperback)
ISBN 9781786126450 (Hardback)
ISBN 9781786126467 (E-Book)

www.austinmacauley.com

First Published (2016)
Austin Macauley Publishers Ltd.
25 Canada Square
Canary Wharf
London
E14 5LQ

I sincerely thank my wife, Jennie, for her help and forbearance, as I spent many hours in my crystal room writing this. Jennie also proofread the initial, finished copy, as her English grammar is far superior to mine. Thank you Jennie.

Let us not forget Sheila, my famous 'medium' friend, for her great assistance, her hours of patience and the remarkable help she has given me, over the years I have known her.

This prayer is exactly as is always said, before my medium friend and I ever do anything to do with the spirit.

The Prayer

Dear Father God, friends and loved ones from the other side of life. We sit, as we always do, in loving expectation, for we do know that you will come with your messages of love, upliftment and encouragement. I ask that I will see clearly, that I will hear clearly, that I will understand what I am shown and as always, we ask, that only that which is good, true and pure can come towards us and may we have your loving protection and your blessing with us at all times.
AMEN.

Foreword

Dear Reader,

I am a medium and have been involved for many years in spiritual work, mainly in the South and South West of England. As I do not drive, I will always be extremely grateful to my dear husband, now himself in spirit, who so graciously drove me to wherever I needed to go, without question, so that I could further my work for spirit. I miss his physical company terribly. That said, I am also known both throughout the U.K. and in many parts of the world, including America and Spain. I feel humbled to know that my work, that covers many angles, has helped many people over the years, bringing great peace, love and joy to many of the people that I have been privileged to work for.

It was during a session, one of many, with Alan, who was at that time writing another book (with the help of the spirit whose book this is), and who is the transcriber behind these books, that we were privileged to meet with the 'author', Aurora. She truly is the beautiful, very amazing spirit behind this book and whose story this is. I say whose story this is, when in actual fact, it is and can only be a very small part of her story.

Aurora has had a great number of previous lives and it would be impossible in one lifetime to tell them all. The basis and objective of this book from her, is to tell you about a couple of her 'spirit' lives. Giving you the connections and thoughts that both she, and we, sincerely hope will show you, that indeed, there is no beginning, as there is also no end. You truly are an eternal being, a magnificent being of light.

Having been privileged to help bring this book about, I know it to be a very magical book. A book that gives us a more than considerable 'insight' to the life of a 'being of light' as you join her, first, as she is, again, about to return to the land of spirit from a place on Earth, that at this time was called Khem. I know it will bring a great deal of joy to many, and hopefully, open the minds and doors of others that will make the transmission of many, as they eventually, just as we all do, make the journey home again to spirit, a very happy one.

Enjoy it all, I know I have.

Love and light.

Sheila R. Webb
Medium.

Setting the Scene

To those of you who have read my previous book '*Their Gift Of Love*', you will already have met and know who Aurora is, but to those of you that are new to my books, please let me introduce you to this truly amazing spirit.

As I started to write another book, currently on the 'back burner' as it were, I had taken a trip to see my wonderful medium friend, as I had sought some friendly advice regarding some of its content. On this particular visit, there had been many before it, we had started our discussions without, on this particular occasion, my recorder. For some strange reason I had forgotten to take it with me.

As we progressed with the meeting, everything suddenly, all just stopped. After about a minute it started coming through again and I was then told I had a *spirit* who wanted, no sorry, had been 'asked' by those of a higher station, to help me in my books. (What you need to know and understand at this point is that this spirit had a choice. She could have said 'no' to those higher spirits and I might never have known, nor felt, this wonderful connection that we now have.) This amazing spirit had, however, agreed to this request from those higher and now wished to contact and speak with me. This was the beginning of what is, and indeed has been, quite simply, a truly incredible and amazing connection and journey, with regular meetings at Sheila's.

From that day on, every time I go to my amazing medium friend, I have always ensured that I have my recorder with me and that its batteries are always fresh. I never know what is going to be said to me, nor do I know how long that particular session is going to last. However, I do now always have some very specific questions written down. It took us a couple of visits to get to know each other, as we talked and she advised me on how I could also get the best from each meeting. I, or should I say *we,* learned what could cause interference or poor communication between us, and I also learned the benefits of having a very specific sanctuary for myself, such as the one I have now set up and from where I always work, when I am working on my own. Like the one that Sheila, my medium friend has, it also has many types of crystals, both large and small. For instance, I have a very magnificent quartz that stands nine inches tall (23cm) and is over four and a half inches across the base (12cm), and that is not the largest crystal I have! These crystals in my sanctuary are very important in the work I now do with my spirit friend, as I also work with her on my own, virtually every day.

During these early days, when this special connection was made through my medium friend, she started to tell me a little of what she did in spirit. It was on about the third visit with her, that slowly a story about Atlantis and the life of the people of Atlantis (that eventually became the book called *'Their Gift Of Love'),* quite unexpectedly began to come through. It was over several visits that I realised, a story was unfolding through her, as I transcribed what I was receiving from her. It took nearly four years to complete this book, but at no time during this period did I have a name for this amazing spirit. All I had been told initially was that she was a lady and had been on Earth around the time she was talking about. Now through this new book we are about to write, I have learned much more about her. How did I know she was, and is, genuine? That's very simple. I *never*, ever tell a spirit anything. I only ever *ask questions* and that is how everybody should be when working with or visiting a medium. Any medium.

The information, some very personal to me, that she has told me about, and then continued to tell me at each subsequent meeting, is incredible. She also, amazingly, told us about something that was just happening in Palestine. The time then was 3.30pm approximately, on the day of that recording. That particular true event hit our news as 'breaking news' at 6pm that evening, being told then, that this event had happened that mid-afternoon. That was the first of many revelations that were to come our way, over the years that we have spoken about and still to come. We were, however, two years into that first story, when I finally received the name that she said that she had been given in spirit and would now always use when we were talking. The name she had been given was AURORA.

Now I had heard of a Princess Aurora before, she was a Princess of the Gods, as the story that I knew went. So I asked her if she was that Princess Aurora. 'Oh no', she said. 'I am not that elevated, but I did work as a hand-maiden for her, and that is why I am being allowed to use the name.' Notice that word *allowed,* because she specified that point. So the result of this amazing connection that had been made, was now our very incredible book *'Their Gift Of Love'*. I am pleased to say that it is now, amazingly, on sale worldwide, ISBN 9780993176814 or through my web site at www.spiritoflite.com and is an excellent thought provoking read for anybody that is interested in spiritual matters.

As we came to the end of that book, we had often talked in a light manner about life in spirit. I had also tried to get her to talk about her life in spirit as a *being of light*, but up to that point not very successfully. Now we were at the end of *'Their Gift of Love'*, Aurora told me that I would never stop writing my books. That knowledge alone was interesting, to say the least. She then let it be known that we would continue to work together, as she had enjoyed our meetings and through me and the questions I had asked, was herself gaining further knowledge. From all this that we had done together, we were now about to embark on another book, this one this time, would be a truly magical book.

The subject matter! Yes, Aurora's life as a *being of light* in spirit. Amazing, now that everything that I had been asking her for, was about to be given to me in the form of a book. It is planned that we shall actually have two of her lives in spirit, so that you can see and understand how eternal life carries on.

We will start first, from the last few hours of her Earthly life in KHEM (now Egypt), and then join her on her journey through the tunnel, as she is about to return to spirit and start another life again as a spirit *being of light* with her new ethereal spiritual body. We will follow that life in spirit and all that she does there, eavesdropping as it were, on her many and very varied conversations with her own angel. A lot will surprise you, as it has me, as they discuss many different areas and topics of life, including things from both the 'Akashic Records' and the 'Book of Probabilities', and all with her angel.

Then, her preparation from spirit, back to an Earthly life that we will follow to the birth. We will then, from that moment of birth, leave her and skip forward in time, to another departure time for her, some 6,000 Earth years on from this first spirit life we have been privileged to learn from. We will now pick up, just as another life time, here on Earth, begins to come to its completion, and she returns to spirit. Following her, first as she completes that life, before her return back to spirit as a *being of light*, again in her ethereal body. From this, we will learn of the connections that create that continuous life in spirit.

I would also point out here that we will also receive help from other spirits, as they give us their points of view on her life at that time.

So, as you have just read, this very magical story will have two departures from Earth, and two arrivals in spirit form as a *being of light*. There will only be one arrival on Earth, as she pops out of her new mother's womb, now back on Earth again after our first trip in spirit. We will not follow that Earthly life, but will skip forward to the end of the second Earthly life. From these stories you will learn the truth of what truly does happen when it is your time to depart this current life you are on and return to the world of spirit. All of us follow a similar path, both in and out of these spiritual lives to our new experiences here on Earth. Sadly, many believe, or have been led to believe, that when you die from this experience, that is it, there is no more. So we hope, that from this amazing book, you will realise that this is definitely not so. All you have to do when your turn comes, as it always does, on time, to the second, and never late nor too early, is to simply 'follow the light' and allow your eternal life to continue, as it always will.

It is sincerely hoped, that you will take from this very magical story, a much greater understanding that you are, as we all are, continually progressing through each experience as an eternal *being of light*. You see, the main reason for this is because the SOUL, which is you, already basically knows everything, except the 'physical' experience of what it knows. As a *being of light*, it cannot experience that which we can, as humans in a finite life. Just as we, as humans, cannot experience life as a *being of light* in an infinite way, which a *being of light* can. I hope that makes sense to you.

There is one very important thing I do need to ask you and it is this. Please, please, be very thankful to our special spirit, Aurora, as I am informed that at times, depending on the memories she is putting out for us to read, it can be 'painful' for her (not in a physical sense), as she relates an experience of her Earthly life to us. As a spirit, they sense pain as they go back into a life that had great sadness in it, and in this case it is being re-lived for

18

us, so that we may learn that death, as we know it, is not something to fear.

We most sincerely hope that you enjoy this magical story as it unfolds. I would like you just to remember, all that you read is indeed *totally true*. It is in no way fictional. Indeed, if you are actually prepared to check it, look at the latter life in the story as she prepares to return for the second life in spirit, that we are covering. (Remember she has had other lives between the two we are allowed to cover.) It might just surprise you, I personally had no idea of the existence of such a place that she has told me about. I was educated in Scotland, so my history of England did not include, in detail, this part of the country. I know I have, through work, travelled extensively to many areas and did indeed live in Guildford for a while (which is reasonably near the area that she talks about), but I assure you, the particular area of Kent she mentions was very new to me and I had to go there after I received this part of the story.

This was, and *is,* Aurora's life story, or should I say a small part of her story, because her eternal life continues. We are only having a glimpse at two small parts of her story. How else would I now be receiving this, if her eternal life did not continue?

So let us now take you back in time and catch Aurora, as one of her many lives on Earth comes to a close. Watch the clock now, as it spins back 100 years, 200 years, 400, 800, 1600, 3200, 4000, 4500, 5500, 6000, 6400, 6800, 7000, 7014, now STOP.

Yes, we are now back-in-time. To a time over 5000 years B.C. A time when the world is in a traumatic turmoil. The darkness is now really starting to rule the world, the time of the light has waned and it will be over 6500 years before it starts to turn properly back to the light, as it still is, even now as 2014 A.D. draws to a close.

As I start to write this story, slowly but positively, it is turning back, and turn back it will; but I know when I finish it, hopefully in the middle of 2015 A.D., it will still be turning back steadily to the light. What I do know is that between now, 2014 A.D., and mid 2015 A.D., many startling facts will have emerged that will have surprised and indeed, even shocked some of you.

We sincerely hope you enjoy this story as much as I am as I write it. Especially in learning just how close Heaven and Earth really are, which may just surprise you as you read on. For those of you interested in spiritual matters in any way, this is a must read.

I have had a great deal of pleasure in writing this on Aurora's behalf and indeed, I too, have learned much as it has unfolded for you. What has also been a very, *very* great surprise, is in meeting not only her own special angel and her *spirit guide,* but also in meeting so many of God's other amazing creatures. These amazing 'spirit beings' that look after so much of God's creation here on Earth, many we thought were just pure 'figments of our vivid imagination'. How very wrong we were, as that turns out, not to be so.

So many of these amazing creatures now adorn many of our gardens and houses as beautiful ornaments. So think on this point. They had to originate from somewhere, so that all the stories that were read to many of us as young children, and are to this day still read to children, could be written, and it is very nice to know they truly exist for us also to enjoy.

I am sure that many of you who know anything about working with spirit, are aware of the need to always ask for 'white light protection', because as on Earth, so in spirit, there is a *dark side*. I did, just a couple of pages back, mention about the 'darkness' that was starting to rule the world. You will find in the story what can happen when the *dark side* tries to connect with a spirit they may wish to capture and use for their own benefit, and how the *light side* stops it. You will also read about how one of the main *spirit beings* was actually marked and how that being was recovered. No *spirit being* is EVER abandoned, no matter how long it takes to get them back.

We sincerely hope that this book will give you peace of mind and let you know you truly are LOVED and will be welcomed with open arms, when it is your time to return home.

So here goes. Sit back and enjoy the ride.

Alan.

A Trip Through Heaven

That is Truly a Magical Journey

We begin this magical trip by meeting Aurora, as her life at this time is sadly, and very unexpectedly for her, coming to its end. Aurora is not aware in any way that she is about to return once again to Heaven. Yesterday, for her, was just a normal day as it began, but things, totally beyond her control or her imagination, rapidly changed. So let us meet her, on this, her last day on Earth, as she stirs from a very restless and troubled night.

Awakening from sleep, yet still feeling very tired and more than a little afraid. Yesterday's terrible, terrible happenings that she witnessed, still running wildly through her mind as she arose from the straw mattress. Afraid now, just to look outside, to what she feared she would see again before her. Creeping to the door and slowly pushing it open, and yes. Oh God! Yes, it had all happened just as she remembered. She had hoped it was all only a terrible, bad dream. A nightmare. But no, she could still see, despite the dust cloud, the massive hole in the ground where the huge pyramid had stood. She still could not believe that such a giant of a building, a beautiful building such as that was, could just be suddenly swallowed up by the Earth.

The noise had suddenly started early yesterday morning, as she woke her child and husband for what should have been just another normal day. After having their usual early morning meal, she had prepared and dressed her young daughter, now ready to go with her husband to the clinic in the pyramid. Although the noise, and now also the very severe ground vibrations with it, had been steadily increasing for the past two days, she knew she still had to get her child to see the special doctor. She was not worried, as they had lived with this earthly tremor several times before. They had been going regularly to the clinic since her little one had been born in the pyramid three summers ago. A child so beautiful, but yet suffering so much, she had found it so very hard to breath in the very dry atmosphere, every single day of her young life.

They had called her Crystal, after the strong, proud, shining crystal that topped the pyramid. The man that she called her husband (they had been together ten summers now), had met her when they were both still no more than children themselves. A tough life, yet as their love for each other grew stronger every day, he had made her happy every day, and found a way to keep them safe and always fed, no matter what befell them. So now they had left her, as they had done several times before, to walk across to the pyramid.

She had started to prepare a meal for their return, when the ground had started to vibrate and shake, even more violently. Never in all her life, had she ever felt it like this. Mild tremors yes, they were a regular thing all through her life and they had just accepted it. This was much more violent, the fighting and violence they had been witnessing recently had been bad enough, but that was nothing compared to this feeling. She managed to get to the door to try and see what was happening, but the ground was vibrating so much that everything in front of her had a terrible blurred effect to it.

Aurora stood holding onto the door frame, her knuckles white as she held on so tight, and now afraid. Very afraid. She could see the pyramid that was just a short walk from their little house. It stood so proud and tall, with its beautiful, bright crystal beacon that sat on the top. The beacon that had guided the sky ships, these massive, disc shaped vehicles that looked as if they could never get off the ground. They were so big, yet they were so gentle as they dropped straight down, it was as though they just kissed the ground. No noise, just a gentle swish from the rush of air as it arrived. The last time they had left, and that was only seven sleeps ago, had made her very sad, as they said they were sorry they would not see her again.

These giants of men and women, the women were more beautiful than any other women that she had ever encountered before, or since. Many of them she had come to know over the summers in her life, as they had come and gone. One man, who had taken an interest in her, had been like the father she had lost as a child. He had understood about her daughter and often would comfort her. She could always tell when he was returning, she could feel him. No, more than that, she would sense him and then suddenly, there his great ship would be, almost outside her door. He had told her when she had asked, what made the great ship move? 'It's all in the thought, my dear, all in the "thought", that they move.' She could not understand when he said they could not come back, for she knew he loved her as if she was his daughter and yet, he could give her no reason. He simply told her to watch and to look out very carefully for her family, but not to be afraid. What had he meant when he had said that to her? Now she thought that she knew the reason for his warning and why he had given her no detail.

The ground, (the same ground that had held these massive circular ships that were even wider than the base of that giant pyramid, yet never moved when they landed in a whisper and when they took off again quietly, but with amazing speed they rose into the air) was now quivering and moving and she became very afraid. The pyramid in the distance, she could see was now shaking violently and she knew from that gut instinct deep inside her, her husband and her daughter would not be coming home to her again, something terrible was happening.

She wept massive tears, she was so afraid for them, knowing they were trapped in that building. Still the terrible noise increased and the ground shook more and more. She was watching the pyramid as best she could, as she stood in the doorway, transfixed at the site of this vast building, the building she had been born in, and her daughter just three summers ago. What now was going to befall her, as her thoughts went totally wild with fear?

Suddenly, and slowly at first, the great pyramid seemed to fall in on itself. She watched it, she could not move, as it slowly sank into the ground and then suddenly, it just totally disappeared. How? How could that possibly happen? How could that building, that was truly as big as a mountain, just disappear just like that?

The ground, for what seemed an eternity, but was actually a matter of only a few minutes, just kept on vibrating, and then it suddenly stopped and all around became deathly quiet. As the dust started to settle, she realised her little house, in this little community, was nearly the last one standing. How? How could this have happened? How could so much devastation and destruction have taken place, and yet her house still stood?

Slowly it dawned on her what had just happened to her husband and her baby daughter. She ran and ran, jumping over big cracks in the ground, stumbling as her feet touched uneven ground. She had to see if there was any possibility that they could still be alive, yet she knew. She knew in herself that was just not possible, but she just had to see for herself. The tears now rolled down her face and she felt that they would never stop.

The sight that greeted her, as she saw where the pyramid had been, was now only a massive, very wide, deep hole. No, it was more a crevasse; a steep sided, very wide, very deep crevasse in the ground. There was no sight of that massive building, not even of the vast, beautiful crystal beacon, that had been bigger than her house, which had sat on top of that beautiful pyramid every day of her life. It was all completely swallowed up with just thick dust, now settling down. It would be many, many days before the dust would completely settle.

Her thoughts now came back to the present, what was she going to do? What could she do? Her life just seemed totally pointless now. What had it all been about? Why?

Had life not already been cruel enough to her? Her parents, taken when she was still but a child of barely twelve summers, then totally left on her own. Now her husband and her child had also been taken from her now totally shattered life, leaving her again all alone and totally lost in her life.

Total exhaustion took over her, there were no tears left, just total devastation at her loss and the feeling her life was now, not just totally worthless, but also *totally pointless*. She just wished she had gone with her husband, as he had suggested to her yesterday morning, then at least she would have been with them. Why had she not gone?

The day had droned on slowly with a few small aftershocks as the ground still tried to settle. She could not eat and at present, there was no clean water to drink, as her water jug had fallen and smashed to the floor. She just sat there at the door. She did not know how long she had been there, there was not another soul in sight. There wasn't even the sound of a child, anywhere, and yet the day before, she had watched the local children as they played out in the sun. What had happened to everybody? Surely she could not be the only one left, could she?

Lonely, and totally exhausted, she lay down again on her straw mattress not knowing what to do or where to go. The day rolled on and now the darkness, as the night crawled slowly by, as she just lay there silently weeping to herself and for her lost ones.

Why, oh, why had she been spared? She asked herself. What reason and what purpose could her life have now?

She had risen early as she had not really been able to sleep. Her mind working all night as she thought and thought about this terrible, unbelievable thing that she had sadly been witness to. The new day had now crept slowly in, she did not know what to do and still she heard and saw not one other living soul. Her neighbours on both sides were dead, their houses shattered, their bodies all crushed as their house had fallen in on them. Practically every house around was wrecked. Late in the afternoon, after she had ventured out to see if anybody else was alive, she had returned dismayed and shocked. So she lay again on the now very dusty mattress. She just did not care anymore what happened to her.

As she lay there, the worst thing was the dust in the air. So thick, it was covering everything and yet she never thought to cover her face. The dust, she thought, that would also be the reason why she had not heard nor seen anybody around. Slowly, she drifted off to sleep. At first it was a troubled sleep, as her mind just would not let go of what she had seen. Then a more peaceful sleep crept up on her, except was she asleep? Was she really asleep?

Now everything around her was pitch black, very silent, she could see nothing in the darkness, there was not even a breath of air.

Slowly, she became aware of what she thought were the voices of people singing, just like some heavenly choir of beautiful voices, way off in the distance. No, no, I am just imagining things, dreaming things, she said to herself, yet the beautiful sound seemed to get clearer and clearer. Then, there in the distance, she could now see a tiny, tiny speck of light, like a single distant star in the sky. I'm in my bed, how can I see that light? There must be a crack in the roof, she thought, and where is that beautiful sound coming from? At first she could not move, so many questions, but no answers. What is this very strange feeling I now have?

Slowly, very, very slowly, the tiny light that she saw grew and grew. The singing, like no sound she had ever heard before. The beautiful, yet somehow very peaceful music grew, as the light now also grew. It seemed so far, far away, yet she knew that she, somehow, was getting nearer to it, or perhaps it was getting nearer to her. Ah, that was it she thought, it was getting nearer to her, she just did not know how. Was the roof above her now also breaking up like the other houses, she thought?

Suddenly, above the sound of the singing she thought she heard her daughter shouting for her. 'Mummy, Mummy, Mummy, come on, hurry up, we are waiting for you.' No, that cannot be. This is just my imagination playing tricks on me, because I am so very, very tired.

Yet still she heard the music, stronger now, and her daughter's voice was clear above it all. How could that possibly be? I know she is dead, they both are, I saw what had happened. They could never have survived that, never.

'Mummy, Mummy listen, Mummy please, look. Come to the light, Mummy, we are waiting. Hurry, hurry, Mummy, please hurry.'

What cruel trick is my mind playing? That simply cannot be. She's dead, I know she is and I never got to say goodbye to her or to my poor, poor man. He was my life, *they* were my life. They were *my everything*. The light seemed bigger now and she had this feeling, she could not explain the feeling she was having, but she felt light, as if she were floating. Now, she suddenly saw that she could look down at her own body, but try as she might, she could not get back into it again. No matter how hard, or how many times she tried. Now she was totally bewildered and her daughter's voice, much, much quieter now, yet it was still there and still with that same urgency, 'Come Mummy, come Mummy, come please to the light, we're here.' The music seemed to have nearly stopped, yet it too was still there.

She looked around to see if the light was still there and it was, but it had become much smaller, again it was just a tiny, tiny speck as she had first seen it. 'Come Mummy, come Mummy, come to the light.' How could her daughter be calling her? HOW?

She tried to get nearer the light, concentrating on it and how she could possibly move towards it. Slowly, very slowly, it appeared to get bigger as she thought about it and the music started to increase. But she panicked again. She could now no longer see her body. Then suddenly, she was back again, back with her body, but trying again and again, she still could not get back in it. 'No Mummy, no Mummy, this way, the light, this way please, please follow the light.' So again, she thought, she could now just barely see the tiny light, but as she thought about it, again it started to grow and then panic yet again assailed her, stopping her in her tracks once more. She saw her body again, except this time she now saw the dust that had thickly covered her face, nose and mouth. Now she knew that she too must be dead, she knew now that she had suffocated. But if that was true, why and how could she see this light? Why could she hear her daughter's voice if she was dead? How could she even see her own body? When you're dead, you're dead, *aren't you*?

Again, her daughter's voice roused her to try to move, much fainter now, but still there, persisting. So now she thought, if she is calling me, perhaps I will be safe. She tried so hard, just to concentrate much more on the light and on that beautiful voice, her daughter's voice. Now the singing, that beautiful sound, also grew in strength and volume. Her daughter's voice still quietly, but more persistently, persuading her to keep going forward, this time to the light. So unsure, so very unsure, yet her daughter's voice, so gentle and lovely, was still gently persuading her to keep going forward towards that light that now grew and grew in size.

Suddenly, now right in front of her was this big beautiful bright white light. It was lighting up everything around and yet she could see nothing *except* this beautiful light. Then, as if by magic, she was now watching her whole life, in every great detail as it passed before her. Yes, everything that had happened to her from the moment of her birth. She saw that she had dropped from her mother's womb into the still clear water, then through all of her childhood she saw something, *no* someone she did not recognise, when she was but a very small baby. It was far too quick for her to realise what or even who it was she saw, as another part she instantly recognised was now clearly passing before her eyes.

Everything she saw was all so clear, as if she was seeing it new, for the first time. Once or twice, she did not know how many, it seemed as if certain specific points slowed down as her mind picked up on them (like the death of her parents), but it never stopped. Everything, so totally crystal clear and in a way, she now understood everything, as she saw it all happen again before her eyes. She saw with disgust the men who had tried to take advantage of her when she was on her own, then her man, her special man, as he first entered her life and how they immediately had a strong rapport.

It slowed again at the terrible time of her miscarriage and she saw clearly just what and how much her man had helped her during this tragic and very distressing time in her life. It slowed again at the time of her daughter's birth and she was actually able to enjoy that revisit, tough though it was for her at the time. Then all that happened from that moment on, with regard to the health problems that plagued her daughter. , As her life now drew near to its end, she saw again the very last days she could remember, complete with the pyramid slowly disappearing into the ground, just exactly as it had. Her last part as she entered the tunnel, she saw herself faltering not knowing exactly what to do, all still so clear in her mind, and then it all stopped as she thought about all she had just seen.

It all seemed strange to her that her total life had, seemingly, just flashed clearly before her eyes and yet, nothing was missed. No, nothing that had happened to her was missed, every detail of her life was crystal clear and strangely, she now understood everything about her life. Now she saw again just the pure white light. Not dazzling in any way, just a pure brilliant white light and a feeling of peace from within. Then she felt that from within the light itself came a positive yet gentle loving voice saying to her, 'You have now reviewed your life as all souls who return do. I ask you, have you done all you wanted to do on Earth, in this life you have just viewed? Do you wish, or need, to return to complete anything that you should have done, or are you now complete and do you now wish to stay here?'

Her simple reply was 'Please, I am complete. Please let me be with and see my beautiful daughter. Please, I ask you, let me be with her.'

The voice, still firm, but very positive, then spoke again to her, but much stronger, more powerful this time, saying clearly 'So be it. NOW let all rejoice.'

Now, before her, this beautiful white light started to change again and she felt a new, very peaceful, loving feeling envelope her, and as it did, so did the way she now felt in herself. Throughout her life she had always felt as if there was a part missing, in a way that had changed when she met her man, yet not completely. She had still felt there was something missing, something more to life, but she could never find what it was she was looking for. Now, as she stood in this wonderful light and yes, she could still clearly hear her daughter's voice, she now felt a great change within her very being. It was as if she was absorbing the power this beautiful white light had. She started to feel whole, complete, all that she had sought before, was now no longer needed. The question had been answered, but how?

It all started to change again, she did not know how long she had been in this light, as time seemed irrelevant to her now. Slowly, in this new light that she was now seeing, forms, no shapes, yes shapes, began to slowly appear before her eyes. Not clear yet, but her daughter's voice, so soft and gentle now, it was as if she was right here beside her. A warm peaceful happy, no, a much more contented feeling now enveloped her, and the shapes, all still before her, as this great feeling of peace and joy strengthened within her. She had never known, nor had she ever felt this feeling that she was now feeling within her very being. Such peace and love, yes that was it, *love*, it was a feeling of pure *love*.

Love is Pure, Love is Kind

Welcome to 'Heaven'

Slowly now, as the beautiful white light gradually changed, she saw before her, first her beautiful daughter and a great relief flooded through her at this wonderful sight. The sight of her beloved daughter now before her. Then, beside her, her man. The lovely man who had given her, not only her daughter, but also so much great joy and happiness and especially his love, she knew now she was safe. His total unconditional love, he had in life for her, now wrapped itself around her. Her first thought was 'How can this be? How can this be possible? How can all these people, some I do not at this time even recognise, possibly be here for me?'

Then, she saw clearly all these other people behind them, her mum, her dad and some other family members, and to her surprise she also saw her near neighbours, who she had last seen when she went to what was their houses. She had seen their very badly shattered and crushed bodies covered by the walls that had fallen in on them. She also saw briefly, at the very back of all these people, a very beautiful lady. She shone like a beacon, much, much more than anybody else and then strangely, she seemed to disappear. How can this be? How am I still alive and how are they all still alive?

'Mummy, Mummy', as her daughter now ran to her as she had never, ever been able to do in life. It had been all she could do to get enough breath to allow her to walk, but never, ever to run. She bent down and scooped her up as she ran into her arms and held her tight, never wanting to ever let her go again. Ever. Her husband now slowly came towards her, knowing how very special that this moment in time was with her daughter. Her very beautiful, very precious, very special daughter. Then he took them both in his arms, the two most precious beings in his life, and he knew now, also for his eternal life. He knew within himself that whatever happened in the future, they would always have a special connection and for a moment, there was just total silence as the three of them held each other, with all the *love* they had for each other emanating out from them, like a great blue-white light for all to see. Then slowly, her own parents came forward and held them all in their grasp, as everybody else slowly came forward, awaiting their own turn to welcome her home.

Suddenly, she started to get this other feeling all over her. What was this new strange feeling? It...it felt like...happiness, like joy. Yes, and peace all rolled into one, yet... it was more than that...much, much more. So what was this, she was now feeling?

Then it dawned on her, it was again that overwhelming, 'all consuming' feeling, a feeling, a wonderful feeling of *love*. It came from all around her, everything, everywhere, giving out this truly amazing feeling of pure *love*. Just pure, simple total *love*. This feeling that emanated from everywhere and everybody, she had never known such a wonderful, wonderful feeling ever. This atmosphere of spirit that was and is, just quite simply, pure *love*.

When all the celebration was complete (because that is what it was, a celebration, but not like any other celebration she had ever known before, of her return home), her daughter and her man now took her to themselves and took her to what would now be their new home, a home that was everything she had ever wanted in life, but she had thought could, would, never be. Such a beautiful, pale pink, glistening, shimmering alabaster building that was now before her, this was to be their home.

Again the same question. That question that had assailed her as she was in that dark tunnel. How can this be, how can all this possibly be? I am dead, yet I am not. I have a body, a body of sorts. I can see everything and I can see it all clearly. *How*? How is this possible?

'What is it, Aurora? What is troubling you? As I can feel it.' her husband asked

'I am finding all this hard to take in. I am dead and yet I am not. I have a body, I still have all the feelings and most of the thoughts I had before and now more besides, how can all this be possible?'

'Ah my dear one, my beautiful girl, let me explain to you what is troubling you.'

'Mummy, Mummy we want...'

'Patience, my dear little one. Let me help Mummy first. Yes, my dear, yes. To Earth you have died, but know now, you never actually ever die, you simply discard the old Earth body like an old worn out overcoat and now you have a very pure body of, dare I say it, PURE ENERGY. Yes, pure vibrational energy, and if I may say it, you're ethereal or spirit body that you now have, is shining very bright, for someone who has just recently come through the veil. Especially after the very traumatic journey you have just had to get here.'

'Mummy, Mummy, we want to take you somewhere special.'

'This, my darling daughter, is so very special to me, me here with both of you. What more could I possibly ever ask for? I honestly thought I had lost you both for ever, I'm still finding it hard to take in what I have just been told and that somehow we are, all three of us, together and anyway, I can't go anywhere in these dirty clothes that I am still wearing.'

'Come, my special girl and just look in here. For you, all the garments that you could ever wish for are in here, if you feel you need to wear a cover.' Aurora looked and saw such beautiful coverings as she had never seen before, all for her and in her mind she said, how?

'Because it is what you wish and what you desire my lovely.'

'How did you know what I was thinking?'

'We now do not speak with a voice, it's all *mind to mind* thought transfer, to who it is we wish to speak with.'

'Mummy please, please, oh please come with Daddy and me p-l-e-a-s-e, say you will please.'

'My beautiful Aurora. Let her take you, as she took me where her angel took her when she first got here, then perhaps we will get some peace together.'

'Whoa! Stop right there. I need to know why were you not together when you got here?'

'She went before me and a child, as I have discovered, more especially a young one such as she is, is always safely collected up into the arms of someone who is specially trained to deal with a child who has suffered such an overwhelming shock, and in her case, totally unexpected. Like you, it took me a while to understand what had actually happened to me and that, although I was now dead to those on Earth, I was not actually dead and I had now returned to the *land of spirit* where we all had originally started from.'

'You say that as if it was a long time before you managed to get together?'

'In Earth time it was several days that had passed before we actually got together. She had gone with her doctor and his assistant, seconds before it all started to shake, so I did not know about her, but as with you, she was here for me the exact time I arrived.'

'Several days...but you only...the pyramid only disappeared two or three days ago.'

'No, my precious love. You were, as also with me, totally unaware of what was happening. Time here does not actually exist, but in Earth time you actually died to earth many, many days ago.'

'But it seems like...Oh! I don't know now, but it doesn't seem like many, many days. It was two days as I just looked around at the devastation and all that happened, then I lay on my mattress and it seemed like forever before I fell asleep, except I did not fall asleep, I started to see that tiny light and to hear my daughters voice.'

'We were watching you as you finally set out on your journey home here to us. Your daughter kept calling you as she had also been calling me at first, shouting at you to hurry up. We saw you, as you, unsure of everything, kept going back to try to get back in your body as it lay there, slowly getting covered in all the dust from the earthquake. When I saw my body I did not wish to go back in there. Please do not ask me to tell you, it was not a nice sight and it actually pains me just to think about it, I knew it was no longer of any use to me.'

'Mummy, Mummy, please come with me now, please, it's very special.'

'O.K. little one, I'm coming.'

'You'll come too Daddy, please, please.'

'Yes O.K. I'll get no peace, so let's all go together shall we?'

'Do you know where I'm taking you, Daddy?'

'Yes, of course I do little one.'

Decision now made, Aurora held onto her daughter's and husband's hands very tightly. She was not letting go of them again. Suddenly, not knowing how she had got there so quickly, she saw this amazing white house. Like white alabaster, as with her own pink house, but more beautiful and shimmering. From where she saw it, it appeared to be a large circular building, this amazing building that now stood before her, glistening, just like the big pyramid she had seen every day in the sun, and in they all went, hand in hand.

She could not believe the light, the purity of it and the truly amazing colours that she was now seeing, all of them so crystal clear, and so many, including many she had never known existed. Nor could she understand the feeling she was getting, the feeling that she could now *achieve anything* that she wanted to. They wandered through what was indeed a magnificent gigantic hall of more colours and more light than she truly ever knew existed.

This amazing myriad of colours, they seemed to emanate from nowhere, yet, at the same time, they came from everywhere. Accompanied by gentle music quietly playing somewhere in the background, all of it just relaxing and taking every bit of stress and tension out of her.

Her daughter now explained to her this was the Healing Hall. All these colours were healing and strengthening her ethereal body, as they did to anyone and everyone who came here. Any time she wanted to come here to refresh, to feel better, or just to be quiet within herself, all she had to do was think of this place and she would be here.

This wonderful music that was playing from somewhere, she did not know where, was just so very gently soothing her as it played in the background. Not intrusive to her thoughts, but very, very soft and gentle and somehow, comfortably reassuring. Not like the music and singing she had heard as she passed through the darkness, which also had been very comforting, an almost indescribable, peaceful, relaxing orchestra of what sounded like mainly strings. How did I know that, strings? How did I know that is what it sounds like?

There was so much to learn and yet, in a way she felt she already knew how this was. How did she...could she, already know these things?

'I know what you're thinking, Mummy. I'll help you, as my angel and my guide helped me, so I'll help you. My angel told me lots and lots of things, it was and it is, so exciting. It's like...like creating my own magic all the time. The first thing Mummy, is that everything that is said is not like speaking as we used to do, it's all as Daddy said, by thought. Everything is simply impressed in your mind, just as you know exactly what I am saying to you now, except my lips are not moving, just my thoughts transferring to you and at this moment, to you alone, as I think of you.'

'So, nobody else knows what you have just said to me?'

'Exactly, Mummy, exactly. Only if I want them to know what I am saying to you will they also hear it. It's magic, Mummy, it's all just magic.'

'And your angel told you all this?'

'Yes, Mummy.'

'I would so like to meet your angel if I can, if I am allowed to, am I?'

'You will Mummy, but you have somebody much more important to you than my angel to meet.'

'Strange, I was just thinking that I haven't eaten in days, yet I don't feel hungry.'

'You don't have to eat here Mummy. You just come here to this wonderful place, this Hall of Colours if you ever feel the need of refreshment, or the wonderful place with the beautiful clear water will also refresh you. Just think, Mummy. No washing, no teeth and no toilet to worry about, and for *me,* no worrying about not being able to breathe. Oh Mummy, it's magic Mummy, it's truly all just magical.'

'Oh, you have no idea how good it makes me feel to see you so happy and so full of life, my beautiful little elfin daughter. Your hair glows like a halo around your head, your eyes and all the colours around you are shining so bright and so strong. I feel all excited inside for you.'

'You should see yourself now, Mummy. You should see yourself.'

'Why? Why, what is wrong with me?'

'Nothing is wrong with you, Aurora, but when you arrived here your colours, in comparison to as they are now, were all muddy. Just as mine were, but now, like your daughter, you shine so bright, *both of you*. Your hair glistening like it has been polished, you look so amazing.'

'Is that what this Hall of Colours does for you?'

'Yes, Mummy. As I told you, it refreshes you and makes you like brand new again. Colour always does that and the people that are left on Earth, they should learn that lesson, to use colours much, much more. They do so much good for you, instead of all that horrible black or dull, muddy colours they always seem to wear.'

'How did you ever get to be so wise, my little one?'

'My angel, Mummy. My angel and the lovely lady who collected me, they told me ever so many things. I said it was, and it is, magic Mummy, *just magic*.'

'It makes my heart swell to see you so happy. I never thought I would see the day this would ever happen for you.'

'You haven't got a heart, as such, now Mummy, but you've got, we've all got, something much better, you'll see.'

'Oh dear. Our little daughter's all grown up now and yet you still look like my little girl, so very petite, so very beautiful, it's all so...so very wonderful. I am still finding it so hard to take it all in, the changes. We don't need to speak, yet we can talk to each other so easily and clearly and the nice thing, I can still cuddle you, my precious girl. I can still hold you in my arms, that is a priceless gift.'

'Come on now Mummy, please. We've got to be somewhere else, there is somebody very special you have to meet urgently now, so come Mummy. Please hold my hand, come on Daddy, you too, take my hand. Let's all walk this time and I can talk to you as we walk, as I have something very exciting to tell you both about and it will definitely surprise you.'

Love, the Greatest Gift There is

Crystal's Journey Back

The trio all left the Hall of Colours through a different door to the way they had entered, and outside now, they entered the beautiful parkway, now before them. Aurora and her man could not believe how beautiful everything looked, so clean, even the grass shone like it had been polished and with a very gentle yellow light to it. The trees, the shrubs, the flowers, they were all magically in full bloom, they had never seen such an amazing sight. All they had ever seen at home had been, basically, sand and stone, and the very odd plant that, somehow, had managed to survive, despite the dry heat of the day. They had often heard people talk about lovely gardens, but never like this, this amazing place, this park, yes it was indeed something very special. So very special.

Our little trio walked slowly, taking it all in and yet, Aurora knew her daughter was waiting for the right moment to tell them something, something she had hinted at before they left the Hall of Colours. She was worried about her, as she realised she could feel the worry that was within her daughter.

'Don't worry Mummy, please don't worry. I feel you thinking about what I have said, when I told you I had something to tell you. Let us all now sit here on the grass a moment and I will tell you what is on my mind.'

'How did you know I was worrying about you and what have you got to tell us, my little one?'

'We are in tune, Mummy. Yes, you and I, Mummy, are in tune. Soon you will, like me, clearly be able to pick up my thoughts, as you appear to be starting to be able to do already, but you need to meet somebody else very special to you first, before anything else.'

'I'm intrigued, my little one, but I know you've got something else on your mind, so please tell me what it is, because I know, that is not it.'

'Mummy, and you too Daddy, I've got to leave you here, as I have to go and do something special that I will tell you about when I get back.'

'I feel, Crystal, that you really need to tell us now, before you go, and who you are going with, to wherever it is you are going.'

'I, Mummy, with my lovely angel, am going back to the pyramid.'

'NO! NO! NEVER! No, I can't, I just can't, I *won't* let you. YOU CAN'T GO BACK THERE. You just can't, please. Please don't leave us, not now, please?'

'Oh Mummy! Mummy, I'm not going forever, I've been asked by some very special *high beings*, beings that you will also meet soon, to go and help a little girl. A little girl who knows me, as we met in the pyramid every time Daddy and I went there. So you see I am going to help someone and that is important.'

'But why you? Why *you* my precious little girl? Can't the lady who collected you get her?'

'No Mummy, that is the problem. She is very, very frightened and she won't come with the lady. They think I can help her as she knows me and they know she will talk to me. You see, Mummy, I was not afraid when it all happened because, well, you remember. I always told you about the...about my angel that used to come to me every night. You used to say I was just dreaming, but I knew I wasn't. Well, she came with the lady who came for me, so I knew, I just knew everything was all right. Look up above you Mummy, you see she is always beside me, always wherever I go, she is watching over me.'

Aurora looked up and slowly this beautiful golden angel, with these amazing wings, all quivering, came clearly into view beside them, and now took the little girl's hand in hers.

'Meet my special angel, Mummy, she is called Rebecca and we are going together on this trip to get this frightened little girl. She's a little older than me and sadly, has forgotten all about her angel. Her mummy, she was very cruel to her and got very angry and hit her when she talked about it. So now, she is very frightened and won't come away from her body. She keeps trying to get back into it, but of course she can't and she just won't come with the lady who has tried so hard to get her to come home, here.'

'Can I help you please, can I not come with you?'

'No Mummy, no. She does not know you, and you are not ready to do this yet, but you will be soon. Now, you have to go to that golden building, see over there, Daddy will take you because he knows, and he knows that he has to go there also.'

'But when will I ever see you again, my precious girl.'

"Oh Mummy! Of course I'll be back, you will see me soon, you'll see, but I must go quickly now, so see you soon.'

With that they were gone, her little girl and her amazing angel, hand in hand. She watched them just simply float away into the ether.

Before you could blink, in Earthly terms, Crystal and Rebecca were now both back, deep inside the ruins of what had been the beautiful pyramid and was also now deep under water. The ground had again shaken, even more violently than it had before, and with a tremendous wave, the sea had rushed in to cover it, as it all sank below the water level.

Rebecca had explained all this to Crystal as they travelled, so that it would not panic her as they went into the very dirty looking water. Slowly, very slowly, so as not to frighten the little girl they had come to collect, they watched her. She was not even aware they were actually now deep under water. Slowly, Crystal approached her, gently speaking to her as she went forward to meet the little girl she knew. She could see the fear in her eyes, feel the fear in her and sense it, as she now tried to make *mind to mind* contact with her. Instinctively, she knew the little girl could not understand what had happened, or what was still happening now. She just instinctively knew she had to be very slow and gentle with her, if she was going to have any success in getting her to come with her. She started to talk to her, 'Hullo, I'm Crystal. Do you remember me?"

'Yes, you come here with your Daddy', she replied and Crystal asked her about why she had to come to the pyramid. Slowly at first, the girl started to talk to her and told her what had happened to her in her young life. Her parents had treated her with severe cruelty and punishment, and because of all the punishment and beatings that she had received, including blows to the head, she now had to come to this place as they had damaged her. She also learned that the lady who had come for her, had not understood what she had tried to tell her, and instead had, at first, told her that she would take her home, *home to see her parents*. She had replied saying she did not ever want to do that. She also said she did not want another beating. No. She had told the lady she was better off staying here, because here she had always felt safe.

So, these two little girls talked and talked as two little girls will, and slowly, Crystal with her great patience, started to gain her confidence.

In Earth terms, they had been here with her for three days so far, as they had talked. They were still there, deep in the pyramid, under water, but, of course, as they were both spirits, time meant nothing to them. Just the same as it doesn't mean anything to any young child, ever, at any time, and water is irrelevant to them as a spirit, as they can pass through anything. But the little girl, as yet, was totally unaware of any of this, she did not even realise she was deep under water.

Slowly, Crystal turned the story around to talk about her angel, who was with her, and invited the little girl to meet her, if she would like. Her first reply was 'My mother told me these things don't exist' and it took Crystal a lot of gentle persuading to change her mind, before she would allow the angel to finally show herself, without frightening her. Slowly, this beautiful, gentle angel that is Rebecca, having now shrunk herself to nearly the size of the little girl herself, gained the confidence of this very frightened little girl.

As she talked to the little girl, to also gain her trust, she also explained that she was now slowly going to grow back to her full size. Then she would be able to carry her safely and securely, back to a safe place where she would be truly welcome, and would always be totally and completely safe. *Nobody could, nor would, ever hurt her again,* she promised her. The little girl was now mesmerised as she watched in amazement, totally spellbound, as Rebecca, very slowly at first, grew before her eyes and became this most beautiful, winged creature you could ever imagine, now so very soft and gentle with this terrified little girl.

As Rebecca gently caressed her and soothed her, a gentle smile formed on her lips and she said, 'You are so lucky, Crystal, to have such a beautiful angel to look after you. I do wish I could have one like her to look after me. I'm sure if I had one she would not want to speak to me after...'

'Oh you will. You will soon and I will introduce you to her. I have met with her and she loves you. Yes, she LOVES you and she knows that it was not your fault. Please know she is also very lovely and gentle, you will simply love her, as she truly loves you. Because of all that has happened to you, she said she would prepare a very special place for you and she will fold you gently in her wings, just as Rebecca holds you now.'

Now the three of them talked gently, all *mind to mind*, although at this stage the little girl did not realise it was *mind to mind*. Her lips were moving just as if she was talking with words. As they now slowly gained her confidence, Crystal and Rebecca, having now heard the whole story, could totally understand the fear that had been instilled in this poor girl.

There was nothing really physically wrong with her, she was not mentally ill, as her parents had tried to make her out to be, she was just totally and completely frightened. Frightened of all adults, as all they had ever shown her was cruelty and total abuse. Abuse in every possible way. She was very badly bruised all over her body, which also showed considerable signs of rape. Totally malnourished and very small for her age. Crystal just could not understand how people could ever be so cruel, so terribly cruel to a child, when she knew how warm and loving her own parents were and had always been to her.

Now slowly, they gently persuaded her to leave the pyramid, or what was left of it, with them, as they slowly floated to the top of the ridge and out of the water, where it had once stood so tall and proud. Still in Rebecca's arms and in the folds of her wings, she saw for herself that all around was devastated, flattened, and much of it now, to her great surprise, underwater. There was nobody else around, not a single living being. These two little girls ran around the few houses, or rather, what was left of them and was still above the water level. They found where the girl's house had been, an area still dry, where she saw her parent's now dead bodies, as they had been totally crushed when the house fell in on them. The girl relaxed at last, as she understood that her parents could no longer ever hurt her. Nobody could, as there was nobody there, not even the men who had done so many terrible things to her. Crystal had wanted to go to her own house, but Rebecca said NO, very firmly. She did not want her to see her mother's body, that she knew was still there, but now totally covered in dust and dirt, and the house itself now a pile of rubble.

Now all they had to do, was to persuade her to go with them, as Crystal was now getting anxious to get back to her mum, who she knew would be worrying about her, despite what she had told her about her trip. The girl, now safely back in Rebecca's arms, also took Crystal's hand and both Crystal and Rebecca started their slow gentle return to spirit and to Crystal's new home.

There was, for this frightened little girl, no dark tunnel, no light to follow. They did not wish to frighten her again, because they could still feel her fear. Rebecca's own natural golden glow shone out as an amazing light as they travelled. All they heard from that powerful light as they arrived was a gentle, tender, loving voice as it said 'Welcome home little one, know and understand that you are truly loved' and she knew she was. The little girl had never been so relaxed, ever. Never in all her young life, yes, in all her young life, had she ever felt as she was feeling now. Once they were back in Crystal's house, the white light gently appeared before her and that wonderful voice, again so soothing and gentle asked the little girl if she would now like to stay. The voice reassured her again that here, she was safe and nobody would ever hurt her again and that she was truly loved.

'Please can I stay here? I don't want to go home to my Mummy and Daddy again. Please, *please*, can I stay here?'

'If that is your wish, my little one, so be it. Know my *love* enfolds you always.'

So, Crystal and her angel Rebecca had succeeded in their mission to bring her over to the light, and the gentle lady who had tried so hard before to get her, now came to her. Crystal assured her that she was safe and when she was ready, she would take her to meet her own angel. To do this, all she had to do was think of Crystal and she would be there beside her. She went, happily together with the lady, knowing that all she had to do if she wanted to see Crystal, or be with her, was to think of her and they would be together again, and through that, she would get to see and meet her own angel.

'Well Crystal, I think the *high spirits* who asked you to go and try to help your little friend, will be very, very pleased with you and with what you did. You have done a wonderful job for such a young one and it pleases me greatly to say so to you.'

'Thank you, Rebecca. In a way, I enjoyed it. I know it was sad, but it was also, strangely, a fun thing to do. Maybe we can help other children.'

Now, she thought, where is my Mummy, what is she doing? I miss her. In the blink of an eye, the speed of thought, they were both outside the golden building as her parents walked outside and they were all together again, hugging each other in ways that, when on Earth, they had never been able to do with Crystal.

Anybody who ever saw them, knew and felt the *love* they all had for each other. What a beautiful sight to behold, these three amazing *beings of light*, together in pure love. Aurora now thought to herself, this is how it should always be between families.

There is a Great *Love*
Here for You, Within
These Pages

Aurora's First Meeting

Aurora and her 'husband', because that is what she called him, although they had actually never married, walked hand in hand, slowly towards that wonderful golden building that their daughter had told them both to go to. What, they wondered, was so special about this place?

As they approached it, they began to see and feel just how special this place really was, the beauty of this building shone out at them from every corner. It was simply a magnificent, heavenly structure that words alone could never hope to describe. This whole building just seemed to emanate peace, happiness, joy, tranquillity and *love* from every part of its being. Over and above the wonderful golden glow that seemed to emanate from every part of this building, as it too, shimmered, indeed as they all did in this amazing place. They knew, that where they were now, in the *land of spirit*, love was the essence of everything, yet this building seemed to have a special feel, the closer they got to it.

At the entrance, stood two magnificent, very, very tall, statuesque golden angel *beings of light*, and who now opened the way, to allow them to pass through into the building itself, saying to them *mind to mind*, 'You are expected.'

Now Aurora thought she knew where all the music and angel voices that she had heard as she came through that long dark tunnel, had come from, as she now heard the angel choir sing and the music play. Never in all of her life had Aurora heard such a beautiful sound, nor felt the amazing sensations that she was now feeling throughout her whole being. It was as if her whole being seemed to be in tune with everything here in this amazing place they call Heaven. They both stood there, just inside the entrance for a moment, now totally bewildered as they saw what looked like a thousand, or even more, golden angels. All singing and it was as if they were singing just for them, that was how it made them feel. It was as if they, these two people alone, were that special and this was just for them.

The singing never stopped, but as they stood there, as if transfixed, another very tall angel called them forward and then ushered them into another massive hall. They could still, much more gently now, hear the music, but they were the only ones there, or so it appeared, as they now stood in this amazing magnificent place. Every part of this hall was a wonderful rose gold colour, the likes of which they had never seen before and different to the other parts of this building that they had seen when they first arrived. That was a vivid yellow gold, and this rose gold section, strangely, had a totally different feel to what they had felt as they entered the building.

All communication was obviously by *mind to mind* but then, it was as if, out of nowhere, a voice now called them forward by name. As they walked forward to the middle of the hall, they saw another two magnificent angels, also tall, but not as tall as the others they had seen as they entered, come forward. One came straight to Aurora and the other to her man and then, suddenly, she was just there, alone with the angel that had come to her. Just for an instant, she felt a panic arising in her, where has my man gone? She thought, but the angel who immediately picked up her feeling, gently said to her,

'Fear not, Aurora, for there is only a great *love* here for you. My name is Daniel and I have been privileged to be your guardian angel from the very, very beginning, and always will be. No matter where you go, or what you ever do in your eternal life, I will be at your side. Sadly now, as most do, you have just forgotten these things, but I know it will all come back to you, that I promise you. Let me also tell you at this stage, that if you wish to see anything that has happened in your previous lives, because I know these thoughts have been in your head, we can go to the "Akashic Record", that is the book of everything. Yes, everything from the beginning, and yet there is no beginning, just as there is no end. However, if you do wish to see it, even if it is only to confirm what I am now telling you, then I will take you there. HOWEVER!

What I will also tell you is this very important fact for you to understand before you make any decisions. *You can only ever live one life at a time. You have lived many lives before this one that you have just completed, but nothing, and I mean nothing, you ever did in any past life, has any bearing at all on the life you have just lived. Nor will it ever have "in any new life in the future". On the very rare occasion that you may wish to look at an aspect of a life you have lived, in a different way perhaps, then that aspect will have no bearing at all on any past, or more especially future life, unless you deem it so.'*

'Thank you, Daniel. It appears that I was given some very false information at one time in my life, because I was told most sincerely, by someone that I now think should have known better, that all my problems that I was encountering in my life were due to my many mistakes from my past lives.'

'How very cruel and very, very wrong, that anybody should tell anyone such total, complete and utter, ridiculous rubbish. You, as everybody else, can only live one life at a time, the end. Nothing is ever carried on to a new life, even if you did wish to view a point at a different angle, the old life will have no bearing on that aspect of that life. EVER.'

'Perhaps I would not have spent so much time worrying if I had known these true facts, Daniel, but I do now know I followed my true path. Tell me why, and how is it, that there is just you and I now in this massive great hall, which surely, could hold thousands and thousands?'

'It does, indeed, hold many people, but there is not just you and I here. Watch carefully for a moment, you will see just how many people there are here, including your man and his angel.' Aurora watched and suddenly she saw that the hall was indeed filled with many, many others who, just like her, were talking to their angels and then, just as swiftly, they appeared to be on their own again.

'What! How is that possible...where have they all gone?'

'I alone, with permission, let you see that amazing sight. Nobody else in the hall will see it. You are one of the very few people who even thinks about that and it is because you are far enough advanced already, in the way that you think, that I was able to show you that scene. If everybody knew that there were so many others here in this great hall, they would never hear what was being said to them and they would never be able to concentrate on what they were being told.'

Aurora just stood for a moment, totally amazed at the sight she had just seen. The hall was actually packed with people, hundreds of them all with an angel beside them.

'That's amazing and yes, I did see my man, but he was totally unaware that we are virtually sitting next to each other on either end of the same dual seat. WOW!"

'You can tell him when you are together again and watch his reaction.'

'I will. Oh yes! I will tell him.'

'You know that we, as angels, do not have, nor can we show, emotions in any way or form, but I was very sad when you, in your human life form as that young child, you quickly forgot me. But I understood, as so much has changed in the way people of Earth now are. The loss of the amazing powers of *thought,* and that also includes the ability to converse *mind to mind*, has made life on the Earth plain so vastly different. It is sad that, as a result of these changes, people do not now *believe* in us. Through the loss of *mind to mind* communication, which was the way everybody at one time communicated, they can no longer converse with us and yet, we are always there beside the person it is we are looking after, every day. If they would just sit quietly for a short while, they would know, they would *feel* us around them.

It is sad that all they ever have to do is ask us and we will do all we can to help them on their path. It may not be instantaneous, but I assure you, they will receive any help that we can give. The only proviso is, that we can never *interfere* with your chosen path. The same actions also apply to your *spirit guide*, who I know you, as yet, have not met since you returned. Normally you would have met your guide before meeting others, but your guide, because she is such a gentle and warm loving lady, just as you are, knew that in your heart you longed for your daughter to be with you. So she held back, but I know she is now anxious to meet with you. Her name, as I know you have forgotten, is Grace, and she lives up to her name in every way with a great warmth of love.'

'It is very sad that I have forgotten her name. Because of what has now happened to the people of the Earth plain, we have all basically forgotten our angels and now I also know that we have also forgotten our *spirit guides*. How very important I now know and understand you all to be, Daniel. What is this about a *spirit guide*, Daniel? I know you have said her name is Grace, but who is she and what is her function in my life? How long has she been my guide and why do we have both an angel and a *spirit guide*?'

'Thank you Aurora for saying that about us, and yes, we are both important, but with different functions. We now also both have a much more difficult task than before, but all of us, never give up. Sadly, we both can only ever help our charge when asked, except if something serious was about to happen and it was *not* on your true path. Then we have the great power to be able to step in to be of, in some cases, very considerable help to you. People who have received help in that way, they often refer to that help as a *miracle*, as something usually happens that could not normally happen.

Your *spirit guide*, let me say, actually chose you. Yes, chose you, as they all do, those that become guides. It was her choice to guide and help you, all she could on the path you had agreed to, before you set out in your life. She had walked the Earth before and she knew the path you had chosen would be a difficult one, and that her job in this life just passed, would not be an easy one in helping you. But let me assure you, she did it very well and she *nudged* you and she kept you on your path, virtually 100 percent and this was no easy task.

Keeping you on your pathway, which is her principal function, was no easy task for her, as you, as you well know, had a very hard time in your short life. Especially when you were left on your own, and many men who knew you and your situation, when you were on your own, had serious designs on you and rarely in a good way.

'You had agreed to a life with many difficulties and I am pleased to say, as I knew you would be, you were strong, pure and true. You will meet your guide very soon and you will be able to discuss all these things with her.'

'I look forward to meeting her, I am sure it will be a very interesting conversation when we meet.'

'I am sure it will be, but I will leave you to that yourself, as I am sure a woman to woman conversation is no place for me. I see that you have changed your covering to a very beautiful rainbow coloured, full length dress, you look stunning. Is this your own thought in the way you want to look, and tell me, did you actually take time to look at your own, new ethereal energy body when you changed?'

'No, I just quickly changed into these things that were already there for me. I did not really have time to think, as Crystal was anxious to go off on her task with Rebecca. As for my body, no, I did not think it would look any different and as they, my man and my anxious daughter were waiting for me, I did not want to keep them waiting. Why, am I now different?'

'If you had looked closely at yourself, you would have seen that you can now see the 'chakras', or main energy centres of your body as they spin. When you were on Earth you always had seven main ones that spun, now you are a *spirit being* you have much more and they also all spin. Each one spins separately and they alternate in the direction in which way they spin. On a man, on Earth, they spin the opposite way, just as they do here if you have retained your thoughts on your gender, something I know you will do for many lives to come. You will see when you get to spend some proper time with your man what I mean, and why they all purposefully spin the way they do.'

'Oh! I'll look forward to that, if we can get the peace to be alone that is. Perhaps that opportunity will happen when Crystal has something to do again.'

'Oh, you will. I will find a way to help you, as it will be very good for you both to have some good quality loving time, alone together. Strange I am talking of *time* and yet here, there is no such thing. Now where was I before we got side-tracked, oh yes, I was talking about how people have forgotten about us. It is very sad for the people themselves, they have lost something precious to them and very sadly, they don't understand. They know and many often feel, yes feel, as if something is missing, they just don't know what it is. Strangely, they not only feel something is missing within them, but many keep looking for their 'soul mate', thinking that is the problem. If only they would just *stop looking* and then just sit quietly and go inside themselves, they would receive the answers that they seek.

All that they really seek is what is called their *higher self*. I will tell you more about that in a moment, so please, just be patient as there is much to discuss. I too, was with you every day, just as your guide was, to ensure that you were always on your chosen path and you were safe, and at times I know we were linked, you and I. I was also very, very close with you when you gave birth to your daughter. I also knew it would be a difficult birth for you and I had brought her angel for her with me, I knew that she would be looked after from the second she slipped out from within the comfort of your womb. That was no easy task for her, and then onto her own very difficult path that was laid out for her.

That is who you met before she, with Crystal, had to take leave of you to do their work. I can tell you now, that they were very successful and that those *high spirits* who asked her if she would help, (because she also had a choice, she could have said no, but she is very like you, strong where it counts), they are indeed very pleased with her. Very, very pleased.

They will return here for you, when you are ready to leave here. Your daughter, as are you, is a very special chosen one. You were indeed, the very special one that was chosen to give birth to her. We knew, *they* knew, you had in you the natural *love* that your soul always carries, and the care that such a special one, as she is, would need when she was reborn. Indeed, you continue to love and care for her even now, after what you yourself have just been through. My dear Aurora, that, yes that, is the sign of a true and loving spirit and mother. Now, let us talk further as we still have much to do. So very, very much to do now.'

'What do you mean by *we* still have much to do?'

'As I have just told you, you are a very special spirit and have qualities that most others, as yet, do not have. You would not have seen what I just let you see, if you did not have those qualities, you simply would not have been able to see that sight, even if I had tried to show it to you. You, before you went on that past life you have just lived, were indeed a very learned soul and that you will never lose. However, before we get ahead of ourselves, let me bring you up to date with all that has happened to you since you returned to us here, so that you fully understand all. I am very aware that when you first met the *'light'* you had some feelings, strange to you then, but feelings that you have now got used to. The feelings that you first had, when you felt as though you were absorbing the light?'

'Oh yes, I remember that. It was a strange, yet wonderful, comforting feeling, as if I was being enveloped. For some reason I felt more complete, and then it changed again, as I then reviewed my life that I had just lived. Why was that and why was I asked if I had completed everything I wanted to do on Earth?'

'Everybody who returns here goes through that life review, and from that review you see what you did in your life and whether you completed everything. That is, everything you had promised to do before you set out on that journey. You would have known when that review finished, if there had been something that you had not done that you should have. You would then have been back a *millisecond* before you died, to allow you to complete your life's path. You see everybody, before they set out on that new life, knows exactly what they have to do in that life.

It's as if you had a picture frame and you knew exactly what that picture would contain, yet only when you had painted it, would it be complete. As the artist, you have choices as to what goes in the picture, although the *subject* of the painting always remains the same. Also, the time of your departure was already decreed *before* you were born, although time is a misnomer. So let me say before you ask, if you still had something else to do and you had gone back, that is because that decreed time was not yet reached. Everything always works directly according to the plan, just as I have told you. It was all clearly laid down, before you were even born.'

'Thank you, now I understand so much more and much that I had forgotten. In that beautiful light, as I began to feel more complete, I seemed to understand more. I then began to see forms at first and then these forms started to take on shapes, as people I knew appeared and some I do not know, but they all knew me.'

'That is because you were not, but are now, complete, from that first experience with light. It's as if there were two of you and the light caused you to join together. You have forgotten that when you go to have a new physical experience on Earth, you also leave behind what is thought of, and known as, the greater part of you and that part is known as your *higher self*, which I mentioned earlier. So now you are all together again, as one complete *being of light*. Now let me tell you another very important fact for you to know.

No matter what was wrong with you or whoever it is who is returning to spirit, whenever you leave your Earthly body and return here, any illness you may have had at that time does not come over with you. You are complete and fully fit, any missing limb is no longer missing, and you are definitely not suffering from any illness or complaint that you may have been suffering at the time you departed, to return.

You will remember I told you earlier, and I am repeating myself here, but it is important you fully understand about this, many people keep looking for their soul mate. Sadly, many people spend their whole life seeking their soul mate, as it were, when all they ever had to do was, as I told you earlier, just sit quietly and meditate. In doing so, they would connect to their *higher self*, and in doing that, they would have found the soul mate they sought – *themself*, or at least the other part of themself.

The *higher self* is the greater part of you that contains your main mind energy, some of which is accessible to you when you sit quietly in meditation. Unfortunately, people do not remember that they have, while on Earth, both a brain and *higher self* also known as *mind energy*. Both the mind energy and the brain energy work for you, either together or separately, depending on what it is you are doing. The power of thought, which sadly is now severely diminished, because man greatly abused it, is mainly mind energy. I say diminished, but sometime in the future it will return to as it was, when man can be trusted again to use it as it is meant to be used.'

'When do we know? Can we ever just use our mind energy as a human?'

'During meditation. Although, you can never shut the brain energy down completely, and I am very pleased to say, meditation was something you did remember to do. I could then tune into you *mind to mind*, to help you on your path, and yes, you can use it, but now most people don't, because they simply do not know it even exists. So the ability gets less and less and yet the power of their thoughts is actually still very strong. Everything that happens in your life is as a direct result of your thought power.'

'You say we can never shut down the brain energy completely, why is that?'

'The only time the brain energy shuts down completely, is when you die on Earth and return to spirit, so even in meditation it is still working, you just have to learn to let each thought from your brain energy, pass by as you meditate. It can be confusing to think that you have two similar systems and yet they are both vastly different. Your brain energy only comes into being when you become a human being on Earth. The object of your brain is to look after your human body while you are on Earth, as a human being, and take care of all the human functions of that body.

The more that you work that muscle, for that in a way is what it is, the better it will do its job. It takes care of all the daily life happenings with your body, so it can be your best friend, or it can be your worst enemy if you do not look after your body.

Now please, let me continue with what I need to tell you. Before you went to Earth on your last life experience you were on, as it were, a very special mission, which as yet you do not remember, that you actually chose to do before you went. You had been, prior to that, as I mentioned earlier, working and learning very hard. Now, those *higher spirits* that worked with you then, are very, very pleased with your progress and at your success in that life, especially in the way that you dealt with not only your own problems, but with your daughter and her problems when she, through you, arrived on Earth. Remember that you, as does everybody, always have that choice on Earth in what you do. Your patience, your love and understanding to both your daughter and indeed to your man, the man you call your husband who also had a choice, have far exceeded their expectations and desires for you.

You, as all do, had many, many choices in your life's path. Your choices were to follow the path exactly as was discussed before you left here, which up until you were twelve summers, you did. Yes, you did to the letter. You never, despite all that happened in your very young life, deviated from that path. It was fascinating to watch you as you dealt with each challenge that was thrown at you.'

'Ah! My life. It did change very dramatically from that very terrible summer onwards, with the loss of both my parents. My father was killed by a bull as he tried to remove its horns. He had taken one off and was about to remove the other but the bull was too quick for him, and my mother, I am sure, died from a broken heart as a result.'

'From that summer, that age, your life now started to further develop very seriously. As you said you had suddenly lost both your parents and you now had to look after yourself in every way. You accepted that choice, you did not sit back and moan, as many others would have and indeed, in similar circumstances, did, but no, you moved on in your life.'

'I had a little help.'

'Yes, we know you had a little help from a very special friend, but then, within a very short time of you losing your parents a young man also came into your life. A young man who was a bit of a rogue, but you could see and feel the good in him, as he never tried to take advantage of your young age, or your vulnerability, as many others had. So with love, your *love* for another human being, you took him into your house and gave him shelter. Up until that time, he had known nothing but cruelty and abuse in every way, he had had to fight to keep himself alive, but his path was destined to meet with you.'

'He brought me hope and much pleasure with his cheeky grin, his presence and yes, his determination. He was fun, but he never gave up his drive, his drive always to give us the best he could.'

'You now had a choice, you could have thrown him out, but you were very determined that you would not allow him to go back out on that rough road again and he felt that. So, through *love*, through kindness and it has to be said, good food, no matter what it was, he grew to love you and what you stood for. He took great pride in the strength he saw in you and through that, his own strength grew. You learned to bond and work strongly together, until you had a very serious miscarriage.

That miscarriage alone, set you both back and he could have left you then, but by now, his love was as strong as yours and he was determined to care for you, whatever. He did not want to lose you and he knew within himself that with care, you would become strong again and he was right. You did, and you still are, strong, in every way that counts. His strength became your strength, until one day he returned home to you from a day's hunting and he saw you *smile* again and his heart melted.'

'I remember that terrible time. I was so scared and so weak, but he helped me and nursed me for many, many long days and often, very long nights and I knew it was very hard for him and I knew I did not want to lose him, ever.'

'Three and a half years ago, in Earthly terms, you gave birth to your daughter and the problems that that now presented you both with. Again, you both had choices, but through love, the love you have for each other and now for your child, the dye was cast, and for three years, you have both lavished your love and care and attention on that child, no matter how hard things got for you.

You not only stuck to your path you...*no that is wrong*...you progressed. Yes, you progressed. Way above your path and far exceeding all their expectations of you, both of you. So now we, or should I say 'they', the *high ones*, because I cannot make choices ever, I can only always ever do as I am asked, either by them, or by you, they would like you to grow even more, so that you can further learn how you can help many, many others from the experiences you have had. Yes, help others, both here in spirit and eventually back on Earth.

This is what they are going to ask you to do, when shortly you meet them again, just as you did before. I was allowed to tell you all this, so that you could have time to think before they met with you and of course, you can now ask me anything you like and I will do my best to answer you truthfully, as always. There is however, one thing I must tell you and it is VERY IMPORTANT that you are aware of this and always do, please, what I now tell you. As on Earth, so also here, there is a *dark side* that will always try to mark you, so it is vital that you ensure, that before you do anything, you always ensure you are fully *white light protected.* Think and listen very carefully to what I am saying to you, because it is vitally important. It is especially important when you, for instance, wish to get in touch with your friends not yet here in spirit.

I know that you have a friend who is still on Earth that is a medium, a good medium, and she may just one day try to get in touch with you. That is when you must ensure you have that protection in full. Do not be fooled into thinking it cannot happen to you here, because they also know how important you are and so they will try even harder to get at you here. Be strong and be in the light, as it will always triumph over the dark.

I know you have already visited the Hall of Colours, that is an excellent place to go whenever in need of refreshment and if you feel that those that would try to harm or mark you are worrying you. It is also used a lot by the women who, when they like to get together for a chat, as many often do, they will go there and get the benefit, not only of being together but of being nurtured at the same time.

I will do everything I can to ensure you are safe, but if you learn from right now, to be aware of all things, then all will go well for you. If you ever feel that you are unsure of anything 'ask for protection', make it a way of life here. If all fails, just ask for me and I will be here. Remember, I never leave your side, so I see all, but I do not, will not, ever intrude. I only act when asked, either by you or the *high ones*, that is all I am ever allowed to do. Now first, I suggest that you have a talk with Grace, as I know she is anxious to talk with you. She has always been your *spirit guide*, as she chose the aspect of you when the great creator first created you in the new beings that he created at that time. He still creates new beings, because remember, spirits often return to their God when, after many hundreds of different Earthly experiences, they feel complete.'

'Is Grace here? I can't see her. Is she here with us now, Daniel?'

'Yes, here she is now for you. Grace, as you well know, this is Aurora, but as yet she does not remember you. I am sure once you have talked, all *will* come back to her about you.'

'Aurora, how nice to be able to speak with you again. You do not remember when last we conversed, do you?'

'Sadly, Grace, no I do not. Yet, when I see you, as I do now, I cannot understand why I do not remember you. You are so beautiful and serene. But wait. You, *you* were the lady that I saw when I first saw everybody and then, before I had a chance to get to you, you had disappeared. Why?'

'Thank you, but I am just me as I have always been and basically, as I was when last I walked the Earth, although it has changed beyond all recognition to when I was last there, eons ago now. Yes, I was there for you when first you returned, but as Daniel has said, we knew you were anxious to be with your daughter, so I agreed with him that I would withdraw and leave meeting you until now.'

So Grace and Aurora started a long conversation, as they got to know one another again. They discussed the life Aurora had just lived, especially the salient points regarding that life, and of course, Crystal, who Grace adored. She let it be known to Aurora, that the *spirit being* that is 'Crystal', had been her daughter when last she lived on Earth and that had been for Crystal, her first incarnation, but not as Crystal. She, in that incarnation, was called Moonlight, and she has had many other incarnations since then and two of these, before this one, have been with you. From this, another long conversation was had, as the two ladies relaxed into each other's company. They laughed and they cried as they recalled events, until finally Grace said 'Daniel and I have a surprise, a special surprise for you, Aurora, that we know you will love.'

At the mention of his name, Daniel appeared and said he thought that Aurora would indeed be very happy with her surprise, which they had been able to engineer and been given permission, from those *higher beings*, to allow to happen.

'I would like first, if I may, to have some time with my precious daughter, please. It is so very nice to see her as she is now and was never able to be in her life, as a human being.'

'You will have as much time, as you put it Aurora, with your daughter as you wish, although time is a misnomer and does not exist here, as you know. You also have many other people to meet, especially after you meet the *high ones*, as you have indeed, as I said, much to learn. Do not worry, I shall be with you every step of the way, even if you do not always see me, the instant your thoughts are on me, I shall be visible beside you. Remember as I said before, that I have never, and will never, ever leave your side. Yes, I never have and I never will.

We do have however, as we said, something very special that we would now wish to show you before you go to your daughter. For this, we had to seek and be given special permission to do this for you, as it really is quite extraordinary that we are being allowed to do what we are now going to show you. Relax Aurora, you will enjoy this surprise, for I can feel you tensing up as you wonder what it is.'

'Now this does intrigue me. What can be so special for *me,* that you had to be given permission to do this, whatever it is?'

'Do you remember these big circular ships that you used to see? They came down from the sky outside your house and the one in particular that was brought by the man who befriended you and tried to help you?'

'Oh yes! He did more than just try; he was, in a way, just like a father to me after I lost my own. Amazingly, I always knew when he was coming as I 'felt' him and as I so 'felt' him, he would suddenly appear, or rather his ship would. In my own way, I loved that man for what he did for me, without ever asking for anything from me. That alone was exceptional, as most men that came to me, especially when I was first alone, I had to fight them off. They soon learned that I was not easy prey. He restored my faith in people with his kindness.'

'Then turn round and look down. Look deep down there, tell me what do you see? What can you see?'

'I see another planet, just like Earth, but I know it is not Earth. It is not Earth, because it appears to me to be a much bigger planet.'

'That is correct, it is much bigger and that is one of the reasons he would not, could not take you there when you asked him. The gravitational pull is so much stronger there than it is on Earth, but look closer, study it and what now do you see?'

'I see people, lots of people. They look similar to those on Earth, but bigger. Oh, and lots of very big buildings, but one area alone seems to stand out for me. Yes, it's as if there is a bright, bright white light down there.'

'That is correct. Now look closer, much closer at the people, study them closely, especially where you see that light, tell me what you see now.'

'Oh! Oh GOD! I...I see my friend...I see him, and look! Now it's as if he is looking directly at me, smiling.'

'He is. He knows, yes. He also knows where you are now and that you are looking at him, and even now, thinking about him. If you relax, you can speak to him *mind to mind,* as he is also very special, but in a different way. He is able to clearly see the fourth dimension, and what you are about to do, is exactly the same as a medium would do, as they relate what they see from the spirit to their client.'

'I hear him in my head. I clearly hear him speaking to me, or should I say, I am clearly reading his thoughts as I don't actually hear his voice. It's just the clarity of what is coming into my head and I know it's not me putting those words there in my head. I know and remember the way he talked, it was slightly different to us.'

'So now we will both leave you for a while and let you speak with him in peace, *mind to mind,* as you are now. While you both have this strong connection, because you are right in what you say, and as you learn more, you will find you will always be able to do this with him, no matter where you are, forever. However, just remember the energies you are using, the level of energies will drop after a while, because you are not yet strong enough to sustain this level of energy indefinitely.'

So Aurora began to converse *mind to mind,* as if he was standing right beside her, this man, from a far-away planet, that in truth had replaced her father at a time when she had needed comfort and support. When she had first been alone and felt totally vulnerable. She also now knew what he had meant when he had talked to her about the 'power of thoughts' and how powerful they were, no, are. She remembered her mother, who also had amazing abilities, all through the power of her thoughts. But that amazing power had not been passed on to her and she had always wondered why, as she did, again, now. As she completed her *mind to mind* chatter with her friend, they said to each other 'See you soon' and Daniel, together with Grace beside him, immediately came back visibly with Aurora again.

'I thought I would, and should, explain about why you did not have the power of thought that your mother had. Because of all the terrible happenings that were, and are now happening on Earth, and will continue for very many years, that power of thought has been taken away. It was taken first from the men, because of their anger and aggression, then from all newborn babies. The male ones first and then to all newborn to Earth, and it will not be returned to the human on Earth for many, many years. That is, not until man again learns, that this power, the power of thought that these people had before they abused it, can only be used for good. They knew that when you went to Earth that last time, you had enough in you to survive your time without it. Now before I forget, which I never do, this is one of those times I was telling you about, the need for protection. I ensured you would have it on this occasion, but these are very important times that you should ensure it is in place, always, OK?'

'Thank you, Daniel. Yes, I will ensure I put that protection in place, and thank you, again. Thank you for explaining something that had always troubled me, I thought I had something seriously wrong with me when I could not do as my mother could.'

'Now you must go Aurora, but please worry not. As you learn more, so you will understand more. Grace and I are always there to help you, so now go. Go to your daughter and your man, as they are awaiting you.'

'Then after that, what happens? Do I go straight to the *high ones*?'

'No, you can stay here awhile if you so wish and enjoy the music, let it seep gently into your very being. It will serve you well and it will help to refresh you, especially after all that energy you have just used talking to your friend. Then, when you are ready to go, you can meet your husband and tell him what we have discussed. Trust me, they will not know the difference whether you go straight away, or as I suggest, you take *time,* as it were, to allow what has been said to you to digest. The choice is, as always, yours, and time is irrelevant.'

'Will he, my man, my special man who has been good to me, will he be with me on my next life, if I do what is requested of me?'

'Ah! I'm sorry, I cannot tell you that. I have not been made aware of any of these facts as yet, possibly because you, yourself, do not truly know what is involved and won't until you learn further.'

'Ah! I see.'

'In truth, as yet, you do not see and I would say to you, do not discuss please, too much with him for a while. Forgive the metaphor, there will be time soon enough, when you have learned more.

'Thank you for your advice, I will tread slowly till I learn more.'

'Good. Now when you are ready, go and meet with your husband, he will soon be wondering what has befallen you. You will find him by the choir, when you are ready, as he half listens and half waits for you, patiently wondering. Your daughter will also be outside when you are ready.'

So Aurora, after she had given herself time to digest what she had just seen and also been told, departed from this great hall that she had come to, together with her man, to meet with Daniel and learn all she had now learned. Her mind was now buzzing with all these amazing things she had been told and indeed seen for herself, especially both her special friend and her beautiful guide Grace. She now set off to find her man.

As she reached where he sat, he quickly rose and took her in his arms, the *love* and great need they had for each other showing, as their energies and colours mingled and shone for all to see.

'It is good to hold you like this, my beautiful girl, so good. I wish I could hold you like this forever and to see you looking so unbelievably happy, especially when with your daughter.'

'Our daughter please, for without you and your *love*, she would not be here.'

'That is true, so let's go and meet her. She should, I am told, be outside on the grass waiting for us.'

So our trio again came together and hand in hand they decided to go home, home to spend a while happily together as, up until now, they had not been able to. They chatted and reminisced, as they slowly wound their way home, past all the amazing houses and buildings they now saw there. They talked about how beautiful, clean and fresh everything here was, it all sparkled and shimmered. So many buildings and yet there was all the room that they could ever want. Nothing here seemed crowded, just beautifully spaced out, clear and full of beautiful colours. Everything about here, this beautiful place they were now in, looked so fresh, just like it was a bright new spring day.

As they walked slowly back, Crystal told them a little of her experience when she, together with Rebecca, went to bring her little friend back home. She told them how the pyramid, or what was left of it, was now deep under water. At first Aurora looked shocked at where her little girl had just been and what she had done, but then she realised that with Rebecca beside her, she was perfectly safe. Crystal told them she thought that, although it was a serious job, it was fun for her to go so deep down in the murky waters and still see clearly everything that was going on. She told them 'There were even fishes, lots of fishes, swimming about down there.'

Then she proceeded to tell them about what they saw when they went running around what was left of the houses. That they had seen her little friend's house and how it was now all flattened and her parents, what was left of them, were buried underneath the rubble.

She said the little girl looked very relieved, as she knew then that her parents could no longer hurt her, they too were dead. Then Crystal said how she wanted to go and see her own house, but Rebecca would not let her. She said she did not want me to get upset at what I might see. Anyway, their house was all just flat now as it had all collapsed in on itself.

After all that, they just gently flew home. She then told them she would soon go of on another spree to get a little boy, but not yet, it was not quite his time yet.

'One thing Rebecca told me, was that my little friend's parents, they were at a lower level in a special place, and that until they understood how cruel they were and what they had done to her and how wrong it was, there they would remain. She told me they had a lot to learn and it looked as if it would be a long job, as they still felt they had the right to do with her as they felt. She was their daughter, they said, and should always have done as they told her without question, and the only way she would do what they said was when they beat her. Allowing other men to use her had put food on their table, not that she got much of that. People can be so cruel Mummy' she said.

'Crystal, I have somebody very special, somebody that I have just met, not for the first time as I have just been reminded, but strangely, you in the past have also met with her. Would you like to meet with her? What she has to tell you may surprise you, as it did me.'

'Yes please, Mummy. You know I love meeting people, now that I can. Oh, you know what I mean Mummy. You know I was shy before because I was not able to breathe properly, now I don't need.

So as always, using *mind to mind*, Aurora called her guide Grace to her.

'Crystal, I would like you to meet Grace, who I know that you actually do know, although I also know you will not remember meeting her. Let her tell you how you already know each other.'

'Crystal, how nice to meet you again, and yes, we do know each other. If I said to you, that once you were my daughter, what would you say to that?'

'But you are a *spirit being* and not, as such, a being that has lived on Earth before, so how can that be possible Grace?'

'Ah! Crystal, I have walked the Earth and indeed, the last time I walked the Earth you, in your first incarnation, were my daughter called 'Moonlight', because you were born on a very beautiful night. The night of a full moon, when it was on the very top of the sky.'

'I wish I could have seen that or at least remembered that time. My memories of time on Earth are not strong and I was not a 'well child', was I, Mummy?'

'No Crystal, you were far from a 'well child', as you put it. Is it not strange that we were both your mummy?'

'Yes, when I think about it, it does seem a strange thing to say, that you are both my mummy, but as I learn, so I now understand. I suppose I could go to the hall of records and see myself as I was then. I'm sure Rebecca would take me if I ask her?'

'You are correct in your thinking, Crystal, but I do not think you would benefit in any way from that experience of looking back to these times. You would find it so vastly different to everything you remember, as in Earth terms you would be going back nearly a millennium and you would gain nothing. The thing to always remember is that the *now,* not the before and not the after, but the *now* is what is always important. Aurora, I feel you have a question you wish to ask, what is it?'

'I was just wondering if you could tell us a little about you and your lives and experiences, or is it because you are my guide that you are not allowed to do this?'

'Just because I am your guide, that does not mean we cannot discuss matters. My job is to help you in any way I can, as long as that is beneficial to your experience and this way, strange as it may seem to you, I also learn.'

'Then shall we, just the three of us, go and sit in the Hall of Colours and chat a while and get to know each other better? How does that sound?'

'Now that sounds like an excellent idea. It's a while since I was last in there, it will do me good and it's an excellent place for you to absorb what I can tell you. Let's go.'

So now the three of them, hand in hand with Crystal naturally in the middle, went off to the Hall of Colours for what was a long and pleasant period, talking about anything and everything, but mainly enjoying each-others company, with Aurora saying she did not think she had ever done anything so nice, ever. A *mind to mind* thought to Crystal is what eventually broke them up, as Rebecca also suddenly appeared to say they had a job to do. A little child needed her help, as she did not want to leave her friends that she could see, but they could only see her shattered body.

So Crystal departed, and Aurora and Grace returned to Aurora's house, still chatting away like two old friends which indeed, is what they are, aren't they?

Love is All There is

The Rainbow Bridge

Sometime later, and remember that time is irrelevant in spirit, our trio all decided they would go further and explore this wonderful place, a place that so far had been beyond their wildest dreams and expectations. Aurora had not yet heard from those *higher spirits*, who she knew wished to see and speak with her. They had both briefly told each other what had happened when they had been with their respective angels in that amazing Golden Temple building. Neither of them being very specific, as their daughter was always by their side. They both knew that they had not been specific with each other, saying 'we'll talk more later, but let us spend some time with our daughter'. Aurora, also had not yet mentioned about what she had been able to see when Daniel let her see the hall they were in as it really was, with everybody in it.

Crystal had now told them all about her trip back to the pyramid and had also explained to them that it was now deep under water. Aurora, was still trying to come to terms with what she had learned from her. She was still horrified at what she had told her, even after Crystal had explained it all, it made no difference to her. On Earth she could now pass safely through anything, as if they were not there, be it walls, rocks or even water. To

Aurora she was still her little daughter. Crystal had also told her parents all about her little friend they had gone to collect and bring home. She told them about the type of life she had led at home and how sorry for her she felt. She felt sad that her parents had been very, very bad to her, saying 'It was no wonder she did not wish to see them again.'

'Where will she go?' Aurora now asked.

'I do not yet know, but I only have to think about her and she will be beside me. I told her that, and if she thinks about me, I will do the same for her. I will go to her if she needs or wants me.'

'That's good. Do you want her to be with us now as we go and explore?'

'Could she, Mummy? Could she be with us? It would be so nice for her to feel she was wanted, properly wanted.'

'You are, for such a little one, turning into a very thoughtful girl. I am so very proud of you and if I may say so, you are growing, you are definitely getting taller. Yes, let her come if she would like to.'

So, in the blink of an eye, suddenly she was beside them, shyly looking up at Aurora's beautiful face and saying 'Thank you, thank you.'

'You are welcome, little one. Very, very welcome.'

Now they were four, as they continued to meander down what appeared to be a country lane, still with all the amazing flowers and trees like they had never seen before. Crystal suddenly said 'Mummy, Mummy, why are there no shadows here in this place?'

'I don't know. I had not thought about it, but if you look around you there is just this incredible light everywhere. But there is no Sun, as we know it on Earth, and it is the direction of the Sun that gives us shadows.'

'Clever thinking, Aurora. I must admit I had never thought about that, but you're right, Crystal, there are no shadows. But of course, there is no Sun either, so no shadows.'

Aurora now reminded them, that if they wanted shadows to play with they only had to think about them and they would be there for them. So for a little while, the two girls did just that, they had their own shadows as they walked and skipped along.

They had walked on quite a bit further, Aurora now deep in thought when her husband asked her, 'What are you so deep in your thoughts about now? You seem to be away in another place and yet, you are obviously not, as you are still here with us.'

'Oh, I was just reminiscing about what our life had been like before we came to this simply beautiful place. In so many ways it still seems like a dream and that in a minute I will wake up, yet I know it all to be true.'

'You're allowed to dream, my precious. It does take a bit of getting used to. Sometimes, yes, just sometimes, I wish we could all sit down to one of your lovely meals, but I know that is just a memory.'

'Don't think about it too seriously, Daddy, or we will all be sitting down to something we can't really do now and do not need to.'

'Our life as we knew it, has certainly changed, Crystal, but I must say, to see you so happy and playful brings me such joy in my heart.'

'I was also just thinking about your beautiful dog you had, my dear, when we first met. I wonder if she is also here?'

'Oh yes! She would love it here, I never did thank you enough when you also took her in to live with us.'

'You did not think I would have left her out on the street did you? She was a lovely part of you and I wanted you all and she was, I know, a very important part of you that kept you happy. Which you would not have been, if we had let her just roam about.'

'You did not have to take either of us in, all dirty and rough. We had been weeks on the road, scrounging food from wherever we could get it, yet you took us in like long lost friends. That always amazed me and still does, despite all I now know. You took us in so lovingly and made us feel at home, right from the beginning.'

'We were both very happy though, weren't we?'

'Oh yes, very, very happy and from that day you always ensured we had food on our table, whatever it was, thank you.'

'A lot of what we ate was from that which you supplied us with. Yes, all from what you were able to go out and catch, so I also thank you.'

'Mummy, Daddy, you have never told me you had a dog. Why didn't you tell me and what was she like?'

'I'm so sorry dear, we just never got round to talking about her, we were very sad when she died.'

'Was she old, is that why she died?'

'No.'

'Why then, did she die, Mummy?'

'Sadly, she was killed by a hunter's arrow, he mistook her for something else, or so he said.'

'Oh! That was very cruel Mummy, very cruel. Did you bury her?'

'No my dear, we cremated her. We thought it was better than some wild animal getting to her and digging her up to eat, which they would have.'

'Wouldn't it be so nice Mummy, Daddy, if we still had her and she was with us here, still running around beside us?'

'That was part of what I was thinking and even more so, now we're talking about her.' As they talked, something very strange started to happen around them.

'Mummy, Mummy, what's happening to the sky? Over there…look Mummy, what's happening?'

'Where do you mean? Oh! I see it now, I don't know. It's like as if a big…no it can't be, it's not raining, it doesn't rain here, how is this possible?'

'All these colours Mummy, mingling and coming out of the sky. Look at them growing, they are getting bigger, wider and longer. What's happening, Mummy, what's happening to the sky?'

The four of them watched, totally amazed at this beautiful sight of many colours, now in the sky before them, as it grew and grew, from out of nowhere it seemed. One end still deep in the sky, but the other, it was now reaching out to the ground before them, and yet, it was not quite touching it. They all ran to get to it. Try as they might to get onto it, strangely, they could not seem to walk right up to it, as every step they took towards it, it moved back away from them, as if it was playing a game with them.

A look of utter amazement was on all their faces, as they took in this quite beautiful sight before them, that to them, could have been a magical bridge. A rainbow bridge, yet a bridge to where and why a bridge?

The more they tried to step on it, the more it moved back from them. It appeared they were definitely not allowed to get onto it, so why had it appeared? Why was it here, what miracle was this for?

Aurora now spoke out loud her thoughts, in fact the thoughts of them all. 'I wonder what this is for and why is it here for us now? Surely, it must have a reason?'

Then suddenly Crystal shouted, "What is that up there? Look…on the top, right at the very top of the rainbow, Mummy, it's moving slowly towards us, what is it, Mummy? Daddy what is it?'

They all now looked up and they saw this dark shape, at first just there, as if it, whatever it was, was watching them. Then, slowly at first, it appeared to start to move, was it actually walking towards them? As it slowly grew nearer he 'knew'. He knew for certain what it was, he just could not quite believe his eyes. 'How can this be, how can this possibly be happening?'

Suddenly it started to move much quicker towards them and then in great leaps and bounds, with its tail wagging like mad and it was as if it was smiling at them, its whole face just alive with excitement.

'It's our dog, Aurora, see it's our dog, our lovely dog. Oh! How is this possible, that she's also here?'

With a mighty leap it sprang, from still quite high on the bridge, straight into its masters open arms, as it had done so many times before in life and licked and licked his face, so very pleased that they had not forgotten her.

Crystal and her little friend stood there totally and utterly amazed that a dog, such a big dog, could ever be so friendly and soft and cuddly. All they had ever seen before were hunting dogs and they were always cruel, but she was so beautiful and just as big, and oh, how she was enjoying her cuddle with her master.

Then it was Aurora's turn to have her face licked, as it, in her mind, said thank you to her. Aurora looked at the dog totally amazed and she said to them 'She has just said thank you to me, I read her mind, she said thank you.'

'Seriously?'

'Yes, seriously. Doesn't that just beat everything? WOW! What a miracle and its own bridge to get here. Oh thank you, thank you, whoever or whatever miracle allowed this to happen for us.'

To that, Daniel now appeared unto them saying, 'Let me explain how she got here. She has watched over you since you all arrived, but as you had not called her or thought of her, she did not come. She began to think that you had forgotten her, as many other dog owners do. She and I are also good friends, as she remembers me from when you were all still on Earth. She saw me then with you, as all animals can see us, but they know the difference. I have watched her here, knowing you would soon be with her again. I told her, but as so many others get forgotten, she was not certain I was telling her the truth.'

'But you Daniel, you cannot do anything else but tell the truth, can you?'

'No, but sadly, she does not understand that.'

'So many things have happened since we all got together again, it's just taking time for everything to sink in.'

'I know that, Aurora, but she unfortunately, again, did not understand. She tried to send out thoughts to you both, and you Aurora, as you are the most sensitive of all of you at present, you started unwittingly to pick them up.'

'So why could we not go on the bridge to find her? That is what that is, yes?'

'Yes, you are quite correct. That is a bridge, but a bridge with a major difference, you see only animals can use it. They can come over that bridge and they also use it to return to their own place. Let me tell you about souls. You all on Earth have, what you know as a soul. That is, the energy in and around you. When you come back here to this place, it is your soul that returns here. You have no need now for your material body, so like an old coat, you have cast it off.

Now an animal has what is known as a *collective soul,* so they all go to the place that is for them and their particular species. That said, for your dog, and all dogs that are human pets, it is slightly different, as they can develop a *partial soul,* shall we say, that's the easiest way to explain it. This means that when you think of them, as you have now done, they can sense it and this is the result, here you are together and as you can see she is absolutely delighted to see you.'

'Can she stay with us all now please, Mummy, Daddy? Oh! PLEASE?'

'Oh yes, as long as you want her here she will stay with you. When you go to your special meetings or things like that, she will go back to her group, but when you want her, she will come wherever you are. She will always use the bridge that will take her right back to her own area.'

'Why are we not allowed to cross over the bridge?'

'Ah, now that is a long story, but suffice to say, to cross that bridge you would never, ever find what you are looking for. Basically, because you are not high enough in knowledge to do that. That does not mean that you would never be able to go over that bridge, because some time in the future that may be possible, but only as you *learn and understand* more.'

'Thank you Daniel, thank you. You are very special and I do appreciate what you are doing for me, for us.'

'Go on now, all of you and enjoy your walk, see you soon.'

So now, complete with their very excited and very affectionate dog, they ambled along the path, enjoying the walk. Aurora's thoughts as they walked, were of wonderment, as to what would happen to them now and what else they would see. As they walked, a new sound started to enter their senses. Aurora voiced their collective thoughts. 'That sounds like water, but surely that can't be, can it?'

As they walked, they began to see what looked like a shining blue path, coming up on one side, so they hurried on to see what it was.

'Look, Mummy, look, it's full of fishes. Lots and lots of pretty colourful fishes, all swimming about in the shiny water.'

They all looked at this new sight, this amazing little river that was now flowing past them, and true enough it was what looked like water, except it looked as if somebody had polished this water, it was so clear and bright with a beautiful blue glow in it. It was as clear as clear can be. They could see all the stones at the bottom, all shining bright like mirrors. Never had they seen anything like this before, the sea water they had seen, in life, looked dull in comparison to this sight. Strangely, their dog made no attempt whatsoever to go in the water, which they did indeed find very strange, as before, when they were on Earth, they could never keep her out of it.

'I wonder why she will not go in the water, Aurora, she used to love to play in it, any puddle, even the sea.'

'Perhaps it is another wonder of this magical place, because the more I see, the more magical and simply amazing it all becomes.'

Our little foursome, together with their dog, walked on, feeling so very relaxed and happy. Further along the side of the little river, they saw another interesting site appear. A tall waterfall, coming down what appeared to them to be a cliff face that had suddenly come into view on the other side of the river. The waterfall was quite wide and the water seemed to be gently falling from this tall cliff face, making very little spray or splash. The fish seemed to be playing in this new water that fell on them, as if it was a fun place for them, some of them jumping in and out as if they were frolicking in the water. They all just stood there for a while watching, fascinated. They walked on further, as the cliff face now slowly dropped down to more of a meadow land on the other side, yet still gleaming as everywhere did.

'Look Mummy, look Mummy. See over there by that tree, what is it?'

Aurora and her man looked over the water to see what all the fuss was about. The little girl was so amazed that she could enjoy being out with people who, strangely to her, never shouted at her, but instead, they made her feel welcome and included in everything they did. These feelings were so very strange to her, after her life that she had had with her parents and other adults that had treated her so cruelly. Why could her life not have had some of this love in it? That is what she felt from these people, love and kindness, a very strange, yet, comforting feeling for her.

'It's a baby fawn and look, there is its mother. Oh, there's more over there, look, lots more.' Said their little friend to Crystal.

'This truly is a magical place, so peaceful and so amazing. How did we get to be so lucky to be allowed to come here to see this place?'

'Aurora, I think you will find that everybody, yes, everybody whose life on Earth is over, gets to come here, but sadly, some take a little longer to realise exactly where they are.'

'Like me, when I was totally lost in that tunnel and did not know what to do or where I was or even how I got there.'

'Yes that's right, you need to talk to Daniel about that, then you will understand it more.'

So again, our four friends started to walk further along the riverside, which appeared now to be curving around the cliff face; the dog running and playing with the girls, who were totally at ease with her. Suddenly, Crystal stopped and looked seriously over to the other side.

'What are you looking at, Crystal? What has got your attention now, my darling?'

'Look, Mummy, look. Can't you see? Look at the stream and the water, see where it's going, it's funny.'

'I can't see anythi - oh! Yes I do see what you think is so funny. Weird. Water can't do that, it's impossible, it just can't do...that, yet it is... I can see for myself. But how is that possible?'

'What is it, Aurora? What are you looking at that is so strange?'

'Look, my love, look over there at the river. See what it is doing. Now tell me how that is possible, because if I did not see it with my own eyes I would say... I don't know what I would say. How on Earth is that possible?'

'I see the water. OH GOD! It's going uphill. UPHILL! That's not possible is it? Now I know why you said "How on Earth", but of course we are not on Earth are we? So I suppose, as we are learning, anything here is possible.'

'It appears that all things are definitely possible, look at the fish playing in it, as they jump in and out. It's so funny, it makes me laugh. It may look like water but it certainly does not act as if it were just water.' So for a little while they just watched, fascinated at what they saw.

Daniel appeared to them again and said, 'This is a four dimensional world, whereas on Earth you only ever see a three dimensional world. So things here are very different for you, so enjoy what you see. Anything else, just ask, I am here.'

Our foursome again carried on walking, looking and being amazed at each different sight, as it appeared before their eyes.

'I'd like to go back to our home now Mummy. Please, can we?'

'Let's all join hands and return as one shall we? All in agreement, say yes.'

'YES!'

In the blink of an eye, they all found themselves back in Aurora's house, just exactly as they had left it.

'What do you want to do, little one?'

'Can I stay with you, please?'

'You can, if that's what you really want to do. Just send a thought back to whoever would be expecting you and tell them you are with us.'

'Thank you. I will. It is so much nicer here, more loving and peaceful, I have never felt so much happiness and love between people before. It truly is a very wonderful feeling, a very happy feeling. I just did not understand what Crystal had tried to tell me when I first came with the angels here. I just wonder what will happen to me now?'

'Oh! Little one, please do not be sad. Just know that you are truly loved by all here, not just in this house, but by all in this wonderful place.'

'I think I know that I am now. It's just so strange, it's something I have never really known and I know there are sadly many others like me. I have met with many of them when I was with the lady I stay with and we all talk. There are so very many, other little children who know, and have known, only fear and pain and hunger, just as I did, and yet, I see you and your family and I see how it should have been, and how it should be for everyone. Aurora where and how did you learn to love others like that?'

'That is the way I am, my darling. My mother taught me and gave me great *love* from the day I was born, and she showed me love every day till the day she died. I am also pleased to say *that love* is still with me here, even now, as every time I see her here, she tells me.'

'She must be, like you, a very special lady to have so much *love* in her heart. I have never felt so much peace as I do when I am with you. It worries me what will happen to me, I cannot ever go back to my parents. I know that, even now, they are not in the same place as I am. I am told that so far, they have shown no signs of understanding and until that happens, they will not be trusted with anything. What will happen to me Aurora? What will happen to me, as I never knew any other members of my family and so I do not trust them to be any different?'

'Nothing bad, I promise you that. Nothing bad *I assure you* will ever happen to you again, not as long as I have anything to do with it. You will always have a safe haven here with us, whenever you want to be with us, you can. We will always have room here for you and also in our hearts, you don't need to ask, just come, little one, *just come*.'

For a while they were all in the same place and the little girl felt a peace in her heart that she had never known before.

'Crystal, Crystal, I'm getting a thought in my head, can... you... can you take me now to meet my angel... please? I think she is calling me, as I think that is the message I am getting in my head and it keeps repeating itself over and over.'

So as the girls, with Rebecca, who now visibly joined them, went off to meet with the other angel, Aurora and her man settled down for a while in total peace. Each with their own thoughts and memories, as they now tried to put together everything that they had recently been through and indeed, had seen since they got here in this magical place that is called Heaven. They had now got used to speaking to each other *mind to mind*, a concept that had never entered their minds before, although Aurora knew her mother could do that, when she was still on Earth. They also told each other all about what had happened when, they too, had gone to meet with their respective angels. Aurora also told her man about what she had been shown when she saw the complete hall filled with people.

At first he could hardly believe her, but then he knew she would not, and could not, make that up. So instead, he cuddled her close and as with all couples who love each other, as these two do, one thing leads to another, as it always had with these two people, their love for each other so very strong. As they now learned about the differences in their own bodies, that are now pure energy, Aurora also learned exactly what Daniel had tried to explain to her about the chakras and how they work together.

As their spiritual bodies now came together for this first time, they saw their chakras all link together, and as the base ones slowly found each other and then linked together, they began to feel and experience sensations and pleasure in a way never experienced before. Great *love* now filled the area with a tremendous white light, a power that made them feel as if they were not two beings, but one, in this wonderful amazing sensation that enveloped them both. They now lay together, in a feeling of peace and tranquillity they had never before felt.

As they lay in perfect harmony together, enjoying each other's company, suddenly he stirred, saying sadly, that he was now being requested to go to the Golden Temple, but she was not to worry, as he would soon be back with her.

Aurora was now on her own and with her own thoughts and memories. Very happy memories of a different time, a time before Crystal had been born and they had the time to learn and just enjoy each other in every way. Beautiful memories, as their *love* for each other had just grown and grown. Then, for some reason, she now started to think about how it had been at night back by the pyramid. As she thought about it, she found herself now outside, looking out at what was now a very clear night sky. A sky just as it had nearly always been back on Earth, in fact she thought she was back on Earth.

As she looked at the stars, she felt she could, if she wanted, just pluck one out of the sky, they were so clear and bright. Strangely, the moon was also now there, looking so big and bright. Her thoughts briefly were 'I never expected to ever see this sight again, it's so beautiful. All that's missing is the pyramid and its wonderful crystal on the top, that always shone like a beacon at night.'

No sooner had she said that to herself, than there it was, that amazing pyramid with that fantastic crystal that topped it, shining like a beacon. The whole pyramid now gleaming, as it always had on a clear moonlit night. 'I don't know how this is all possible, but it is so perfect, so clear so... but of course, it is what *I am thinking,* that is why I am seeing this. Oh! How wonderful is this? How wonderful this really is, magic is not a good enough word to describe it.'

Now a new feeling entered her thought senses. I've felt this feeling before, she thought to herself, usually just before the big circular ship arrived, that special ship with my special friend. She scanned the sky, but it was not there, why should she be feeling this now? She could not see it, yet she could *sense* him. How? Why HIM, Why NOW, after how I have just been with my very special man, who I truly love? I need protection, somebody is playing with me. Yet still she felt his presence.

'Listen Aurora, hold still please, do not be troubled, I can read your mind, it's me. I'm so sorry I can't be with you, as I am not allowed to come to you where you are now, but you know when you think of me, we can always speak.'

'Is that who I think it is? Yes, it is you my friend, my special friend, my other father, isn't it?'

'Yes, Aurora. You already know we can talk. Look at the moon, you will see my face as I project it to there for you.'

'I can see you clearly in my mind now, will we ever meet again as we did before?'

'I cannot tell you the answer to that, my dear, ask Daniel, he may be able to tell you, as I am not privy to that information.'

'Do you not travel anywhere now?'

'Do you remember me telling you, we also had one other planet that we would sometimes go to?'

'Yes.'

'We are about to go there now, but you will still be able to talk to me like this if you want to, wherever I am.'

'I do want to, please, I do like to talk with you. I know that I miss you, you were so kind to me, always so kind and affectionate, I do miss that.'

'Thank you Aurora, think of me as I will think of you, as I travel.'

'Are you going now? I do not want to leave you again or to lose you my special friend.'

'Remember Aurora, we are always able to make contact *mind to mind* wherever either of us are, so in that respect I will never leave you. You now know you can always make contact like this wherever we are, so yes, in that sense, I will never ever leave you. I must go now as others are waiting for me. Speak again soon. I love you, my lovely girl, you are my special princess and you will always have a very special place in my heart.'

'You have never told me that before. Take my love for you with you. You are, and always have been, very special to me. You gave me a reason to live, a reason for just being, always remember that, you are special.'

The connection and that very special feeling, slowly dissipated, but Aurora was certain that they would, one day, see each other again. At least she knew now, for certain, that she could still speak to him from anywhere now. A peace and a *love* settled on her as never before, so very different to any other *love* she had ever known. She thought, I am learning that *love* comes in many ways, I did not know nor understand that before, yet now I know why he came to me then. He knew, he felt my *love* and my happiness that was within me and for no other reason.

What now, she thought, as she went back into her house, what's now in store for me? No sooner had she settled down in the house again to think, when Daniel appeared before her, saying 'I need to talk with you, Aurora.'

'Yes, what about Daniel?'

'Since you returned home here, apart from when you first arrived, you have not had an opportunity to meet with all your family, your soul group, and that is important. Yes, it is very important that you get to know more about them, before you start the studies that those of a higher standing wish you to have.'

'When do they, my family that is, wish me to go and see them?'

'Why don't we go now, Aurora? They are expecting you and they are quite excited that you are going to see them.'

'They know I am coming already?'

'Of course they do. You should be aware by now that these things are instant, it is all in the thought, you already know that is how everything happens here. Simply by the power of your thought, just as what you just did was, you just need to truly accept, that is how everything is here.'

'In some ways, I am still trying to get used to the idea that everything is as quick as that. It's such a vastly different way of life.'

'Here, take my hand and we will go. I know all this is coming as a bit of a surprise to you, yet, deep inside you, you are fully aware of all this and so much more. Just as we actually do not speak with a voice, as everything is impressed on you, *mind to mind*.'

Before Aurora had a chance to reply, they were already there. In her mother's house, known as her soul group's meeting place, where a large gathering of people were waiting for her and all anxious now to speak with her.

'Ah! Good, my darling girl, you have come at last to see us all, this is so important, so very important. Thank you, Daniel, for bringing her to us.'

'I will leave her here with you all, I will know when you are done and I will appear for the next item.' With that, he was gone from view, leaving Aurora wondering what all this was about, especially what the *next item* he had just mentioned was all about and was it from, or with, Daniel?

'Aurora, my dear. Welcome to my home, this is the regular meeting place for all our soul group.'

'What do you mean by "this is our regular meeting place"? This is your home isn't it?'

'Let me explain it, so that you will be able to understand what this meeting is all about. Firstly, yes this is my home, but you know, here in spirit we do not really need a home as such. Well, certainly not like we did on Earth, but most of us do have our own, what we call home. These are places where we can, if we want, or need to be, in our own space for a while. Of course your father and I enjoy our own togetherness here on many occasions, for obvious reasons.

For you it will be where you and your man get together for the same reasons, and of course, with your daughter, should you wish her to be with you in your own family time. You can all then have your own time in your own space as it were, although time is a *misnomer*, there is no such thing as time here.

I would like you also to know, that *you* are part of a soul group. This soul group, that we here, are all part of. Not all are here, because there are some people who are currently working, studying or doing other things, such as still being on a life's experience on Earth.

There are a great many soul groups, more than I know in numbers, but most soul groups usually always stay together and work together. If and when, well, not actually if, you plan your next trip to Earth, we will all meet here many times as you plan it, so that we can all work together to ensure that each one of us who has to, plays their part. Just as you will learn to play your part, in the lives we choose to experience.'

'You make it sound as if we were discussing a play for the arena.'

'That's a wonderful way to put it.'

'So what do we do, now that I am here with you?'

'We will talk, as everybody here wishes to have their own time with you, get to know you again and how you and they have benefited from the life experience that you have just completed. Those who had a part, and there are many, no matter how small it was, in your last experience they will want to know how that played out for you, did you actually achieve all you set out to do, or not, as the case may be.

'I know you will have reviewed your own life, as that is virtually the first thing you do before you actually said yes to staying here. As you know, you would have said no to staying here, if you had not completed what you set out to do.'

'What about my daughter Crystal, where does she fit in with all this?'

'All in good time, my dear, all in good time. Meanwhile, there is a physician who wishes to talk with you about your birth and subsequently Crystal's birth. Here, let me introduce you, although I am very sure that you will remember him.'

'Ah! Yes, I do recognise you, yes, yes, I do remember you, from when I had Crystal and how you helped me during that traumatic time. I wondered if you... were you with Crystal when everything happened?'

'I was, together with another specialist who was treating her, and I was also present at your birth, Aurora, when you also gave your mother a very tough time, as you struggled to enter the world. You had been so very restless, yes you were in a hurry to get out, so much that you got all entangled in your cord. It was around your neck and around an arm, you gave us all quite a fright, we thought we were going to lose you, but you proved to be a fighter even then.

It would also appear, from what I know of you, that fighter is the operative word, as your life has not been an easy one for you. It may please you to know, that as I was with Crystal when the earthquake struck the pyramid, I did all I could for her. I knew her father would be frantic, we talked when he first came over and I was able to console him.'

'Thank you for that, I know I was more than frantic as I watched the pyramid just disappear into the ground. I could not believe my eyes that such a thing could ever happen.'

'It must give you great pleasure to see your daughter now, she runs about everywhere, she is never still. She tells me she has been back to the pyramid, what a brave little girl she really is, and yes, there she showed her true strength.'

'Yes, she went back with Rebecca, her angel friend, to bring a little friend of hers, who was too frightened to leave the ruins. Crystal, childlike, thought it was great fun. I will not tell you my first thoughts on that trip, before she went.'

'So, what are your own thoughts, now that you are all safely here in this place of wonderment, what have you been doing?'

Aurora and the physician talked for ages, about every subject common to them both and as they finished, Aurora moved through the rest of the people who were desperate to talk with her about all her experiences, especially where each of them were involved, as they each shared their memories.

She had now, after talking to everyone else, including Grace, her *spirit guide*, been talking to her mum for a short period, when she felt a gentle tap on her shoulder and turning round was surprised to see Daniel behind her. 'Oh! I was not expecting you yet, why are you here Daniel? What is wrong, is Crystal OK?'

'Relax, Aurora. It's just time we moved on to your next visit and I need to talk with you seriously about this next one.'

'Why? What is wrong? Why do you need to talk seriously to me? What have I done or what is it that I have to do now? You are worrying me Daniel, what is it please?'

True Love Never Dies

Daniel's Surprise for Aurora

'Come Aurora, come walk with me and please, just relax. Always, please just know, that there is nothing from me you need ever fear. I could not ever harm you in any way, so when I say we have something to do, be positive about it, do not fear it. Now I have a story to tell you, a very special story that will surprise you. Let us now walk slowly to the Healing Halls as we talk. I do know you have been there before, but last time you did not walk, you simply went by Crystal's thought for you. I know you will enjoy the amazing walk through these magical gardens that we are now about to enter.'

So they slowly wandered forward, towards the magnificent gardens that appeared before them and stopped by the amazing big wrought iron style gate, at least that was what it looked like to Aurora, who now stood there before them. It appeared that all around this area was a fantastic red brick type wall. The brick had a mellowed appearance to it, in that wonderful rose pink colour that old brick takes on, giving it a life of its own.

This was the first time she had ever seen a red brick wall ever, it was just so very unusual in its design, where did that design come from she wondered. But wait, how did I know it was 'brick'? This is a word I have never, ever heard before; and a 'wrought iron style gate'. Where did these words spring from? I know that we could have a pink wall, because I have seen them mix blood with the lime wash they use, but what I have just thought about, these words, these things, gates I thought. How do I know these things that I have not seen nor heard before?

Daniel now turned the big round handle, that looked like a big church door handle, and slowly opened the massive gate and closed it gently behind them. As he gently closed the gate, suddenly before her, all the flowers, the trees and the bushes that they had seen as they entered from outside, they all now magically blossomed together. A show that could not possibly happen anywhere else. It was as if all the seasons were all at the same time and the colours were as you could not imagine the beauty of. Aurora just stood with a look of total amazement on her face, at such a wondrous sight that had now appeared before her eyes.

Never before had she seen, many of the flowers that had somehow magically appeared before her. In her life on Earth, although she had heard of some, she could not remember ever having seen such an incredible sight as this. As she watched, totally amazed, some of the trees now started to bear fruit, fruit of all colours. Now she could hear the tinkle of a waterfall and turning around, she saw before her a beautiful, angelic water fountain.

The fountain was so tall it looked as if it stretched to Heaven, even though she knew she was already in Heaven. The angelic cherubs, just like little toddlers, but with small wings, all stood there. Each had their own stepping stone, as they went higher and higher, all with water pouring from each one of them into the fountain, such a truly magnificent sight. The water again, as had been the river, so clear and shiny blue, as if it was polished.

As she looked closer, she could see, what at first she thought was a form of net all over the ground. Then she realised it was not a net, it was a tiny strand of water from the fountain, going to each and every plant. Be it a flower, a bush or a tree, they each had a tiny strand giving it life, you could say refreshing it, as it were. Then she noticed that they were not alone here in these gardens. Others were walking around and as they walked they trod on the water, yet their feet did not get wet nor did they leave a single foot print. They made not a single mark anywhere.

'Come Aurora, please. We must walk and talk, as we go to that large, pink alabaster building over there. That building is the Healing Halls which you were in before, although I know from here you do not recognise them as such.'

'What is it you wish to talk to me about, Daniel?'

'It is very important first, that I get you to maximise the healing colours over you as, where we are going after that, you MUST be fully protected in every way. You will find, as we go through this place, as you enter each section you pass through, the colours will change. The first colour you will meet will be aqua, to bring you peace and calm. You must not rush this, or indeed any of the colours, make sure you get your full measure every time you enter a new colour.

'You will know when you have had enough, from the feeling you get from each different colour. The second one is the blue spectrum, beginning with azure for protection and then into the more blue spectrum. You will also go through a beautiful rose pink colour that will build your feelings of *love,* because I know that you will wish to show great love. You will also benefit from a very rich plum colour, which will help you overcome the challenge you will face when you first arrive at our destination.

'When you complete the trip through all the colours, you will round off with the full rainbow spectrum, such as you have never seen before. I must also tell you, that I shall be with you every step of the way in this task that you are shortly to embark on. My wings, they will always be around you. With these wings, I can and will, shield you. But I need your total assurance, your promise in fact. I must stress upon you, that whatever happens and whatever you do, please, when we get to where we are going, you must stay inside my wings, until you truly understand and I tell you it is safe to leave. So please, I need you to fully trust me and to promise me now, that you will do these things I ask, with no questions until we get there. Will you please promise me and trust me fully? It is very, very important for us both that you trust me.'

'I will do as you ask, Daniel, although I do now feel a little afraid of this task that is ahead of me. But I know within myself that I can trust you implicitly.'

'Do not be, nor ever show you are, afraid, Aurora, that is important. Just please, trust me to keep you totally safe until you understand and I tell you it is safe to leave my wings. Now, come with me up these steps. Here, hold my hand, I will help you and I know when you leave this place, this Healing Hall of Colours, you will feel so vastly different.'

As she took each step they climbed, Aurora felt a little lighter from all feelings of apprehension that she had felt just a moment ago, as she had listened to Daniel and all he had to say to her. As they now arrived at the top, this magnificent pink building spread out before them, the amazing stained glass doors, which also shone with many colours, now opened to let them enter.

It was a massive, beautiful, round building from this side that they now entered, with crystals and artefacts of all colours, shapes and sizes before them, and lots of what appeared to be like beautiful stained glass pillars. As the light simply poured in through the massive clear domed circular top, the colours that emanated throughout this building were truly amazing.

Now she knew she was in a truly magical building and knew from all the feelings inside and all around her, that without a shadow of doubt, everything that happened in here was good, simply all *good*. Then suddenly, she also realised that she could hear music, a wonderful tone of beautiful peaceful music and it too, gave her strength. She could feel the strength from the music enter her. Never had she known such peace inside her, it was as if every part of her was glowing bright and clear.

Daniel now spoke to her, *mind to mind* as always, saying to her, 'Come with me please, hold my hand. As I explained to you, there is a way we must go through these colours together, so that you are fully able to maximise their benefit to totally refresh you. We will then seal each of these colours around you, so as to ensure you have complete and total protection. You must now also ensure that whatever you do, or wherever you go, both now and always, you have put the very necessary protection always in place.'

'But why is it so... necessary.'

'Patience, Aurora, all will become clear very soon. Please, just do as I ask of you, I assure you, you will be fully aware of everything when the time is right and you will understand it better.'

They slowly went through all of the colour spectrum, including many colours that she never knew even existed, and each colour seemed to have an effect on her that she could feel. She could not explain these feelings, she just knew that every single one of these colours had an amazing effect on her and they also cleared her thoughts to one of pure simple *love*. She felt all this love emanate from her.

Now she also saw where the wonderful music was coming from. Before her eyes this magnificent orchestra was now sitting in front of her and all these people, or were they angels? She could not define them clearly. All with instruments of all shapes and sizes and types, and she knew these people were very special, for although they had no wings, they did have that very same angelic look about them that Daniel had.

Some appeared to be male and some were very definitely and clearly female, yet this glow that shone from them, she could not define. How do you, can you, she thought, get all these people together like this? There were so many she could not count them, and to play with a sound that was so utterly amazing, so totally enchanting.

Gently the sound now changed as they played, with a new resounding effect on her, every part of her seemed to tingle as if she, herself, were a part of that wonderful music. Then slowly it changed back and she became more serene and at peace again. The sight and sounds from this building, she found almost impossible to describe, this had to be the most unique building ever, anywhere.

Aurora's thoughts were now trying to relay everything that had happened to her and the wonderful incredible things she had seen and heard since she had arrived at this place they call 'Heaven'. There was so much in, what to her was, such a short space of time, *but was it?* Time, she now knew, no longer existed here, but she could not put her thoughts any other way. She never thought that a building could ever have such a dramatic effect on her, or indeed anybody, yet she could feel and see the effect it was having on her, as her own colours glowed.

She felt now that she could do anything. Never had she felt the strength, the courage, the *love* and the peace she now felt, all at the same time, and still the colours played on her, as the music gently slowed now, like a lullaby. She could picture in her mind, herself, as she had been with her daughter, her beautiful Crystal as a baby, as she had many times in her young life, cradled her in her arms to help her sleep.

'I can see you are now fully strengthened and ready for the next part of the surprise I have for you. Come, let us leave this place, take my hand.'

'Must we hurry? It is so very peaceful here, I would like to enjoy it a little longer, if I may, please?'

'Yes, you can stay as long as you feel the need, but I know you will be very pleasantly surprised, if not a little shocked, at what I have to show you when we journey on to our next stop.'

So Aurora stayed just a little while longer in the atmosphere that was this amazing place, except now, her thoughts were on what Daniel had just said to her. To her surprise, a reply came into her head saying 'You will never guess, you are not aware of all the facts yet.'

Aurora then sent a thought back saying 'When do I have to go to see the *higher spirits* that you told me about?'

'All in good time, my dear. They did consider calling you in first, but then they just thought it would be better for all those concerned, not least yourself, when you actually know what you are about to do, if you did what I have been asked to do with you first.'

'This gets more mysterious every time you speak about it. I suppose we had better get going then. So, Daniel, where exactly are you taking me?'

'Let us do what I first suggested and walk there, this way I can still talk to you and it will be so much easier for you to understand what you are about to see and hear.'

'Ok Daniel, take my hand please, so that we stay together and I'll let you begin.'

'We are, Aurora, about to meet somebody on what we in spirit call *a different level* to you, but it is important that you meet him and we believe, no sorry that is wrong, *they* believe you could, no, *can* help him.'

'What do you mean by *a different level*? Are we going to a big building where we have to climb a lot of steps, because surely here that would not be necessary?'

'Let me please, first explain what I mean about levels. First of all, when we talk about levels here, we do not mean floor levels, together with loads of pointless steps. We are simply talking about *levels of learning* and *levels of understanding,* and that aspect covers many levels. You will be surprised to know that you are actually now on a much higher level than most, when they at first return here.

'When you first returned here, by the very nature of the way you returned and your understanding when you met your family, especially your daughter, you did not ever question anything, you simply accepted things as they were. You knew *within* your very being, that this is the way it is. For you, your daughter was foremost in your mind, and when you saw that she was now perfect and also very happy, you slipped into the level that you are now. Had that not been the case, and if that had not been realised when you first arrived, things for you would have not been the same, as you met with your family. So, in that respect, your daughter was an enormous help to you.

'She, being of a much younger age, accepted things as they were when she first got here. Of course Rebecca was, as she always had been, with her constantly and they were still at a level of togetherness, because you had not rejected that friendship when she had told you about her angel friend. That was also another feather in your cap, so to speak. Her little friend though, because of her mother's attitude and her father's cruelty, had long since rejected her angel. That was part of the reason why she would not accept her situation and come with the lady that was sent to help her.

'The *higher spirits* thought, that if they sent Crystal, through the *love* that she had received from you, she would make it easier for her friend, as indeed she did. So, you see now why your daughter is thought so highly of. You are not aware, but she is currently trying to help a little boy from another country who, again through fear, will not come. I already know she is winning him round, as after several Earth days she has got him to come out of where he was trying to hide. He is totally unaware that he is actually now, no longer of Earth. We know she will bring him home safely and she will be back before you. I will tell you when she has returned.

'Now to get back to what I was trying to tell you. I want you to also know, that when you were in these great Halls of Colour, you were not only receiving healing, you were also receiving *instruction. Instruction and learning* that was being impressed on your mind, before you meet somebody that I do know is actually very special to you. Although as yet, you do not know, or rather you do not remember, that he exists. However, he still knows deep in his mind that you exist, but you need to *re-awaken* this knowledge within him. This person, this man that you are about to meet, is actually *your brother.*'

'My...brother? But... I do not have...a... brother. I...was an only child...was I not?'

'So you have always been led to believe, Aurora, you were never told the truth. Unfortunately, your brother was stolen from your family when you were barely one summer old. Your mother managed to hide you, as a band of men from another country came. They took him for their king, and they would have taken you also, if they had found you. I ensured that they could not see you, although one of them actually stood right beside you. My wings do make good protection when they are needed. They took your brother to make him a gladiator. That was something we could not stop, as that was an agreement he had made before he was born. You will learn more about that later, as you learn about life planning.

'He has been very cruelly treated since he was taken and was taught to be a very strong fighter in the arena, where he had to fight not only men, but tigers and other big cats. He has won many fights and was very brave in the ring. On the day he died, he had won two fights already, killing four others. Two men, he could always deal with easily, but the King, he wanted him to fight a group of four men in the arena.

'It had never been done successfully in the arena before, the record was still three to one and had never been beaten. He managed to kill two with his speed and skill and was in the process of seriously wounding the third, who would have killed him, when the fourth one, cowardly, came behind him with a ball and chain. He was not quite fast enough and it hit him fatally.

'They then set the tigers on that man, as that was not supposed to happen. A true gladiator *never* came from behind and your brother would have killed all four, had he come from the front. However, it was his time, and so now, the coward thought he had won his freedom by killing him. The crowd bade for his death, saying "death to the coward" and they released the tigers. They now made his death slow and painful, as the crowd intended.

'Your brother, because it had been totally instilled in him that there would never be an end to his fighting, still believes he is in the arena and his *thoughts* are what is keeping that situation going for him. He keeps on playing the last fight, time and time again, and in Earth time, he has been doing this for twelve summers now. No matter how hard others have tried to get into his thoughts, they have not succeeded.

'So you see, from this Aurora, there is no soul ever that cannot be saved. It just sometimes takes a little longer, depending on how they were indoctrinated as a child. His total beliefs that were instilled in him were, that death simply did not exist for him and that he would have to fight till the end of time.'

'Now I know what it was that I saw when I did my life review and did not understand. It was such a quick passage as I reviewed that part, but now it makes sense to me what I saw. It was, very briefly, my brother that I saw.'

'Yes, that is who you saw, but it was purposefully cut short because of this visit that was, even then, planned for you.'

'So where, if this was all planned, please tell me, where exactly do I come in to this equation, Daniel? How can I possibly help him?'

'They know that somewhere in the back of his mind he will still remember you. He fussed over you and really looked after you when you were such a young child. You were a perfect pair of siblings, despite how young you both were then. He also knew you were not strong and he would not tell the soldiers that you were there, he kept very quiet and did not, would not, ever give your hiding place away to them.

'Those of a higher understanding never give up on any soul. They believe, that if anybody can get through to him and his soul, *you* can, and bring him out and back into the fold again. Your mother does not know he is here and because of his state of mind and his indoctrination, he cannot hear her calling him, as she tries so hard to find him. She has searched the Earth long and hard, as she is not even aware yet that he is dead to Earth.'

'I'm so sad for my mum, but I understand.'

'I knew you would be when you knew and understood what had happened, all that long time ago.'

'Tell me honestly, Daniel. Do you believe that I can do it? That I can go in there for him, bring him out and back to us again?'

'I know you can, and I would never have agreed with those who seek your help if I did not think that you were able, and more than that, also very capable of winning him over. I have seen how strong you can be despite everything. Yes, despite everything that has been thrown at you in your life just lived, you always fought through and won. Oh yes, you are strong. Yes, you can do it if you want to, but do not do it for that reason. Do it only if you *feel inside* that you can.'

'From what you have said, he saved me once, the very least I could ever do for him, is this. For he is who *I know* to be my brother, and I know you will help me achieve what must now be done, not for me but for him.'

'Let me take you to him, but on the way I wish to show you others. Others who are caught up in similar positions, in as much as, because of the life they lived, they also cannot believe that there is any form of life after death, or that they will continue doing what they are doing, until the end of time on planet Earth. There are many, many sad souls like this. It is sad how, since the terrible change that took over the people of Earth, they have been lied to in so many ways and told so many untruths about what life should really be like. All so that they can be controlled by their evil masters or rulers. It is also sad for me to say this, but it will be many thousands of years before it turns back, but it will. Yes, it will turn back.'

Aurora and Daniel arrived at this area and Aurora saw for herself, the numbers and types of people from all walks of life. Both male and female, from the very highest to the very lowest forms of human life, who were by their thoughts, and by their beliefs, all trapped this way, because of all the untruths they were told. She also now met some of the helpers, souls from her own spirit level and above, who were trying to help these poor souls. She also learned from many who had been helped, including one who had once been trapped in a similar way to her brother and was now trying hard to help others. Sadly he didn't have the skill needed to help her brother from the arena point of view, and of course Aurora would not be approaching it from that aspect.

His task currently was indeed a very hard one, as he well knew. What had happened to him, was exactly what he was now trying to help these others to escape, or should I say, be released from. The man he was currently trying to help, had been like this, in Earth terms, for about ten years. He had been told by the people who had enslaved him, that he must do exactly as they told him and never to be afraid of death, because he would never die. Instead of death, he would receive seventy beautiful virgins, all for himself and of his choosing, as a way of thanks for being a faithful servant and fighter. He had died in a fight, as his keeper knew he would, a man feared by many, who was getting him into fights constantly.

This man, as she now saw, did indeed, through his mind only, have seventy virgins all lined up for himself. Except, he never actually got close enough to touch them, because they were all figments of his imagination from his indoctrination, and they simply did not exist. When they finally get through to him, as they will, no matter how long it takes, they will simply all just disappear from view.

Aurora was now told by Daniel, this was something that happened to many men, as it was used to lever them to do as they were told. 'I could show you over a thousand men who are in exactly the same way as this man was,' he said, 'and sadly it will be this way for many men for a long, long time to come. Let me show you another situation that may surprise you, but again happens often. Look at this man, he was a KING and yet look at him now.

'His life was full of greed, he always had to have everything and as far as he was concerned, everything was his. He ensured that none of his followers ever had anything, they had to give it all to him, or die. Now look at him. He is dead to Earth but does not know it, and he cannot understand why all these people he sees before him, his subjects, have it all and he cannot get hold of anything. They just will not give it to him. Greed still controls his thought pattern. They are at last just beginning to see a small glimmer of change in his thoughts, but he has been here for over fifty summers of Earth time now.'

Aurora could not believe that so many men, and also in some cases some women, could ever be so foolish as to believe all this that they were told, yet she knew it to be true and could see it all for herself.

Eventually they arrived at where her brother was, and as with all the others, she could see how he had made his own scene and where he was now. Not understanding in any way that he was dead to Earth, but that he still had to fight on and on and on, as he recreated his own scene, time and time again. They watched and studied him carefully, trying to get through and into his mind, but as Aurora said to Daniel, 'It's like he has built a solid wall in his thoughts.' Aurora tried everything that she could do to break through to him, time and time again, from all different angles as she studied him, but to no avail.

'Daniel, we have been trying this for so very long now and it is not working. I have lost count of the number of times he has gone over and over the same scene time and time again, you see, there it starts again. I feel the only way I can stop this, is that I am going to have to go into that arena *myself* and face him. I can think of no other way. I know in myself he cannot kill me, I also know and understand that he cannot hurt me in any way, no matter what he tries to do to me. True?'

'That is very true Aurora, but you must know beforehand, that he has had to kill other women in the ring, because the King *told him to*. Any woman ever found in the ring, yes, in the ring, has to die, this was his instruction. So Aurora, he will not think twice about *trying* to kill you and so, because of that, you will have to face full on as he swipes at you with his sword.'

'But he can't kill me, can he? If he swings his sword at me, even if it goes straight through me, it cannot harm me if I do not *allow* it. I can therefore, just keep on walking steadily forwards towards him, talking to him all the time, until I finally get through to him and I *will,* and I know you will be beside me at every step, apart from the fact that to him, he can never see you because to him you simply do not exist.'

'I can see you have been clearly watching him and giving this a lot of very deep thought, Aurora.'

'There is no other way. I must do that, and do it *now* or we will be here forever. The only thing I would ask of you is this. I know he will strike me with his sword. I know in myself he cannot hurt me. However, I want you to do a test strike on me, so that when he does strike at me, I am not taken by, or show any surprise, because I will already know what happens. Which should be nothing, so will you do that for me please?'

'Two things Aurora, I must first inform you about. The first, by the very nature of my existence, I cannot do that to you with a sword, it just cannot be. However, secondly, and much more important to you, is the protection that I can give you. Yes, I know he will attempt to strike you, because as you already know, he has previously killed women who have entered the arena. At all times my wings will be around you, although he will not see them. He will only see a bright golden light around you and that he will not understand. Whatever it is he does, or tries to do to you, if he does strike you, it will feel as if a feather is tickling you, so try not to laugh and you will be able to continue walking towards him.

'You may want to play him a bit, until he gets used to the idea that no matter what he tries to do, he cannot swipe you down. You must show no fear in any way to him, for that is the only way he can hurt you. If you *allow* him through your own fear. Talk to him anyway you wish or feel you can get to him, but please, show great patience and *love* in what you are doing, it is not a race. Remember, time here is irrelevant. Remember, it took Crystal three Earth days to get the little girl to move, it may take you a lot longer than that, as we have already been here the equivalent to twenty one sunrises on Earth.

'So do not allow your mind to think of time, as I have just told you, that from an Earth time point of view we have been here over twenty one days already. Here, time just does not exist, although I know, sometimes your mind still wanders a little. Think only of the job in hand, remember that time is totally irrelevant to your task. So now do you feel up to the task ahead of you, are you ready to enter the arena?'

'He is my brother. I know if he knew that, he would not wish to hurt me, so I know that I must be strong; strong for him as he was once strong for me. I know you are with me and I know what I have to do. I will not rush at him, but we must time my entry to the arena in such a way as there is no break in his actions. I do not want the cycle to begin again just as I enter the arena, so it must be just before he is struck, so that we can prevent that strike from happening and so stop the cycle.'

'Good, Aurora, good. I can see you have thought much about this, so let us now make a start and to do that, we must tune directly into his mind. I can do that easily as I have tuned in through his own angel who is here, although you, as yet, cannot see him so you will not get confused and I will help you there also.'

'Ah! Now I see his angel, although only very faintly, more as a light than as you are, but I cannot yet tune into my brother.'

'That is because he is using his energies trying to help your brother, and it will take some time before you are able to tune into your brother, as he is not receptive to your, nor anybody else's, thoughts yet. His mind set is solely on the fight, just as he was trained to do.'

'I know from what you have told me, he was called Saul by those who took him from us, but what name did my mother give to him please?'

'Clever. I can see how you are thinking clearly about this. This pleases me. I now know for certain you will be perfect at this task, you are giving great thought to what to do and how you do it, just do not rush it, please. Your mum called him Tirri. He may, or may not, remember that, but yes, try it once you have really got his attention. Now what do you see? Please tell me so I know if you are properly tuned in to all that happens for him.'

'I see the whole arena now filled with people...now I can even hear the cheering as each event happens.'

'Good, if you can hear all that, you are properly attuned. Now, wait until this series finishes and as soon as it starts up again, we will proceed with the plan.'

So they patiently waited and watched the events go through their cycle one more time. Then, as it all started again they prepared to enter the arena at exactly the correct point in the events. At the appointed action, Aurora found herself now facing her brother and the look on his face told her he, at first, could not understand what had happened. Then they both heard the King shout 'Death to the woman' and he moved forward to her and lifted his sword to strike her.

Now she knew for certain how much her brother had been indoctrinated and that his thought pattern was still reacting to exactly what he knew the King would say.

'Stop SAUL, stop! You cannot hurt me...ever, for I am your *sister*... your sister of long ago whose life you *protected and saved* when I was but a baby.'

He smote at her with his sword to strike her down, but she stood firm against him. To him the sword went straight through her and she said again 'You cannot kill me', except she shouted this time 'TIRRI, you cannot kill me for to Earth I am dead already.' Again he took a swipe at her, but although he saw the sword go right through her as before, she did not fall. She kept going forward to him, speaking gently now, calling him gently by both names, slowly at first, now only using the name his mother had given him.

Slowly they worked around the arena, again and again, as he kept on trying to take her down. Now she knew and understood why Daniel had insisted on a maximum healing session for her, as they now completed their sixth turn of the arena and started their seventh, but still she would not give in.

'STOP TIRRI, STOP! Talk to me please, do you not remember your little sister, who you so bravely protected? Think Tirri, think back, please. Put your sword down and come into my arms, please,' and for the first time, he faltered. Again he heard the King shout 'KILL HER. KILL HER', she too heard that, very clearly this time.

Perhaps she was now, at last, actually linking directly into his thought process, as again he started to try to smote her down and again, they went around the arena once, twice, three times now, since that first falter. Now the audience noise seemed to be getting fainter to him, and this woman in front of him, who would not lie down, now began to look more alive than ever to him. She kept coming forward, speaking to him all the time. What was she saying? He could barely make it out. Is she calling my name?

So tenderly she kept calling him. Reminding him who she was and who *he* really was, using his Tirri name, not Saul, trying so hard each time to remind him *who he really was.*

Again and again, she gently told him she was his little Aurora, his little sister, as she said again and again to him, she loved him. A word he had not heard for a long, long time. I... AM... YOUR... SIS... TER... AURORA. She now saw a change in his stance. Was she, could she, at last be getting slowly through the fog of his mind. He was starting to think, she thought at last.

140

She really was now, just about tapping into his mind. She could almost feel his mind now fighting hers, so she tried even harder, concentrating much more on him. TIRRI, TIRRI, listen to me, please? Now she had a new thought. If only the music I heard in the tunnel would, could, slowly replace the noise of the arena audience for him.

As she watched, she gently heard the music start, the same music she had heard. Her thought power was working much better for her now. Slowly, he started to crumple down on to his knees before her. The audience noise totally stopped and was replaced completely now by the soft gentle music and amazingly, she also saw that now, the audience was also starting to disappear, growing fainter and fainter. The arena was shrinking away. She watched him, as she very, very slowly moved forward, not ever taking her eyes off him or his eyes, trying to get clearly into his mind. To wipe away these pictures he had been holding onto in his mind of the arena, with the strength of all her *love* for her big, strong brother who, so long ago, had kept her safe and free from harm. Free from those who would have taken her for their own evil purposes. He was now on his knees looking up at her, trying to focus on her and what she was saying.

Now she stood over him, still gently telling him that he was *loved*, he was precious, he was special, very special. Slowly, he looked up to her face. She felt that tears were flowing from his eyes, as in a way, she felt they were also flowing from hers, yet she knew that could not be. Slowly, she knelt down beside him and took him in her arms like a baby, gently rocking him, and slowly, she felt all the fight, the fear, the anger and the aggression all move away from him.

His armour, his helmet and the sword he had held, they all simply just vanished, as his mind finally let them go. In her mind and her thoughts, she now held him tight and took him to that magnificent garden. That garden that held the great healing halls and he found himself now on the grass in that garden, still held tightly in his little sister's arms, but with total silence, peace and tranquillity all around them.

'Aurora, my beautiful girl. I am so very, VERY proud of you. You have succeeded where so many, many others before you have tried and failed. I always knew you were my very perfect, very beautiful and very special princess.

I know there will be many who will now learn much from the success you have just achieved, as you worked hard to bring your brother back into the fold. Great patience and *love*, the natural *love* you hold within your very being that is so, so important to everything, that it just shines out from you constantly.'

'Thank you, Daniel, and thank you for your guidance and amazing help and most importantly, your protection. I could not have done it without that.'

'Go now, heal your brother, take him *by your thoughts* into these great halls. Then, take him home. I will tell no other, Aurora, till you get him home. This is one surprise I am looking forward to seeing, as nobody has any idea what you have just done. But let me tell you before you go, I know now that you could have done all that you have done with your brother, *without my help.* You are that strong, my very dear one.' Daniel, although still around as he always is, now withdrew from their sight.

Aurora held her brother in her arms and awaited the questions that she knew he wanted to ask her. She could now read his mind clearly, as he at last opened up to her, *mind to mind,* but she did not disturb his thoughts with a reaction. She just let him know that he was loved.

Slowly, he moved against her and again turned to look into her face. To him, it was the most beautiful face he had ever seen and her eyes, yes, her eyes that shone so bright. She smiled and her face lit up with the warmth and love she had for her brother. He felt the love she had for him moving into him, warming him, yet he still was not truly understanding how all this was, or how this could be. How had she been able to come to him? He thought. Now he realised, just how he must have hurt her with that sword, he must have hurt her he thought, it could be no other way, yet she did not show any sign of that hurt or injury. Her eyes were full of love, how could this be? How, he thought, could all this possibly be, that I could hurt her so terribly, and yet, she indeed showed no sign of hurt, nor of pain, just a great love for him, how? Am I dreaming all this, am I just dreaming it?

'Where am I? Please tell me where I am, are you really and truly my little sister, Aurora? What has happened to me, where is this place, how did I get here? Please tell me.'

'Tirri, Tirri, Tirri, my big beautiful brother. So many questions, but thank God you have come back to me. Yes, thank you God, thank you for this priceless, priceless gift.' (God answered her in her mind 'You have done well and brought him home again, in you I am very proud.')

Now, Aurora, using *mind to mind* spoke to her brother. 'Tirri, you were killed in a battle in the arena, but you were a very, very brave man. Now, because of that and because I was told about what had happened to you a long time ago, and where you were, I came for you. You are here beside me, in Heaven, where we all, every one of us, return to when our time on Earth, in that lifetime we have just lived, is finished. This place I have brought you to is a healing place, or at least the gardens to the healing place. Watch the flowers, as they will now all blossom just for you, just as they did for me when I first came here to these gardens with Daniel, before I came for you.'

He watched, amazed, then suddenly a look of great fear came into his eyes. Aurora saw the sudden change and then, from the corner of her eye she saw the dark cloud above forming and for less than a second she also knew fear. Then she shouted, DANIEL, DANIEL, DANIEL, QUICKLY NOW, I NEED YOU NOW.

Only True Love Can Wash the Dark Clouds Away

The Dark Side Threatens

Daniel was instantly there and he too saw the gathering dark cloud forming and he knew they were coming for Tirri. 'Cover him, Aurora and keep asking for *white light protection* for you both, but keep him covered.'

Now the two great angels that normally stood guard at the doors to the Healing Halls, both grew in size, getting bigger and bigger, until they formed a great canopy over Aurora and Tirri with their wings. Now the angel that is Tirri's guardian angel, became very visible saying to all, 'NOT THIS TIME, you are not getting him back.' Suddenly, above the great winged canopy, a mass of white light angels and a mass of those of the *dark side*, grew closer and closer together and a great gale blew, as Aurora felt the dramatic change in the vibrations.

Aurora could feel the wind as it whipped up, even beneath the winged canopy. Have faith Aurora, show no fear, they will not get you I promise you. Aurora spoke gently to Tirri, saying be strong, have faith my big brother, you are safe, stay within my arms. Still the gale blew stronger and stronger, it was like a hurricane as it whipped up everything it could, as those from the *dark side* tried to get to Tirri. Aurora could see the darkness through the winged canopy and she thought to herself 'You will not get through, you will not get my brother. I will not let you take him again.'

'Good, Aurora, keep that thought, keep it going, it's helping, keep it strong.' As she heard these words from Daniel, so Grace now appeared visible to her, helping her protect Tirri.

On Earth at this time, a major hurricane was now blowing, with very dark, thick black clouds and torrential rain, that seemed to be covering most of Earth. People could not remember a storm like this ever. For seven days this raged with tremendous damage everywhere. Trees were uprooted that had stood proud for many, many years, and towns and villages were ravaged.

Several large earthquakes, followed by giant tsunamis, meant the coastlines and the landscape were now changed forever. The Earth shook on its axis and moved a degree, causing extreme panic everywhere, as people did not know where to go to be safe. Thousands lost their Earthly lives, as even more damage happened and a great fear took hold. Many places had not seen daylight since the storm began. What would have been the seventh day came and went, as those before it and then the following morning the first glint of a break happened, as the cloud, at last, started to break up.

As that day wore on slowly, suddenly, by the time the sun was at its highest, a small break in the clouds let the sun through and as the rest of the day wore on, the sky brightened. The wind, although still strong, had eased and the waves lessened. Night followed a similar pattern, as the sky slowly cleared to let a very weak moon show through, but not yet clear enough to see the stars. The following morning saw the wind rise again and everybody feared the worst. What was happening to the Earth, was this the end?

'How much longer is this terrible thing that is happening to us, going to last?' was the question on everybody's mind.

As the day drew to an end, the wind started to drop again and by morning, as if by some miracle, the sky was clear again, everywhere. People came out from their hiding places and could hardly believe what they saw. The bright sun and clear skies, but also the total devastation, everywhere they looked. The whole face of the landscape had changed forever and the question on everybody's lips was, WHY? What had caused this total devastation?

Tirri now stirred in Aurora's arms, saying 'Thank you, Aurora. Now I know I also have the strength to fight them, they will not get to me.' In his mind, although his lips moved, he shouted out 'YOU WILL NOT GET ME, I WILL NEVER COME WITH YOU AGAIN. MY PLACE IS HERE NOW, WITH MY SISTER AND WITH THE LIGHT. BE GONE, I AM NOT YOURS TO HAVE. I BELONG HERE.'

Slowly now, the wind eased and Aurora saw the darkness recede, but still she held her brother tight. To her horror the darkness started to come down again and she thought even harder about the power of the white light and what she knew the angels, these big powerful angels were doing for her and her brother.

At last, she again saw a glimmer of light shine through, but she knew better than to relax. Only when Daniel returned to tell her everything was safe, would she then relax her hold on her brother. At last the light shone clear and bright and she watched these two magnificent angels, who had grown so big, now reduce in size to as they always were. They now bowed before Aurora and her brother saying 'Now you are safe.'

As they resumed their stance outside the great Healing Halls, which they had also covered with their massive wings, Daniel now appeared before them, saying to Aurora, "My beautiful brave princess, what amazing strength you have just shown in what you have just done. I am humbled to be allowed to be your guardian angel.'

'He is my brother, they were not getting him again, ever. I would give my eternal life first, before I would allow that to happen to him. Thank you, Daniel.'

As Aurora, now kneeling on the grass holding her brother, looked to the gardens, she now saw exactly that this had happened before, for Aurora herself, the first time she had entered here. Now it also happened before their eyes for her brother. A smile appeared on his lips as he watched this amazing event happen, just exactly as it had for Aurora.

He now told Aurora, that he had been told he would never ever stop fighting, but now he knew, they were wrong, and he knew in himself he would never ever fight again. He took his sister in his arms and just held her, still studying her face, such a beautiful face with a smile that just lit up that face and melted his heart. They talked for a while, as she explained all that she knew now. Not only about him, but also about her life, her daughter, her special man, the pyramid and what had happened to it, and about their parents.

He remembered the pyramid and could not believe it had just disappeared into the ground. She told him she would show him, but all that could wait, there were other things they had to do first. She told him that by her thoughts, she would take him with her, very gently into the Healing Halls, explaining what would happen to him as all the colours would then work their magic on him.

At the entrance to this beautiful pink alabaster building, just as before, the great golden angels that stood guard over them during that terrible happening, now opened the large stained glass doors to allow them to enter and said to him, 'Enter now in peace and may God be with you as you bathe in this, his great colour palace. Let the music now play and soothe this man's weary soul.' They again bowed before him, as he entered with his sister into these great Healing Halls, the beautiful music again played, just as Aurora and the angels had asked.

As they started to walk in through the colours, the music, so soft and gentle, began. The great choir of angels also started to sing a gentle lullaby that brought peace into his soul. First she took him to the pink quartz crystal area, where the colour gently flowed all around and through him. Great love and peace now settled on him, as a spectrum of colour from this pink crystal and then through to a very nurturing gentle green, then onto a light blue for his throat. Indigo also gently covered him, then gold and the amazing white light followed, as they had gone through each of these sections. Then a change back for him, as an aqua colour now brought him great peace and calm, into azure for protection, sapphire and then blue, as the healing continued as he went through them all. The music that changed at each colour change, continued to play for him.

Purple, lavender and violet, bringing his mind and soul balance, as all the full spectrum of colours continued to work their own individual magic on him. Then that magnificent rainbow wash, also worked its magic, and to finish, the pure white light followed, to complete his healing.

Now a white light, such as he had never seen before, so brilliant and clear, enveloped him. To his surprise, what he now saw before him, startled him for a moment, as he suddenly began to see before him, something he never expected to ever see.

His whole life now started to play out exactly as it had been, he saw first his birth and his young childhood. Now came a fleeting glimpse of a baby, a baby that he knew was Aurora. Then suddenly, he saw the soldiers come, he watched, horrified, as they injured his father, grabbed him, and dragged him, as he kicked and struggled for his life and for the life of his family. He also saw, when he had not told them about his sister, he had not told them, despite what they did to him.

Now he watched as he was learning to fight, being trained as a gladiator and then him fighting in the arena. Everything that he saw, he saw in great detail, as if he was sitting in the arena watching 'himself', as he fought and killed many men. Then, to his horror and shame, he saw the first woman he had killed, as she had mistakenly entered the arena. She was totally defenceless, but the King had ordered him to kill her and sadly, that is what he had done. He felt the shame in his heart for what he had done.

She was not the only woman he had killed. He also did not like the fact that he had also killed animals, as they too were, in a way, defenceless. Then, to his horror and shock, he saw Aurora now stand before him in the ring and he watched and felt the horror at what he was now doing to her. Then, very suddenly, his life came to an end, as he saw himself in Aurora's arms on the floor of the arena. The white light still held him, he could not move and suddenly a voice spoke loud and clear from this white light saying, 'Are you complete, have you done all you had to do?' At first he could not reply and again he heard the question being asked, 'Yes', he simply replied. Then the voice spoke thus, 'Let all rejoice, as this dear, precious soul returns to us and to the light once more. Let his healing begin.'

In Earth terms, he had been in these great Healing Halls for an immeasurable time, as time, now to him seemed totally irrelevant. He had slowly healed, not just on the outside, but more especially, deep on the inside. A great feeling of peace and happiness, feelings he had not known for a very, very long time, now returned to his weary soul.

Tirri now turned to his sister, who still stood beside him and had done so, all through his review, although she herself saw none of it. It was not hers to see. She felt his heartbreak and he took her in his arms as if she was the most precious, most priceless gift he had ever received, which indeed, as far as he was concerned, she was. He held her close, whispering in her ear, except as Aurora knew, it was *mind to mind*, 'I don't yet fully understand what miracle has brought this about, nor how you had the strength and the courage to do not only what I have just seen you do for me, but also what amazing strength you had for me in these gardens. I say *thank you* Aurora, thank you sincerely, for this miracle that has brought you back into my life. No greater gift than this could ever have been given to me, ever.'

'To see you here before me now, knowing what you did for me as a very young child, no more than a baby, you shielded me and you protected me when these same bad men who took you, would have taken me also. I know I owe you my life and in turn my daughter Crystal's life. I would never have had my lovely daughter, if you had not done as you did and protected me, I now feel complete Tirri. I feel totally complete, thank you for your gift of my life.' So, the long parted brother and sister got to know each other, as they went back into the garden for a while and just sat there together, talking. In Earth terms, it could have been days, weeks, months, even years that they were there, as they talked about, not only all that had happened since they met, but everything else. But time does not matter in spirit, as *love* is the only currency that matters, in that wonderful place.

As they chatted on, slowly Aurora started to get a thought in her head from Crystal, 'Where are you Mummy? Where are you Mummy? I am missing you. I can't locate you. Please, Mummy, where are you? Please answer me, please speak to me, PLEASE.'

Aurora did not reply immediately. Instead, she said to Tirri, 'I am getting a strong message in my head, that my daughter, Crystal, is missing me. I need to get back to her, but most importantly, I am going to take you with me. Here is what I suggest we do, but only if you agree?'

'You know better than me, Aurora, what needs to be done. I will agree to anything you say, what is it you wish to do?'

'I will first do something very special for you, dear brother. Please turn around and look up slightly and then tell me what it is you see. Take your time, but watch very carefully.'

Tirri slowly turned around and two very amazing things happened. What at first appeared to him as a bright white light, enveloped him like a big soft cloud and then, it was as if his being totally absorbed this cloud. He felt a great change within himself, a change that, even now, brought him more great peace and warmth. It was the only way he could explain it, and as he relaxed into this amazing feeling within him, slowly, above him, this magnificent angel appeared before him and spoke to him, saying only to him, 'I am your guardian angel and it is, and has been, my privilege to be with you always, as I have been since the very beginning. What you just watched and felt happen to you, was your *higher self*. That part of you that you left behind when you went to your last life experience, it has now returned to you, as you became one again and so now, you should feel complete in every way.'

'Strangely, I do feel more complete. As yet though, I do not understand what you mean by *higher self*, but I know that either you, or my sister, will explain it to me later. Did I not also see you when we were in the gardens and that terrible dark cloud descended on us?'

'You are correct. I was there with you, as always. I needed to ensure they would not get you a second time, as they had when you were a gladiator. That was not supposed to happen, but I was powerless to stop it. I also thank the other angels who helped me, as in that task I could never have done that on my own.'

Aurora, thanking the angel, now spoke to her brother saying quietly, 'I will ask Crystal, to get those immediately to us, to go to my house and when they are all there, she will let me know. We will then go immediately there. Meanwhile, we shall remain in these beautiful gardens and talk. When Crystal lets us know they are all together, then we will speedily travel there.'

'It all sounds good to me. I'm still just more than a little confused about everything and can't seem to take it all in.'

'Talk to me Tirri, please, just talk to me. Tell me what you are feeling. There is no rush for you to be anywhere. If you do not feel ready yet, as I know it is a lot at first to take in, we will go at your pace so that you are relaxed, always. Meanwhile, just sit with me here and relax.'

'No, we should go now, your daughter is anxious for you to return to her, and I know with you by my side I am happy and comfortable, knowing *all is well.* I would not wish your daughter to be upset unnecessarily so, on my behalf.'

'Trust me Tirri, please, you will soon understand and we will help you. In fact, if I know my Crystal, she will soon have you completely under her spell and totally organised.'

'How old would she be Aurora?'

'She was three summers old, getting near to four summers, when first we arrived here, but now, she is so different, yes, so very different to then. She was such a frail child back on Earth. It does my heart good and makes me so happy to see how she is now and growing. Let me tell you about her as we walk slowly to my house.'

But, before Aurora had a chance to tell her brother very much about her precious daughter, she had received a message back in her mind from Crystal herself, informing her, that they were all there already at her house and very anxiously awaiting her news.

'You will have to wait Tirri, as I am told everybody is now there. I know that you, as everybody does, will simply love her. I know she is my daughter, but she is very special and has a way with her that will enrapture you. So now, take my hand and we will go, but we will stop just short of the house. Then we can gently walk up to the door as I'm sure, no, I know, that they are expecting me to just pop up in the room, as I would normally travel there by thought and would not go in through the door. Now, are they in for a big surprise?'

So suddenly, in the blink of an eye, from these magical Healing Halls and the gardens, they were now just a short distance away from Aurora's house. Inside they could see that everybody was clearly there, all excitedly chatting away to each other, trying to guess at what was going to happen when Aurora arrived. 'Are you ready, big brother? Because if you feel you are able, we will now go in using the door and join everybody that I know is inside there.'

In they went, slowly through the door, Aurora first. The look of total astonishment that was on everybody's face as they entered, was a sight to see.

'Who is this?' Aurora's mum asked, as she did not appear to recognise him.

'Do you not recognise him Mum? You, more than anybody else here should. Look closely Mum, look very closely.'

'It cannot be Aurora, can it? I...I...I just don't believe it can be. Is... is it really my own dear son? How

157

and why are you here now in this place? Please, let me hold you, PLEASE.'

'It is Mum, it's your own dear son, who you never thought you would ever see again. I have brought him back to you.'

'How did I not know, how did I not know he was here? Oh, TIRRI!' She swept him up in her arms and you could feel the strength of her love that she had kept safely in her heart for him, as it immediately began to flow freely into him.

'How did you do this Aurora? You didn't even know of his existence, we could never talk about what had happened to him.'

'It is a long story Mum and I will tell you all, but now is not the moment for that, just enjoy him being here, please. He is still more than slightly bewildered at everything.' Locking her mind so that just her mother would hear what she said, she told her, 'He has been in a very sad place, *a very sad place.* Don't ask questions yet, please, it will all come out in good time, just enjoy this wonderful, wonderful moment.'

Crystal sat stunned, for she never knew, just as her mum hadn't, about Tirri. As they all sought to hold this brave man, now among them, this stranger to them all and yet, he did not feel a stranger to them, they knew that he was family.

'Well Aurora, a job very well done. I think,' as Daniel now appeared before them all, 'a very amazing job very well done. I can tell you they, the high spirits, are more than pleased at your amazing success.'

'So this is why I could not contact you Mummy. You were hiding, you were on a secret mission of your own and we never knew. That's naughty Mummy, naughty. You should have told us.'

'In truth, Crystal, I did not know myself, until I was nearly at the place Daniel and I were going to. I will tell you all about it later. However, little one, I hear you have been travelling again, were you successful?'

'Of course I was, Mummy, of course I was. Rebecca and I, we are the team, the dream team.'

'I'm so glad and you look so happy, you obviously enjoy what you are doing.'

'Who could not enjoy what we do, Mummy, when you see the faces and, most importantly, that they know they are now safe? Especially after what they have had to suffer from these terrible people, Mummy, it is so sad. Mummy, you never ever said you had a brother. Where has he come from and why is he here with us now?'

'Crystal, my dear precious girl, so many questions, questions that I promise I will answer later. Let us just enjoy the fact that, after suffering greatly at the hands of others, he is now back with us. What he needs now is *love* and peace and affection. These are things in his life he has not known for many a long day. All I want him to know and be shown at this time is that here, all love him, so that he can feel at peace.'

'Can I please go and speak to him? Will he want to speak with me, because I just want to give him a great, big hug.'

'Of course you can, that is if you can prise your grandmother away from him. She has missed him and thought that she would never see him again when he was taken from her, so long ago.'

'Oh Mummy, that is so sad. Why was that?'

'Later my dear, later. Just go and speak with him, but be very gentle and nice please.'

Crystal joined the many people who also wished to speak with him and the first thing she did was to give him a great, big hug and kiss, saying 'I LOVE YOU.' He did not really know how to respond, so he tried to do the same back and told her he knew she had been a very brave girl. Then he managed to just chat to her about her, asking lots of questions, that Crystal was only too happy to answer for him.

Slowly, he got around to talking to nearly everybody, when his own angel became visible again beside him and explained to him, that those of a higher status wished to speak with him. Would he please go with him to see them. He simply said, 'See you later Mum' and was gone.

So now, as he had left them, the group all returned to their own places and Aurora, her man and her daughter, were left to talk about all that had gone on for each of them, since last they were together. Crystal told them all about the little boy she had gone to collect and what had happened to him. Her man told them he had been sent for, and had a session with the *higher ones*. They had impressed on his mind, things he needed to know for some work they would like him to do. He said that at this stage, he could tell them no more, as he, himself, did not yet fully understand everything he had been told and that he was going back for more tuition later.

Then it was Aurora's turn to tell them about her trip to get her brother and all that it entailed. It took some time for her to relay all that had happened and of course they were full of questions. They were both shocked and amazed with her replies, as she told them just what he had been through. Aurora received a great, big hug from them both, as they learned just what she had had to do, as she herself had entered the ring and fought to save him and release him from his mind entrapment.

As they talked, Aurora now received the much awaited call from the *higher spirits*. They wished to speak with her, would she please get Daniel to take her to them. At that, Daniel immediately appeared, took her hand and they were gone.

Aurora now found herself back again in the great Golden Halls, where she had come to meet with Daniel, but this was not in the rose gold hall, she was in before. This was a smaller hall that she could see clearly all around her. Before her there was a long table and several very elderly people sat along its length, all appearing to converse with each other. Suddenly, one of them turned towards her and called her by name, telling her to sit before them, as they wished to discuss matters with her. At first they told her to relax, as they could feel her stress and distress at what, she felt, was some form of ordeal, especially as Daniel was now no longer in sight.

At this, she visibly relaxed and was now told that they were about to impress her mind with several matters that they wanted her to think about. She now sat quietly as she felt the impressions from each one of them, as if each one was talking to her. It took her a few minutes to unravel the joint conversation, so that she could understand what they were each telling her.

When they were finished the one who had acted as spokesman, told her that they were amazed at what she had been able to do for her brother, and all through her own efforts and her *love*, without any direction or guidance from them. They believed her level of understanding was indeed, much, much higher than they had at first thought.

They then informed her, that they would like her to speak to a congregation, in the great Meeting Halls that Daniel would take her to, about her experience in what she had done with, and for, her brother. How she had, through her own thoughts, actions and efforts, succeeded in her very hard task, where very many before her, had sadly failed to succeed.

It appeared that several others, mainly men, had tried to get through to him, but none had had any form of success or ever a glimmer of a result. She also learned that she had been the only one who had dared to enter the ring with him. They informed her she could return to her home and think seriously about what they had asked of her, but not, at this stage, to discuss this with anyone else, as they only wished for her input into these matters they had discussed. They also informed her they would notify her when they had arranged the meeting in the place they had told her, with the congregation they wished her to speak with.

Daniel now appeared before her and gently took her hand, they both bowed before the table and took their leave of the group she had been speaking with.

'I know, Aurora, that you have no idea just how high these people are, you were just speaking with, but let me just tell you, they do not come much higher than that group of people. They are among the very *top group* of elders. That should tell you how proud they are of your achievements. They even commended me for believing in you as much as I do. I still say to you, I know you are a very clever, thoughtful girl, and the level of *love* you have and show, far exceeds the vast majority of people here. I cannot put into words how proud I am of you. What I can tell you, is that sometime in the future, I do not know when, that level of *love* will be sorely tested. I believe you have at least a couple, if not more, other Earthly lives to live before that.

'My only advice to you is learn now. Learn as much as you possibly can, take it all in to your inner being and I know all will be well for you. Soon you will begin plans for your next life on Earth and you will be fully involved in the planning, or should I say the setting up, of that life. But not yet, as that life is still a good way off. It takes considerable planning and many other souls are involved, as you will learn. However, you have much work to do before all that comes to fruition. Now I suggest that I take you home and when you are all together again, I will take you to another amazing place that will have you enthralled with what you see. NO, before you ask, I am not going to tell you, you will see.'

So they slowly walked back to Aurora's house, still talking all the time as they went. At first the house was empty and that gave her a little time to consider all that she had just been made aware of. Then she heard, or rather felt, Crystal come bursting in, all excited about her latest adventure. Almost breathless (which cannot possibly happen) with the excitement bubbling within her about her trip just completed, she proceeded to tell her mum all about two little girls she had brought back to their mum and what had happened to them all.

'They had all been out in a boat, Mummy, but their mum had fallen overboard when a massive wave struck them and injured their father. They had been on the boat for a long time and they died because of lack of water, but again, they did not know they were dead and did not want to leave their dad. Although they could see their own bodies, they knew they were somehow still alive and they knew their dad was still moving and mumbling when another boat found them.

'When Rebecca and me arrived for them, they were all on the sands and then they took their father away, lying on a board. We found them just sitting there waiting for a dad that would probably never return. When they first saw me they thought I was there to play with them, until I told them what had happened to them.

'So Rebecca and me, we just took their hands and whoosh, we were all back here. It's so funny what we do, although I know it is serious to those left. If they could just see what is happening and know they really are safe and not really dead. Why are people so afraid of death on Earth, Mummy, when they are not really dead at all?'

'Crystal, sadly it will be a long time before people once more, learn and accept that this is all just part of a spirit's travels through an eternal life, as it sets out to experience what we cannot experience in a spiritual environment. People used to be much more aware, so death on Earth did not frighten them. Sadly, some very bad people from the *dark side*, have managed to take control and they now, through fear, control practically everybody. All that control is through the fear that they have had instilled in them. I am told it will be several thousand Earth years before it even begins to turn back, as it will. But sadly, a lot of very bad things will happen first, before that happens or it even starts to turn back to the light

'Why is this, Mummy, why will it take so long?'

'It will not seem long to us, while we are here in spirit, because as you now know, time here does not exist. Part of our physical experience that we can only ever have on Earth, or any other planet like Earth, is to learn from our souls' viewpoint, the different experiences of a physical life.

'If somehow, we can always learn to tune in to our *higher selves* and learn to follow our gut instinct during the time when we are on Earth, then that will help us to understand. Sadly again, this is something that we, here in spirit, know will be lost. Lost to those on Earth, for a long time, as those who now seek to control all those on Earth, try to ensure through fear, that people ignore their own gut instincts and only follow what they are told by these so called superiors. Who are far from superior, more like inferior, as they take the people backwards in their learning, as they forget more and more about how life should really be.'

'But that, Mummy, *is silly*. There is nobody that knows you better than you, yourself. *We* all know that here, why should it be different on Earth? When we know that we start our life there with the freedom to choose for ourselves, and that choosing happiness and joy and *love*, by helping others to do the same, brings lovely things to us automatically. That is the way things work and if we are cruel to others then we, ourselves, will suffer as a result.'

'You are so right, my darling. How did you get to be so knowledgeable in your young life?'

'Rebecca and I have been speaking a lot because, as you see, I am getting a big girl now and I have been asking her a lot of questions. One thing she told me, when I asked her about your brother and what happened to him, she said there are a lot of people who are in similar dark places such as he was, before you courageously got him out from there. Some are in even worse, much darker places, because they have done terrible things. Because they don't understand what they really did yet, they have created their own bad place and there they will stay, until eventually, they begin to realise what they have done. Then they will receive help.'

'Yes, that is true my dear. Nobody is ever left, there are always people working with them and eventually, slowly, they will find a way back, but then they have a lot to learn to put that right. It is actually very hard for some people to understand how things happen here, but nobody is ever abandoned, ever. It can sometimes take eons before they make any improvement.'

'Thank you, Mummy, for helping me to understand, thank you.'

Now, before Aurora had a chance to further discuss with her daughter what was planned, she was summoned to appear before the *high ones*. So, in the blink of an eye, she had left her daughter and was now sitting in front of the *high spirits*. Here, they told her she was now to go to the central meeting hall that is beside the healing centre. It was there she would tell her story, regarding her brother and how she was able to get through to him. So releasing him, from what were the bonds of his own making, through his thoughts, because of the way he had been treated in life.

She quickly arrived at the great central meeting hall, with Daniel at her side, as always, to an assembled group of helpers, whose job it was to also do what she had done with her brother, and were now patiently waiting to hear from her. When she arrived in the hall, she was shocked at the great number of people who were now present before her. Daniel assured her, she would be fine and just to tell it as it was. As she finished her speech, which was actually all *mind to mind* and not talking with words, there was great applause for her and for what she had achieved. There were many who wished their own private word with her, before she was able to return again to her family and take stock of her own situation. Daniel allowed her time to assess what she had just done, reassuring her she had done well and that when she was ready, they would go on the trip he had mentioned before.

'Now my dear little one, who is now not so little, Daniel told me, before I was called away, that he would like to take us all on a very special trip. Shall we see if we can get Daddy and then ask Daniel, if it is a good time to go on his special trip?'

'Do you think he would allow my friend to come with us, Mummy?'

'I do not know. Shall we ask him and see what he says? Daniel, are you here, please?'

'Where else would I ever be, Aurora, but by your side? Yes, if she would like to come, she is more than welcome. Why don't you ask her?'

So Crystal asked her friend by *mind to mind* communication and before you could blink, she was with them and both were all excited, like two young ladies, as they both now were, ready to go out.

'Where is Daddy, Mummy, is he coming?'

No sooner had Crystal said the words, than he was with them, also ready to go on the trip. They all went out into the beautiful light and held hands together with Daniel.

As they started to walk towards the magical gardens they had previously been in, Crystal said, 'We've been here before, Daniel.'

'Ah Crystal, we are not going where you are thinking. This is a very special trip we are going on and I have been requested and given very special permission to take you all there. I know you will all love it when we get there, but it is also for you all, a bit of a learning trip. I was just about to tell you about all of it, but then I decided it would be better, and much more exciting for you, to see what is in store. So patience little one, patience and all will be revealed to you. What I do know, is that what you are about to see and, who you are about to meet on this trip, will truly surprise and amaze you.'

TRUE LOVE

A PRECIOUS GIFT

Daniel's Amazing Trip

Our trio, together with Daniel, and Crystal's angel, Rebecca, now clearly visible to them all, set of together with Crystal's little friend, all taking each other's hands. Daniel had Aurora on one side and Crystal on the other, then Rebecca, who also held the little girls hand. Her angel was also with them, but was seen just as a ball of light beside her. In her other hand was Aurora's man on the end, as they began this magical journey. Although not at present visible as angels, there were also two other angels always with them, because wherever you go, whenever you are doing anything, your own angel is always beside you, even if not visible. These two were, at present, like two golden lights, taking up the rear as they followed behind.

Daniel said to all of them, 'Come, let us all fly together on this magical trip and let me tell you, *mind to mind*, what is about to happen, as we journey. As you can see, we are now flying very low to the ground on Earth. Now as you all know, when you are alive on Earth as a human being you cannot see the fourth dimension. That's the dimension that *we* all live in now as a *spirit being of light*, as a human you can only see three dimensional objects. That is why people never, or rarely ever, see spirit people, although we really are always among them. Some mediums are fortunate to still be able to see us, but that is very rare these days, most have lost this ability.

'It is sad, that at one time, virtually everybody could clearly see the fourth dimension. It will happen again in time, when the people of Earth revert back in their beliefs, that we all do exist. It is strange that everybody talks about us being 'up in Heaven' yet, as you can see, and now know, we are not *up* anywhere. We are actually all around them and clearly with the people on Earth, in the same space, but not *time*, as time, as you know, is irrelevant to us. It is only because we are fourth dimensional that they do not see us. One day, far, far into the future, on Earth, similar to as it is now, people will have little machines that they will carry with them, and these little machines will be able to pick us up. Initially as spirit orbs of light, but eventually they will pick us up as we actually are, a *spirit being*. Then, when that happens, they will know for certain that we all occupy the same space.

'Now, as you will see, we are travelling over lands that none of you believe you have ever seen before, and in the life you have just lived, that is quite correct. I am sure you are noticing the great difference in the landscape and of course, you can also see people who are totally oblivious to us as we pass them by. Yes, you little girls, I can see you can see a funny side to that, with the wide grins on your faces. It is much greener here than you ever saw it in 'Khem', where you had your last life, and there are lots of trees and bushes, now beginning to appear to you, that all grow quite naturally here. Now let us slow right down. See that little crop of trees just in front of us? Well, let us now stop just before them.'

They all gently came to a stop before the trees, still not truly aware quite what they were doing here, or even why they were here. Daniel, through *mind to mind*, spoke gently to them, saying 'You are now about to see some amazing little people and they are called *faeries*. They are very special spirit people who have and do, an amazing job that never stops. Look carefully at these little things growing in the earth, they are called snow drops. Study them for a moment and quietly, very quietly, tell me what you see happening before you?'

Crystal, little bright eyes, was first to see them, 'Look Mummy! See that tiny little girl there, with her little wings fluttering, she's painting the flowers white and shiny, see? Oh! There are lots of them, all busy painting, can we speak to them, Daniel, please?'

'Just give them a minute to know we are here, we do not want to frighten them away. They know we are here and one of them will look up in a minute, when they see we mean them no harm. Normal human beings, they don't see them, so they get treated roughly and knocked away, as people pick or tread on these flowers. They have to be very alert when humans are around.'

So they watched and quietly waited, until one little girl turned round and said to Daniel, 'Why have you brought these people to us? Why are they different to normal people, who just tread on us if we are not quick enough?'

'These people, they are now just like us, they are all now *spirit beings*. Look carefully at them and you will see that what I say is true.' The little fairy approached Crystal and fluttered around her and then around each one in turn, until she was satisfied all was safe. Satisfied, she now called out to the others, who were all working here, and they gathered all around our little group, studying them closely. The little one, who first came to speak, now moved to Aurora, saying 'Your lights are very bright and shiny, you are nearly as bright as your angel. You must be very special, to be so bright.'

'Thank you, little one. I am Aurora, do you have a name I can call you?'

The little faery answered, saying 'We are all Snowdrop, because we all do the same thing. We are collectively known as Snowdrop.'

'How do you speak to each other when you all have the same name?' Aurora asked the little faery.

'When you speak to your daughter, do you always say her name, Aurora?'

'No, little one. When we speak *mind to mind* we just know we are speaking to each other.'

The faery responded, 'So it is with us, we know whether we are speaking to all, or if it is just one of us we wish to talk with. It is also true that we do not speak very much. However, if you listen, you will hear or feel the vibration, as we are always singing.' Aurora listened quietly for a minute and yes, she could feel and hear the gentle singing.

Daniel now spoke, saying 'Thank you Snowdrop, and thank you, all. We must travel on as we have far to go.'

The little faery replied, by saying, 'Thank you. I will pass it on you are coming, so you will be expected. Crocus is down that way and you are now expected. Bye.'

Daniel now spoke to the others, 'Now you are seeing something, or should I say seeing little people, that you will rarely see in Heaven, for although they are there, just like your dog, and in fact, all the different types of animals, they have their own *special place* in Heaven, where you cannot go. They can if they wish, come over to your side, as some regularly do, as they work on the flowers you see in the gardens.

'They have been there when you have been in the gardens, you have just not been aware they were there. When we get back I will show you, but we have a long, long way to go before we return. Let us now go down this path and we will meet Crocus, who will now be waiting for us at our next stop.' Our little troop journeyed on.

'Crocus, I see you, thank you. Please let me introduce my companions to you.'

Crocus replied, saying 'I received Snowdrop's message and I was surprised. We get very few friendly people to see us, most just pick our flowers and then trample all over us, with no idea of what they are doing. There is, however, one little old lady near here and she can see us, she comes to talk with us nearly every day. We keep a watch out for her, as she lives on her own and we are able to stop bad things happening to her. There is always one of us at least, in or around her little house.'

Aurora now spoke up, saying 'I am Aurora, you are very beautiful and your colours are amazing.'

Crocus replied, saying 'You are who I thought you were, Snowdrop said to look for the lady with the very bright lights, and your lights and colours are very beautiful, as are your daughters.'

'How do you know which is my daughter?'

'We all know Crystal well, although she does not yet know us. We have seen her on her travels when she has come back for a young one who will not leave when they should. There is not much goes on around the world that we are not aware of, through our network of all the different types of faeries.

'You see, we are connected to all the faeries everywhere, who look after all the plants, the trees and all the blossoms everywhere. It is very sad that people have forgotten about us, but we do have a very, very important job to do and the colours would not be right if we did not do our job well, nor sadly would the trees bear fruit. Most importantly, the honey bees would have nowhere to go if we did not do our job correctly, and there would be no honey.

'The colours must all be clear and correct, the stamens have to be absolutely perfect so that the pollen is good and pure. We are all, that is, every faery for every plant, busy all the time. So you see, although I only do crocuses, we have to know all the colours of crocus, that way we all get our times and our colours correct. Some are all mauve, purple, yellow or white, and some are splashed with different colours. There are so many, it would take me a long, long time to tell you them all and you, sadly, do not have the time.'

'I am sorry we have to go again so soon, but I love hearing what you have to say. I can see you are happy in your work, as you paint all these pretty colours. I hope you get a chance to speak to Crystal.'

'I will before you go, but know now, this is not work, it is our life and as you can hear, we are all happy as we sing our songs and chat to the birds that come to see us. Although, some birds are naughty and pick the heads off. Thank you for coming to speak with us. Where are you going to now?'

'I do not know, only Daniel knows where we are going. It is a surprise for us all.'

'I think it will be Daffodil next, they are just a short way down that lane, you will see. Let me say to you, although I should not, we will meet again soon, as you start the work you are about to, and I will look forward to that. See you soon, goodbye.'

Aurora came away smiling to herself, thinking, the future sounds good.

Daniel gathered them up again, but not before Crystal had a chance to speak with Crocus, who had spoken with her mum. They went down the lane and sure enough, it was Daffodil next, as they again stopped and talked and learned more and more. Then it was the Dandelion faeries, who were also sharing a field with the Daisy faeries. There were so many of both, that in this field you could not count them all, as they flitted about. They also saw here in this field a few buttercup faeries scattered around. For our little group, this was a whole new experience as they had never seen colours around the fields like this before. They passed on to Wildflower, Forget-me-not, Wild Rose, Harebell, Cornflower, Geranium and Poppy, stopping at each one as they went, some for longer, as they all had a lot to say to each other.

'Daniel, please can I ask you what the reason for this trip is? I feel...no...I *know* there is a lot more to it than you have told us.'

'Aurora, why did I not realise you would soon start to believe this was not just a special trip? You are quite correct in what you say, in some respects. For the girls and your man, yes, it is a special trip, only so you can spend some quality time with them. Otherwise, you would have been apart for quite some time. Now I know time is not a factor here in spirit, it just does not exist, but if I tell you we have been on the Earth plain now for about a full season and we are about to enter the hot season, you will know just how long we have been travelling so far.

'Our next stop will be the apple orchards, so that you can see the Apple Blossom faeries and you will need to pay a lot of attention to them. This will then be followed by a trip to the orange trees, so that you can meet the Orange Blossom faeries, where again you will need to pay particular attention to what they tell you. As you are beginning to learn, there are different faeries for every type of plant, be it a tree, a bush, a wild flower or whatever type of plant you can think of. Every single one has its own faery, who looks after their own plant type.

'Let me just name a few for you before we travel on. There is the Foxglove faery, the Sloe faery, Crab Apple faery, Wild Cherry faery, Strawberry faery and there is a Queen of the Meadow faery. There are well over two hundred different faeries, that all do a very important job because, without them, there would be no flowers, there would be no fruit on the trees, and the countryside would be a very sad place indeed. You asked why you are on this trip. The *high ones* wish you to learn as much as you can, because they have a special job they would like you to do. They feel you have in you the *love* that is needed to carry out this task, because it does take someone very special to do the work they have in mind. Someone not just with *love,* but also with *great patience,* two of the qualities that you have in abundance, my precious girl.'

'Well, first of all I had an inkling from a faery who spoke to me, as she said "I will see you soon", but why me? I do not feel there is anything so special about me that can make them think that I can do as they ask.'

'I've just told you the answer to all that. They don't just think, they *know* you can do it and they feel that you will actually enjoy doing it. What they wish you to do is, from spirit, to get in touch with all the people. Such as, do you remember the little old lady that Crocus spoke of?'

'Yes, I remember seeing her around, when Crocus spoke of her. She was tending her garden with such tender loving care and everything in it was so lovely.'

'Exactly, and that is how all plants, shrubs and trees should look, especially if they are to grow fruit each year. This is part of the task they now wish you to do. You will be joining a band of several others, who are also special like you, and do the work that is also now being asked of you. You will see they are all of the same loving quality as yourself. They all deeply understand the importance of *love*, the great understanding and importance. The tender loving care that can produce rich and fruitful rewards, as far as all the work that you will do.

'Never, ever underestimate how very important *love* is to everything, no matter what it is or where it is. Many people are looked on as simply being mad, because they talk to their plants with *love*, but you will find their plants are always much brighter, healthier and better quality plants. *Love* is as important on Earth, just as much as it is in *spirit*, which as you now know is the true currency of spirit. If only people would recognise this and not be afraid to show *love*.

'The people you will be shown and will meet with, know the importance of what they do. They also know it is a difficult task, and they, these *higher spirits*, are hoping that with your mind, you can impress on these people that you will be shown, to try even harder to spread the word. In the work they wish you to do, it is only by impressing on the mind of these people, that you, we, or they, can successfully get that message across and that, again, can only be successfully done during that person's period of quiet meditation.

'The people that you will be working with on Earth all do meditation, because of their beliefs and their *love* in what they do. The *higher spirits* know you are not afraid to show your *love* and that is why they know you will be successful in this work.'

'I cannot believe that people can be afraid to show *love*. It is part of me and who I am. So, at least now I have some idea of the task ahead of me, but trying to impress things on people who are still on Earth, that must take a lot of energy and effort, especially with the thought pattern on Earth as it is now?'

'Yes, Aurora, but as you now know, *you* are a very *special one,* a chosen one and there are few of you that have this special talent, this special ability such as you have. It is vital that people, as many people as we can get to, learn to *love* their plants, trees, shrubs and all things that grow this way, so that they do not, for lack of *love* and attention, die off. Let me also tell you, we have now been, sight-seeing is the way I would put it, for, in Earth terms, over two and a half seasons of the four seasons they have. We are coming near to the end of the trip and will complete it by the end of the third season.

'Now, from there, I shall take you all back to your home and then you and I will go back to the special gardens we visited before. When there, you will get a chance to meet those little people you did not see when you were last there in those gardens. From these very special, little faery people, for in their own type and learning, they are way above the ones you met while we were on our travels, you will learn the great importance that is given to these special ones and why, sometimes, you may need, no, *will need* their help in your tasks.

As I said we, or should I say they, the *high spirits* also want you to help in the task of bringing some of the few people left on Earth at present, as it nears their time to return here to us, in spirit. We know that some who have already died to Earth do not wish to, nor will they, come easily through the veil, because of their reluctance to leave all they love. We believe that, together with at least one of these little people always with you, you will succeed, where most others have failed, in bringing them home.

You see, I have watched you. On every occasion that you had to meet the different types of faeries, you showed a genuine love, and more importantly, interest and understanding in them, and were able to hold a good conversation with them about what they did. Now if you are to help with bringing these people, like that lady you met, you need a good understanding of them and what they do, so that they will *trust* you and so return with you to spirit. The little faery you take with you on each trip, will help you to get closer to them, because they will recognise the bond between you and these precious little people.

There is also another serious point I would make and it is this. Sometimes, it is a child who has to come back, but they already knew about and saw the faeries, so when they died, they could see these little creatures. As they already trusted them, they are now very reluctant to leave these little people and come back home here. It is because they feel safe with them, usually that is something they never felt when they were at home with their parents. Can you see the monumental size of the task they wish you to undertake, while you remain in and as, a *spirit being of light*?'

'It is strange, I did wonder about what the work could be that I was being set. I know I have a great *love* of children, and love being with them, but now I can understand about these people, such as the lady that we met and her level of understanding. Also, I now understand why she tries to get the very young children to see and meet these little people. I think…no…I *know* I am going to love this work, as it is so close to my heart and how I feel about everything, and the *love* I have for not only the little children, but now for these little people and what they do. Somehow, we must find a way that children can always be made much more aware of these little people.'

'That will happen again more when things start to change back to the light, Aurora, and the children will be made more aware of them again. It will restart slowly, but it will happen. But first, we have to deal with what is now. I know that you will practically always be dealing with children when you are here, or come back to spirit after other lives. Now, we must get on and complete the trip and return you all back home again. However, I would also add that when we get home, home is the only word I can use that will let you understand how we are going about things, I will have another surprise for you.'

'I do not feel as if we have been travelling for as long, nor as far, as we have travelled. I know from what I have seen we have been to so many different places on Earth, much more than I ever knew existed, and I have been amazed at what I have seen. All the things I have learned about as well. I never even knew that such things as faeries, these beautiful little people, ever existed, and to see the amazing things they do to all the plants and especially the fruit trees. When we were with Orange Blossom, I was shown how they treat the fruit so that it is perfect and made *so* juicy, as they fill each orange, apple and grape and all the other fruits.

'Many of these trees had dozens of faeries working on them. I feel so privileged to have been given this opportunity to witness such amazing sights, such amazing things, things that people on Earth just take for granted, often with never so much as a "thank you". How much more do we have to see? In a way, I don't feel as if I ever want to finish this trip or to leave these amazing little people. Why did we not know more about them while we were alive on Earth?'

'Everybody at one time, knew all about them and as you saw, there are still a few, mainly women, but not always, who still are aware of them. Fortunately now, because of all the sad and terrible changes on Earth, they have learned to keep very quiet about them, to *protect* them, and will do for many years to come yet. But as I told you earlier, they will come to the fore again when Earth turns back to the light. You will see, it will happen and *you* will probably be part of that. Now we must think about getting back. As I said, we have much to do and you still have other things to learn.'

'You said I have much more to learn and that you have another surprise for me. What is that?'

'All in good time, Aurora. All in good time. See, there we are again, mentioning time, which of course does not exist. Yet I know when I say time, it helps you to understand what I mean. Yes, I have another surprise for you, because as you will now understand there are a lot of God's *special creatures* that you were not aware of, and yet, they all have a special place in God's creation. They all have their own work to do and yet it is not work to them, it is simply their life.

'The specific object of this trip was to make you aware of, and get to know, some of these other special creatures and what they all do. When we go back, as I said, I will first take you to the very special gardens that we visited before, and you will then meet with some of the very *special faeries* I told you about, that look after those very special gardens.'

'I am sad now that I did not see them when we were there before. Why was that Daniel? I thought I was pretty tuned in to most things these days.'

'You are very "tuned in" as you put it, but as you were not aware, even of their existence, then you were not expecting them, and so, you did not see them.'

'That makes me very sad, especially to know that such lovely creatures as they are, are just totally, through *ignorance*, ignored. Yet they have such an important job to do for all of nature everywhere. Why, oh why, does it have to be this way?'

'Sit with me, Aurora, a moment longer and let me tell you some very important facts about life and why things happen the way they do, so that you may understand better.'

'Thank you, Daniel. I would like that.'

'Sadly, that question you asked, for me is a very difficult question to answer specifically, as to why things are the way they are. Perhaps that part is a question that you can put to the *higher spirits* when next you see them. They may be better able to answer that. We however, the angels, that is the type of angels that I belong to, as there are many different types and levels of angels. It is our job, that is the angels on the level that I am, to look after each one of the humans, and, there is one of us to one human, although, we can also help others if the situation so arises. However, we are not allowed to understand many aspects of the human life, nor can we ever interfere in any way, except when something serious would happen that was not meant to happen to that person. We know that each one of you when you depart to Earth, have a *set path* to travel on and it is our job, together with your *higher self*, to ensure you stay on your chosen path.

'This is often a very difficult thing for us to do, because as you know, when you are on Earth for that life's particular experience, you still have *free will* to do what you wish. Usually, when you start to go wrong you will get a gut feeling that will nudge you in the right direction, often from us, but more usually from your *higher self*. Most times people will follow that nudge, but sometimes not, and that is when the trouble starts for many.

'Sometimes we and the *higher self*, together with their *spirit guide* who is also always with them, we can find a way back for them, but not in every case. When this happens, sadly, these people are very open to the pressures of the *dark side*, such as that which happened to your brother. Although, it is true to say, he was mainly on his chosen path with regards to the actual abduction. It was after that, when everything for him changed, it did not go the way that was meant, his leader had turned very much to the *dark side*.

'Thanks to your deep *love* and understanding, it made it so much easier when you brought him back to us and the light. The leader, I will tell you, is now dead to Earth and is suffering the consequences of his actions. It will be a long time before he learns that what is happening to him now, is as a direct result of his actions.

'You will be very pleased to know that, your brother, is progressing very well and will, as a result, now be able to help many others who find themselves in a similar situation to the one he was in. He has actually asked if he can help that man who was his master, to see if he can do for him what you did for your brother. That takes a very special kind of person to be able to do that. You made your brother that kind of person by your actions. So perhaps now, from all I have told you, you can now understand why I cannot answer your question directly for you.'

'I can, but that must be so hard for you sometimes. Especially when you, or whoever it is, know they, their charge, is straying away from the path they should be on.'

'Not hard, because we understand the way it is. We do not have the ability for all the different feelings and the emotions the human being has. Because of this we can do our work so much easier. We do however have to be very, very alert, and very often we ensure that something that a person thinks, is bound to happen to them. If what they see before them, does not happen to them, we have the ability then to interfere. We do have, as I said earlier, the power, a very great and a very strong power, to sometimes change the outcome of an event. Then people talk of a miracle, which to them it was.'

'So the pyramid, the earthquake, how did that happen and all the people who were in it that suffered, was that their life's true path?'

'Yes and no, is the answer to that question.'

'It can't be both, Daniel. How can it be both yes and no?'

'First, let me explain to you something you actually already know. You know that when it is a person's time on Earth, yes *their own time* on that particular trip on Earth, it has come to an end. Then something, yes something, will happen to ensure that the event happens exactly at the moment decreed. Nobody ever goes too soon, nor are they even a second of Earth time late. However, the method of their departure may change, due to circumstances that are not in their own control, such as all the terrible upheaval that is currently taking place on Earth at this moment. That is simply because the *dark side* is prevalent and anger and aggression are everywhere.

'There is much fighting, and the thought chain is all on that anger and aggression. Yes, there is a thought chain, just as there is a thought bank, where every thought that ever was, is held. The Earth itself is feeling all this and hence the results you are seeing and feeling. Oh yes, make no mistake about that, the Earth has feelings, you may not truly understand that, but it is true and it reacts in many different ways to these feelings.

A simple way you can see the Earth's feelings, when you throw a pebble into a pond or pool of water, watch the ripples spread out. The hard earth has the same effect, when something big strikes the land, the ripples go on through the ground and somewhere an earthquake results. In many years to come, *man-made* explosions will happen on Earth, that will then cause great earthquakes and massive, great waves called tsunamis. They will both cause great destruction and loss of life, because they do not, or should I say *will not*, accept what I have just told you to be the cause of these happenings on Earth. The Earth is a vibrating, living being and it is through these vibrations that these things will happen.

'A lot of the power of thought for each individual has now gone, but the *collective* power of thought, that is still very powerful. The *instant power of thought reaction* that the great people of Atlantis had, will not return for a very, very long time in Earth terms, but yes, thought. Never underestimate it. It is still very powerful in many ways and people get the results in their lives now, because of their own thoughts. What I can tell you is that six people, yes, just six people, with true *love* in their hearts, is so very much more powerful than a thousand with anger in their hearts.'

'Can the *higher spirits* not change the levels of anger and aggression that are around and put them back to where they were before, so that people can again live in harmony as it was?'

'God, that supreme being who is above everything, gave the people free choice, the freedom to choose their own path, and this they have done. So now, it is up to them to find their own way back, and they will, it will just take, on Earth, *time,* as with all things on Earth. But be assured, it will happen. The time of *Aquarius* will come back to Earth.

'You will remember I told you about the 'Akashic Records', the record of everything. If you wished or needed to, you could see and read about a happening from a time on Earth say, a million years ago, or even the life before this one that you so recently completed, then that you could do. Now there is also another book, shall we call it a 'Book of Possibilities'? Yes, a 'Book of Possibilities', that's a good name for it that you can understand. Well, it does exist. These are things that will happen sometime in the future. Yes, things that will happen. However, it is just that the exact moment of that happening is not specified. It is usually only given within a period, or as those on Earth would put it "a time frame". This is why, on Earth, when some people say such and such will happen, their mistake is quoting the *date,* as this is not a given time, *ever*. So yes, they are right and they are wrong. Yes, that will happen, but highly unlikely at the time they specify. There are too many other things involved for it to be that specific, including the way it will happen.'

'Daniel what you have just told me is so amazing.'

'Let me also tell you, that even though many people will sometimes, many times in the future, think they have "invented something" or "created something" new, they have not. They have simply linked into that *thought bank*, a bank of thoughts of everything that ever was, or will be, and from that bank they have produced their version of whatever they have thought about. Be assured, everything that ever was, or will be again in the future, has been before, in some form. There is absolutely nothing new, now or ever. It truly has all been done before, just in a different version and again, that will never change. Let me also tell you, that when people meditate on something, this is what they can tap into, that *thought bank*. Yes, a thought bank truly exists for all to benefit from, if they have the *patience* and the *will* to tap into it.'

'That is incredible, Daniel. Just how old is everything? I mean, what you have just said, in a way, seems so far-fetched and yet I know that you cannot lie ever, so I know what you have just said is true.'

'How old is everything? That is very simple to answer. With regard to everything, THERE IS NO BEGINNING AND THERE IS NO END. It is as simple as that. Just as to your *eternal life* there was no beginning, and there is also no end to it. What you can do with your eternal life is, if you feel your soul has achieved all you ever desire and wish for, you can just be with your God. But at some future time, and that sadly is the only word I can use, as time is something you understand, you may wish to start another learning experience in spirit, and so, you would again start to go to some planet to build a new set of experiences. So you see, you will never stop, ever. It will just be up to you to ensure you *love*, yes *love*, what it is you do and the experience will be that much greater. That is why *love* is the most important product of the universe, it truly is the currency of the universe. Everything, yes everything that is now, or ever was or will be in the future, is built on that one amazing building block, the building block of *love*. A sad fact to mention is, that although this is totally true, that *love* is the building block, it will not seem true when some results are realised, depending on what the end result is, because the wrong kind of love can destroy.

'I know you are now thinking, how can that be possible, but let me say to you, there are two sides to everything, if a person has the kind of *love* to build, say a war machine, he will build it, although destruction will be the end result. What I can say is this, true *love*, meaning happiness and joy, is very much the stronger *love* and this type of stronger *love* will always win in the end.'

'WOW! What you have just said to me will take some, um, 'time' to digest.'

'Yes, but now Aurora, we have talked enough. We must get everybody back together and set about completing this journey that we have embarked upon, and return to your home. From there, you and I will then go to the gardens together. Now, where are they all?'

'I think the girls have wandered off, but we can soon get them back. Crystal, where are you? We have to go.'

In the blink of an eye they were all back together. They gently skimmed the Earth, now completing all the places they had yet to visit, missing not one single faery, out of well over two hundred different types, then reviewing all they had seen, and so very soon they were all back in Aurora's house.

Daniel and Aurora then took there leave of them again and went quickly to the special gardens to begin the next phase of her learning with these special faeries. First she met 'The True Queen of the Faeries' called Queen of the Meadow and two of her very important helpers, the Travellers Joy faery and the Lords and Ladies faery.

Many others could be seen in the background and the thing that surprised Aurora, was the brilliance of these faeries' colours compared to the ones she had seen on their travels. Their colours here were so much stronger, so much brighter, so much clearer, even. She also learned that, wherever she had to go to, would depend on which faery would be needed with her on that trip. However, the Queen faery would also join them. With that in mind, she had to meet them all in this special garden, and talk with them, so that none were strangers to her. While there, she also met with other *spirit beings* like herself, who already did some of what she would now be doing.

As she completed meeting all the special faeries that actually resided in this special place in Heaven, only for them, she learned that her real work would now begin. Her work in spirit now began in earnest, as she was soon called upon to receive a little girl. So, with the correct faery beside her, she set off to collect her. The little girl had fallen in a pond where she had been playing and as she had always done, she had been talking to the faeries that were with the flowers by the pond, when she fell in.

Now sadly, she did not realise she was dead, having drowned in that pond and was now a *spirit being* herself.

She did not want to leave the faeries she was still with, by the pond, as they were more than just friends to her. Aurora found her happily enough and gently talked to her. Soon, with the little faery and the Queen faery, who she had also taken with her, they were on their way back, with the little child happily and safely in Aurora's arms and both the little faeries perched on her shoulder.

Now back, it was Aurora's job to trace any family she had, so that she could be reunited with them. That was not as easy as she had thought it would be, but eventually, she did find people who would have been grandparents of the little girl and a true and positive connection was made. The girl went off with her grandparents, feeling safe and happy, knowing she could still go and see her little friends in the gardens.

A successful result, and also a steep learning curve for Aurora, was now completed. She just knew from then on, that this was work she was going to thoroughly enjoy, and enjoy talking to Crystal about. The next trip, however, would prove to be a much more difficult task for Aurora. It was an elderly lady who had spent a lifetime with 'her faeries', as she called them, and had no desire ever to leave them.

Aurora's time, and more than considerable patience, which amounted to more than three weeks of Earth time, eventually rewarded her with the result she needed, and this lady would turn out to be another *spirit being,* who would help in the same work that Aurora was now involved in. Happy in the environment that she was now working in and with many successful collections now behind her, Aurora was somewhat surprised to find she was suddenly being summoned by the *higher spirits* to a meeting. That resulted in another talk to many others who were interested in what she did and wished to join the band of others in this task.

Having now got many of these experiences of this type under her belt, and that meeting out of the way, she thought she would go home and relax for a while. When she arrived back home again, who should suddenly show himself? None other than Daniel, with what appeared to be a smile on his face. 'Now Aurora, you will remember I told you before we went to the special gardens, that I had another surprise for you, as you still had much to learn?'

'Yes, I remember what you told me. I thought the first two trips were what you meant, they were both more than a bit special, especially the second one.'

'Oh no, Aurora! You're not even close with what your next lesson...no not a lesson, it's more, an exciting experience. Perhaps the one thing that may surprise you is that, yes, we are going on a trip, but it's a very special trip and your daughter, Crystal, is coming with us to help in this particular task.'

'Crystal? Now I am intrigued. So where are we going, and what are we going to do now?'

Love Is Kind

The Unexpected Review

Now Aurora was both confused and surprised, at what she had just been told by Daniel and was even more surprised when he told her they were all going to the sea, back on Earth. He then spoke to her with his serious tone, and said 'Aurora, you will remember I told you about the 'Akashic Records'. That record book, although it is not a book as you know a book to be, is held in the great building that holds all records from the very beginning. This is the only way I can put this so that you can understand, because as I have told you, there was no beginning, just as there will be no end.

'Now the reason I wish to take you there, is because I want you to remember something from a very long time ago, in Earth time. A time when you lived on Earth, in what were very different times and a very different situation. This was a *happy* time for you, so it is a memory that I know you will enjoy. I would never, ever take you back, nor ask you to visit an unhappy time, as I know that would be a very painful experience for you.

'The reason I wish you to go back and re-learn something is, well...let us go there and when you see what I want to show you, from this, you will then understand why we are doing what we are doing, when I tell you where we are going.'

So Daniel and Aurora went to that very large and truly magnificent, shimmering, azure coloured building that is the Hall of Records and seeking one of the recording officer spirits that maintained these records, they were able to quickly find the one that Daniel was looking for. The officer took Aurora and Daniel to a very special type of area, so they could now be alone to tune into the old memories and thoughts that would allow them to view this old life that was Aurora's. Except, back then, she was not known as Aurora. They sat down together and suddenly Grace was beside them saying 'I think it beneficial, Aurora, that I join you in this, as I may be able to help you.' They sat together and gathered their thoughts and allowed this life review, from over 4,000 Earth years before her last life in Khem, to start.

She saw first, her birth at that time, as she slipped from her mother's womb into the area by the shore, that was a specially built pool, full of clean, blue sea water, that was refreshed daily by the tide. As she grew, she found as a very young child, she was never out of the sea. Always swimming about with all the fish everyday, as she frolicked in the water.

She was as much at home in the water as a sea person, as she was a normal human. Fascinated totally by all that she saw and then, to her surprise, she learned that there was a certain big fish, a dolphin (the dolphin was known as God's angel fish by her people of that time, because they could all see a wonderful bright aura around these big fish, when they were jumping out above the water), that she discovered had taken a great liking to her, even as a very, very young child. Every time she went into the water, it was there, close beside her and ensuring that she was always safe, almost mothering her.

It also taught her many tricks that she could now do in the water. It helped her to learn how to breathe, so that she could dive for long periods under the water very safely. (Grace commented that this dolphin was treating her, and had in fact treated her like she was her own baby.) Aurora saw what a great, fun life it had been during her young years in this place. She watched as she grew older in that life and learned how to catch fish. She stood quietly in the water and then tickled them as they relaxed in her hand, so her family always had fresh fish to eat. Her father had a sort of strange, almost circular boat that he fished with, which had a sharp, very hard point, at the front. Very useful when there were sharks around. He also used it to transport others around to other islands nearby. She also learned that he made no charge for this, and in fact, nobody ever paid for anything. They all just helped each other in every way they could. Nobody went hungry and nobody ever hurt anybody else.

Another big surprise for her was how deep she could go, very safely with her dolphin always beside her. She also taught her that if she went very deep, she then had to rise slowly so she did not suffer as some who went diving did. On one of her dives with them she found a cave which was deep down in the cliff face near to where they lived and this became a favourite place for her.

What did surprise her, was that the dolphin knew she could get air there in that cave, as the water did not fill to the roof of the cave, and the dolphin could also get air there. On this first occasion to the cave, her mate, who also often swam with them, kept close beside her. This place where she lived was a beautiful lagoon, full of bright colours and the water was almost crystal blue and clear, as was the sky.

It was when they got to the point of her visit to the cave, that Daniel now tried to stop the review, because as far as he was concerned, they had reached the point where she now knew all she needed to know, for the task that he knew was ahead of her. Aurora, however, had other ideas, as she was really enjoying watching this life. She was so very happy in it. Now, however, she was about to find out why Daniel had wanted to stop it where he had.

One of the things that had surprised her, as she reviewed this life, was that nobody by the sea ever wore any form of clothing or protection, except when it was very stormy, and that situation was very, very rare. All their bodies were so beautiful, so toned and firm and a very gentle tan colour. What also surprised her was that everybody had such great respect, not only for themselves because of the way they were, but more importantly, for everybody else. Being naked there, was just a normal way of life, but from this way that they were, she now learned a lesson of what could happen in the water if she was not careful.

She reckoned she must have been about twelve summers old at this point. She had gone into the sea to swim with her dolphin friends, but on this occasion, they had tried very hard to stop her getting into the water. Finally they gave up and let her in, and off she swam. The two dolphins, however, never left her side, swimming unusually close to her and suddenly, as she swam, she, totally unaware, started to leave a little red trail behind her. Her first warning something was wrong was, not that she was leaving a trail, as she could not see it, but when she saw the shark aiming straight for her.

Suddenly, as if out of nowhere, the area was now filled with many dolphins and now *two* sharks trying hard to get to her. The dolphins fought these sharks with great speed and efficiency, to try and keep them from her, as she turned and raced for the shore. She had barely reached the shore with the help of the female dolphin and started to run, as one of the sharks misjudged the wave of water that was carrying them and beached itself on the sands. She turned as she heard her dolphins 'speak' to her. They were both now standing on their tails in the water, almost shouting in their high pitched squeak at her, scolding her and telling her off.

Two thoughts now occurred to her. The first was, she knew life was precious and because of what she had done, the shark, unless they could get it back in the water, would surely die. Unfortunately, they told her it was too dangerous to try and get it back into the water. However, it did now become a meal and a great celebration of her safe escape from its jaws.

The second thought was, she now remembered what her mother had told her, as this was the second time the *moon period* had taken her. Of course, it was the last of the old moon today, and all the women here were fully in tune with the moon's cycles, as they all slept, basically, in the open and were therefore all influenced by the cycle of the moon. She remembered she had been told, that she should not, could not, swim in the sea at this time. It was very dangerous for her, and now she had learned just how serious it could have been, if she had not had her dolphin friends swimming close with her.

She watched and waited every morning, until she saw that the moon cycle had passed and then she was straight back in the water, giving her dolphin friends, who were as always, waiting for her, a great big hug and kiss for what they had done for her. Almost every day of her life, that she could, she swam with them. It was just magic for her, a truly magical memory that Daniel had allowed her to see. It was a good memory, a really good memory to have looked back on, but Aurora knew there was much more to this than her just seeing this life review memory, beautiful though it had been to watch.

It now took Daniel some considerable effort to get her to leave this review, because she was watching something that was so lovely, so moving, as that life had been a very happy life for her, in a wonderful place and time. What she also discovered after that review was finished, was the fact that she had had *three* other lives between that one and the one she had just completed. That surprised and amazed her, but she was not allowed to review any of them, as they were not relevant to what she had to know about now; nor, as Daniel implied, were they lives she would necessarily want to see again.

'Well Aurora, I know that you have just enjoyed that life review experience. I am glad that you have been able to see that, that life, was a very happy and rewarding experience for you, and as you saw, it was a long and peaceful one. The other thing that perhaps you did not notice was that, even back then in that life, your great *love* for all things, even the shark that nearly killed you, shone through for all to see.'

'Thank you for allowing me to see it, but I know there was more to that experience than me just reviewing an old life, Daniel. So, why have we just done that? What was it for and what is the real reason for me seeing that?'

'Aurora, you have been very privileged to see many of God's creatures. Creatures that very few ever get to see in the way you have been allowed. This is because the *high priests* know you have abilities way above many others, and can cope with difficult tasks with great *love* and never show anything else, but *love*. For the tasks, or should I say the work that you have been asked to do, this is very important. Trust me, if you were not up to these tasks, you would not have been asked if you can do them. Remember you always have a choice.'

'I know I do, but I always really enjoy all that I do. It is such a great pleasure to be able to bring someone home safely, so what more could you ask for than that?'

'There are many who would not agree with you, even though they are here in spirit, but they have much to learn and that is why you are, so often, asked to talk to others. Let us now move on.'

Love is Gracious

Aurora and the Amazing Sea Creatures

'Well Aurora, it is time we set off on this work you have been asked to do. But let me first say to you, you are about to meet with another of God's very wonderful creatures. This very amazing sea creature that has great similarities, both to yourself and that wonderful place that you have just had the pleasure of reviewing.'

'I gather that it has more than something to do with the sea, based on what you said before we did that life review, Daniel?'

'You are quite correct, Aurora, but before I tell you more, we must get Crystal, because you will remember I told you she was coming with us on this trip. So, let's go and get her, as this will be a surprise to her. Nobody, as yet, has said anything to her about this trip and I know she will be overjoyed that she can go with you.'

As they arrived back at Aurora's house, they found Crystal chatting to her friend, who is not so little now and is indeed, taller than Crystal. 'Crystal, I am sorry, but you will need to say goodbye to your friend for a while. You, together with your mum, and also with Rebecca and I, are about to go on a very special trip to bring three people, who do not want to leave where they are, back home again.'

'Oh magic! Mum, we have not done this before, have we? Where are we going to, is it somewhere exciting, somewhere different for us?'

'Now I already know, Crystal, that you have already been underwater and not only when you went to collect your little friend. You have actually done several other trips that also involved you going underwater. So I know this will present no fear for you in this trip, as we are again, going deep underwater.'

'Mum can't swim! CAN SHE?'

'Now, Aurora. You have just seen yourself and how amazing you were in the water before, so I am sure that you will have well and truly remembered about the water and have no fear about the trip we are going on. So yes, Crystal. In answer to your question, she knows she can swim, she has also seen just how good a swimmer she really is.'

So now the four of them, Aurora, Daniel, Crystal and of course the angel Rebecca, set off together with Daniel leading the way. Aurora thought to herself 'I don't think Grace is very far away, I feel her near me', and in her mind she had the reply 'I am close.'

'Do you see those big rocks down there at the edge of the sea? Look closely and tell me what you see.' Daniel asked.

'Ah! I see the rocks,' Crystal replied, 'there looks to be two ladies sitting on them, reclining in the sun.'

'Look again very closely at these two *ladies* you see, are you sure they are ladies, Crystal?'

'Yes, of course they are, Daniel, they've just got no clothes on. BUT they appear to have fish tails!'

'So they have, Crystal! What are they, Daniel, or should I say, who are they?'

'These, Aurora, are the creatures, the very special creatures, that I told you we were going to meet. They are going to take us to those we have to collect, as they are very deep underwater and now far from land at present.'

'But I know this place Daniel, I know this is the place I have just watched myself swim in, in that life-review that we have just done.'

'You are correct, Aurora, this is the same place. It is slightly different to how it was when you lived here and that is because of several severe cliff falls over time. The sea has worn down the cliff faces, but it is the same place, so let us now set down beside the ladies, the 'mermaids', as that is what they are called. 'Mermaids' and 'water sprites' are the creatures God gave to look after the sea, the rivers and all pond waters. The water is their life, and these two mermaids (you could call them water angels, for that is indeed, what they really are), they have been keeping our friends safe for us, so that the *dark side* could not get to them. They too, are trying very hard to get souls who have lost their way back, to go with them. Now you know how important all your work is, and why we need to be very vigilant at all times with your protection that I told you about before. Now let us speak with these ladies, as I know they are anxious to speak with you.'

Daniel introduced them to the two beautiful mermaids, and beautiful they really were, with truly amazing colours running down through their tails, that changed colour as they swished them in the water. Daniel said, that it is this beauty that makes them so good at what they do, not only for us, but for the good of all the people they collect for us, to take back safely.

What they had done on this occasion was to, at first, persuade two men, while they were still alive, to follow them into a cave and try to keep them alive. Because of rock falls, they were now very much further from the shore than when Aurora had last lived here. The boy that had been alive for a while in the water with them, had now died. He had been unable to hold his breath for long enough when they dived and the men had been unable to revive him when they got him into the air in the cave they were taken to. The water was not cold, but he had swallowed a great deal of sea water.

Thanks to the mermaids, they had lived on fish for a few days, but they would not leave the boy, who was a son of one of them. One of the men died, the cold air in the cave had got to him and they had no means to light a fire. The mermaids had done what they could to try to persuade the other to leave with them, but he would not go on his own, as the boy was his son. He could not understand at this point what was so special about these mermaids, how they could do all that they did. He did not realise they were *beings of spirit* and not as he thought, although he was not entirely sure what he thought.

Sadly, he also died, not only from the cold, but the sadness in his heart, first at the loss of his son and now his friend. It was at this point that the thought message from the mermaids finally got through to those in spirit. All three were now dead to Earth, yet not aware of it, and they did not wish to leave these beautiful people they were with. They thought they would be safe here, forever.

The two mermaids now guided our four friends towards the cave, but before they got there, Aurora was met and greeted by a couple of dolphins who made a great fuss of her. Aurora now remembered the way to the cave herself, from watching that life review. They found the two men and the boy sitting quietly on the rocks in the cave, who could not believe the sight that suddenly appeared before them, as our friends entered the cave and subsequently also exited the water to be with them.

It took a very long discussion between them, before first of all, they accepted the fact they were now dead to Earth, then to persuade them that they too, were actually now spirits, *beings of light*. Then, to enter the water with them to leave the cave and return, not just out of the water to dry land, but back home to their friends in spirit, who now awaited them. Crystal, together with the young boy, who had been much quicker on the uptake as to what had happened to him, had been the first to enter the water and they soon disappeared from view. Aurora was not worried, *mind to mind* was working for her. Shortly after Crystal had left, they finally all joined hands and made for the tunnel back out to the open sea and swam to the rocks where the mermaids had previously been sitting.

Aurora knew they could have done all this, simply by the power of her thought, but she did not wish to frighten them. She knew they would be more relaxed if they simply swam to the shore, that being something they both knew they could do, and understood they could do. They all talked for a while, of course it was all *mind to mind,* but the two men and the boy at present did not understand this and their mouths worked as if they were using words. Not until the men and the boy felt safe enough to leave the safety of the rocks and what they knew, would they all start on their journey home.

They finally said their goodbyes to these two wonderful mermaids who had helped them, and Aurora to her two dolphin friends, who had stayed with her all the time she was there. She kissed them goodbye, as they squeaked at her with excitement and she took the two men, one each side, knowing that, although Daniel was no longer visible to them, he was still beside them, as was Grace, who had kept quietly in the background. Crystal had not stopped with the boy at the shore, but had simply taken him straight back to spirit and the light, dealing with everything very matter-of-factly. Aurora soon went safely and speedily with the men to the end of the tunnel, by the great white light, saying to them she would meet them on the other side when they came through the light and get them safely to their friends, who were now awaiting them on the other side.

That was Aurora's first, of many trips with the mermaids, as she was soon to do several other trips in the water for others. Others who would not leave, for their fear of the unknown. The experiences with the mermaids would be varied and not infrequent, but all with their own unique problems, which Aurora soon found easy to deal with and very often with Crystal by her side.

It did not surprise Aurora, to find that the two dolphins were always close by her, whenever she was in the water. One trip with Crystal, had been after a severe earthquake followed by a massive tsunami, where a great swathe of land had been completely washed away and a vast area was now totally submerged. There had been many helpers with them on that trip, as many hundreds had lost their Earthly lives and needed help to go home to spirit. Their own local witch doctor, who to them was their God, had told them they would all perish in hell when the earthquake started. They had quite a job to sort that out, but as always *love* wins in the end.

At the end of another trip with Crystal and having ensured their charges were safely with their family, they set off home to find Daniel appearing before them as they arrived. 'Successful trip once again you two, but now I need you, Aurora please, to come with me, as you have someone else to meet and another trip shortly to make.'

Crystal shouted at Daniel, saying, 'We have only just returned from a trip, so why does she have to go straight away again?'

'Ah! Dear Crystal, in some ways you are correct in asking, but these decisions, as you know, are not mine to make. I can only do as I am asked.'

'But this is very unfair. I would like some time with my mum to talk about things. Can't she stay with me for a while, please?'

'Sorry Crystal, sometimes somethings can't wait. They have a specific time to happen. There is that word, time, again, yet there is no such thing.'

Sadly, Crystal hugged her mum saying to her, 'See you soon, Mum.'

Love

It Can Move Mountains

The Crystal Caves

"Well Aurora. You have now met many of God's truly, very amazing creatures, who have all been able to help you on your travels. The result of all this, together with your *love,* has made your work here a great success, but now it is time to meet another one that will surprise you, and a really jolly fellow he and his friends are.'

'How many more of God's creatures do I still have to meet, Daniel?'

'This Aurora, is at present, the last one that you will meet. God has a great many; so many, that you could never hope to meet with them all. What is important is that you meet with the ones that can help you and all of us who do this type of work that you do. This one that you are about to meet is actually a very, very important one, not just for you, but also for all the people on Earth, for both now, and indeed, for the future. Yes, even more so in the future. They have a very difficult and very, very important job. Indeed, the future on Earth could...no, *it does* depend on how they do all their work.

'We are about to embark on a trip deep, deep into a mountain and a crystal cave within it. Now, as you already know, all *crystals* are a very important part of the Earth's structure. In fact the main crystal that is extremely *massive,* yes, massive is the word I would use, is at the centre of the Earth's core and its make up, in its own superstructure, is what's holding planet Earth on its axis. In its make up are two poles and they are like the centre pins that hold the Earth steady on its course, as it spins. They do move fractionally, constantly, because the crystal moves within the body of the Earth. But yes, that crystal is what really holds the Earth steady on its course and will do, as long as the Earth survives.

'Another great and very important crystal on Earth, is the giant crystal that ran Atlantis before it fell. That crystal, or a major part of it, is at the bottom of a very, very deep part of the ocean, probably the deepest part anywhere on Earth. It is also very strong in the work that it does, and it still holds the *portal,* the gateway, that the people of Atlantis used to go between the two worlds. When people on Atlantis had completed the experience on Earth that they were there for, and they knew their time on Earth had been completed, they simply walked through the portal, or gateway if you like, discarding their Earthly body as they went. Just like an old cloak they were now finished with.

'Some very high people on Atlantis could come and go through the portal as they needed, to complete their tasks. That I know, you will find very hard to accept, but I promise you, what I say is true, I cannot tell a lie. Sadly, when Atlantis fell it was because the people of Earth had taken a great step backwards, and as I told you, it will be a very long time before that ability returns, but it will. The Earth's *Time of Aquarius* will bring that happening very close again.

'Another interesting point I would like to tell you is this. All the people of Atlantis, yes everybody, they had their very own crystal. Everybody had one that was given to them at the time of their birth, so that it was not only special to them, but it was specifically tuned to them. It was the crystal for their birth period. For instance, blue agate or amber, both come under, and can influence, those that are born in the period of Leo, as is marcasite. Lazulite or jade can influence those from Gemini, as does celestite. Or perhaps it's a blue coral for the Sagittarian and Aquarian periods, although there is a lot more to their own crystal than just that. There are also specific crystals with regard to the chakras. So, a person who is born to Earth, the responsible expert at the time in Atlantis, would know which specific crystal suited that newborn, to help them on their chosen life's path. As that person grew, they learned, or rather were taught, how to tune their crystal into the main one that ran Atlantis, to help them in their life's path.'

'Oh Daniel! I am very lucky to have such a great angel as you and all that you tell me, indeed teach me. How do you know all this? Is it all because of what you know through the 'Book of Probabilities'? Why, or how, is it that this little one, as you call him, the one we are about to meet, is so very important to all that you have just told me?'

'Perhaps, in a way, I have phrased that wrong, as all God's creatures are very important in their own way, but this one is of *prime importance,* because of the tasks they do for Mother Earth. This particular lovely creature, who is actually full of fun, has a lot of the time, although time is a misnomer, to work deep in the ground mainly in the dark. Very dark for humans, if the human does not carry a form of light. Where we are going, natural light does not exist. However, this very clever little fellow can see clearly in light or dark, to him it makes no difference. The other thing about this magnificent little fellow is that temperature also makes no difference to him. Hot or cold, to him it is all the same.

'All through planet Earth there are vast natural caverns. These caverns are mainly the homes to these beautiful little creatures, as they walk through all of Earth, going about their work, constantly tending to all of Earth's natural resources. Throughout Earth there are a great number of different types of substances, which the people of Earth will, over the period of Earth's life, discover they can use. Some to help them in their tasks, some to heat their homes, there will be hundreds of uses they will find for these substances. Sadly, not all will be for good, but that will be their choice. Working underground is a dark and not very safe place to be, as many will find. The ground is always moving and there is a lot of water trapped throughout Earth's superstructure and that is always a grave danger to man, working underground.

'However, one thing I will stress to you, although it is dark most of the time underground where we are going, certainly to the human being at least, we are not moving over to the *dark side*. I simply cannot ever do that, so you may relax with that thought that I know was troubling you.

'Now, with regard to the 'Book of Probabilities'. Yes, that is what it says in that great book, and I know all that it says is true. Except, as I believe I have told you before, it cannot tell you the exact time, as you well know, time does not exist here. But again, as I have said before, everything in it will happen, but when they happen, that is subject to many other things. As the humans on Earth go through each phase, the results of each, is a direct result of how they have done in that phase. That is why nothing can be specified, as some people who claim to be *psychic* on Earth claim. They could be a hundred years out or even a thousand, all they are doing is guessing.'

'From what you are telling me, it sounds as if a great many so called psychics, are not *true* psychics and that is so misleading to the people on Earth. Another way, perhaps, to control people. Are we are now going to go underground, Daniel? I know I can do this, as I know that I can still see, even if it is dark to the human eye, can't I?'

'That is correct Aurora. As a spirit, as you now know, light and dark do not truly ever exist for us, unless you call it up, as we are all truly in the *light.* So you are right on both counts, Aurora. Yes, we are going underground and yes, you will have no trouble seeing. It makes no difference to you on Earth now, where you are. Nothing is ever *solid* on Earth to you now, you can, as a *being of light,* pass through everything, if you so wish. This you know from your own experiences as you have gone about your work, and if you remember, you did call up a dark night when you remembered the night at home, back when you were living there.'

'Yes, Daniel, you are so right. I did call up that picture and I also saw my friend's face in the moon. So where are we going to this time, Daniel and when do we leave?'

'Now, if you are ready, Aurora. However, would you like to go to the Hall of Colours first? We have done a lot recently, and it is important that you refresh yourself from time to time. It is a long time since you were last there to do just that, and I think Crystal was very aware of that fact. That is one of the reasons why she shouted at me.'

'Perhaps, Daniel, that would be a good idea. I do not feel as if I am shining as bright as I would like to be, especially if we are going on a trip such as you have just described to me. So yes, let us go there first. I also think you are correct in what you said about Crystal. She has grown into a very thoughtful lady and I am so very proud of my beautiful daughter and of her achievements.'

So they both set off to the Healing Halls, walking slowly as they went through the garden area, conversing *mind to mind* as they walked, about some of the past trips they had made. They were often stopped by others they met, as they walked through these beautiful gardens that the halls were set in, talking to all those that they met. What surprised Aurora, was the number of faeries that now stopped to talk to her as they walked, and even more so, when the Queen faery came up to her and said, 'You will love the jolly little fellows you are soon to meet Aurora, they are wonderful, all of them.'

'How does she know who I am going to meet, Daniel, before I even know myself who it is?'

'Ah, Aurora! That is because these two beautiful creatures very often have to work very closely together, and of course, they all talk to each other, just as you do when you meet with friends. Such as we are doing now, as we walk through these gardens.'

'So, in many ways, we all, as God's creatures, are the same or similar in our habits?'

'Yes, that is a brilliant and true thought Aurora, indeed we are all like that. Us angels also do the same when we meet one we have not seen for a while. So now we have arrived, let us go inside these halls to refresh ourselves and prepare for our next journey. It will be a tiring journey that we will soon set out on.'

Aurora, with Daniel by her side, slowly walked through the Healing Hall of Colours, feeling a great benefit from them, as she went through each colour again. She could see in herself the changes and the benefits of doing this, something she had taken for granted on her previous trips here. Now she thought to herself, 'I should not take all this for granted, it is so special to be able to do this and feel the great benefit we get out of it.'

Daniel, reading her mind, said to her, 'It is just the same as when on Earth you eat; that refreshes you and is what enables you to carry on with your life. It is the same with the colours here. It is as if they were the meal, except you are not actually eating anything.'

'Yes, you are right Daniel, in that respect, but we should never, ever take things for granted, be it here in these halls, or on Earth when we, or they, eat their food. An attitude of *gratitude* in life, indeed in everything, is very important and a better way to live, whether we are here in spirit, or as a human still on Earth.'

'Sad, that now so many people on Earth take everything for granted and yet, everything they receive is actually a gift, a very precious gift from God. But they now no longer see it as a gift, for some strange reason they see it as their divine right. How very, *very* wrong they all are in their attitude to these precious gifts.'

"How do you think we can change that *attitude* Daniel? Because change it we must.'

'Ah! Aurora, let me assure you that it will in the future. It will change, but as I have told you before, it will take a long, long time in Earth terms, before both attitude and everything else begins to change, but yes, change it will. There will be on Earth, over the next few thousand years, and especially the latter hundred centuries, many different conflicts all over the planet; some very serious as everybody tries to say their way is the right way. This point of course is never correct. It is just bullying, so that they can have it their own way.

'Now in the 'Book of Probabilities' it states that, just before things really start to change, what is likely to happen some way, is that there will be two very, very serious events, close together, on Earth. In fact, it is through these events, when they happen, that the change will start, but as I say, they are many, many years away, and much nearer to the 'Age of Aquarius' that we talked about. Only after the second of these serious events and the impact from the seriousness of these events, will it then very slowly start to change for the people of that period, as their general *mind set* starts to change.

'The first event, if that is what you would call it, will see the deaths and disfigurement of many, many young men, and some women as they try to help the men in their time of great need. The second major happening will be as a result of the first event, as a man, who will be a great orator, tries at first, to get his country working again, after they have lost that first conflict, and other nations try to rule them. His success in what he does, will run amok and the *dark side,* who he will be sadly connected to from his very young life, because of the way he was treated as a child, and he will also be in and out of prison at one time of his life. He will succeed in getting the men working again and his country moving away from stagnation, but sadly they will make war machines and as a result, his own ambition will be to rule the world through fear.

'Another great and very serious conflict will arise, and like the first, will also result in a world-wide conflict. Again, millions will die at his hands, until he is finally defeated, as he will be. After this terrible period, as the people struggle to rebuild their shattered lives, the new, young people of this period on Earth will start to rebel and find their feet, as they discover they have not been told the truth. They will realise that again *greed* and *avarice*, such as that which has come to the fore on this planet recently, have caused these immense changes we have just seen, before and during your last visit. Your last life on Earth, is more than ever, going to be the root cause of their problems again on Earth.

'However, the young will be more interested in trying to teach *love and peace,* after all the very terrible things that have happened, and will be continuing to happen. This will be the very small start of the great changes that will happen, as the 'Age of Aquarius' nears.

'All this, as I have said, is in the 'Book of Probabilities' that I told you about some time previously. It will happen, these changes, yes, it will all happen, but as always, no time is ever given. Let me also tell you, that great place Atlantis, that fell just before your time that you have just lived, will again rise up and be as it was, when the great changes have happened. It is, I am told, even now, already beginning to form in the ether, and is, and will continue to be, worked on until the time is right for it to appear again on Earth, as it will. Yes, as it certainly will. There will by then, probably be only one language on Earth, as that was what was first envisaged when everything began, when the Earth was born and man was placed on it.

'The great portal that was on Atlantis, that people whose time on Earth was finished just simply walked through, this will again be the case. People will know when their time is over, through illness or some other reason, and just go back through the portal doorway.'

'Should I read this great 'Book of Probabilities' while I am here in the ether, Daniel, should I get to know more?'

'If it is ever important to your next life, the part that is important, you will be given to read. So no, you have enough on your plate as it were, at present, but it is nice sometimes just to talk about the future. I know we angels do not have, nor do we show emotions, but it does excite me to know what wonderful times do really lie ahead for Earth. Now, Aurora. I think it is time we were moving on. See, there is that word *time* again and yet it just does not exist, but I know no other word to express what I mean. This is why it is very difficult for those not in spirit to understand much of what is said. The finite, such as is on Earth, and the infinite, as we are now, are so vastly different.'

'So much change ahead for everybody on planet Earth over the next major period, Daniel. It will be a very different place when all these things you have talked about happen. Now, where are we going, Daniel, where is our destination and who are we going to meet when we get there?'

'So many questions, Aurora, but you are right to ask them. We are, as I told you earlier, going to a cave. A crystal cave where many men work, digging out crystals to sell. There has been a serious fall inside the cave and a man is trapped, or rather his *body* is, but he will not leave there, as this place has been his life for so long. He does not know any different, so he is with who we are going to meet, so that we can bring him home.'

'What has happened, Daniel, in the cave to cause this fall?'

'Greed and carelessness in truth, all caused by the owner of the cave. His workers do not matter to him. All he wants is the end product to sell and make more money for him to hoard.'

'That is terrible, Daniel. Does he not realise his workers are the ones who allow him to have what he seeks?'

'He does not see it that way, as greed clouds his judgement and his mind from the truth, just as it does with so many others in a similar position. Now take my hand and we will go swiftly to them and see what we can do to bring this man who has been killed, home to his family who await him. They know of his demise, but his mind is shut off from what is correct. In fact, he never knew them while on Earth as a human being, so he does not see them trying to get him home. He thinks they are all dead, but he does not understand that he too, is now dead to Earth.'

Aurora and Daniel speedily arrived at the entrance to the great cave in the mountain side and slowly wound their way down the pathway, deep into the cave. They knew they could have gone straight through the mountain to the scene of the accident, but they did not wish to frighten the man. They were very, very deep inside the cave when they came across a huge cavern that was covered in clear white quartz, this creating its own form of light. Many paths led off from this cavern, but they knew which one to take, as they journeyed on, deeper into the cave. They came across the start of the part that had caused the fall, and now they had to pass through what, basically, was a solid pile of rubble and crystal material. This they did and found they still had not reached the man they sought.

Going further in, they passed through more rubble and eventually they found the man they were looking for. He was being guarded by a little, white-bearded man in a red jacket and red trouser-like garments. On his head was a soft hat with a white bauble on the end and a little pick in his hand. 'Aurora meet Mr. Gnome. He and his two companions, yes they do all look alike, they have been looking after this poor man we have come to collect.

'As you can see, he is now sitting outside his body, knowing that something is wrong, but still, he will not leave his friends who he has worked with, all his working life. He is one of the very rare ones now, men that have been able to actually *see* the gnomes, and they have helped him achieve all that he has done. Through them, he has found many magnificent crystals for his boss over a very long time, but in truth, has had little reward for what he has achieved. His boss knows of this fall, but he is not bothered. Life to him is cheap, as long as it is not his own.'

They chatted to the gnomes and the man they had come to collect, about all that he had been doing, for as far as the man was concerned, his entire lifetime. He had actually started as a young boy working in this cave for over forty summers. Daniel also told them about how and when this mountain had been formed, way back when the Earth was still in its infancy and covered by many volcanoes and the first of the very large animals that were now a long time extinct. He told them how the heat formed the crystals, as it cooled after a volcanic surge had blown great holes in the tops of the mountains. They then started to talk to the man about taking him home, but this took much longer than Daniel thought.

Eventually, they managed to persuade him to come with them and all three of them went straight up, actually through the mountain, just as Daniel had described it. Exiting into the open air at what was the top of a great, snow covered mountain top, they now looked down and only then, did Aurora realise just how deep inside the mountain they had been. The journey was now completed in the blink of an eye, to the welcoming white light where the life review for this man now took place.

After he came out of the white light, it took a while for Aurora to find and sort out the correct family and soul group for this man. Even with her daughter Crystal's help, it had been like trying to find that needle in the haystack. It turned out he had been found, dumped in a bundle of rags as a newborn baby, by a travelling band of warriors. They, in turn, had taken him and handed him over to some old lady they had come across on their travels. It was really a miracle that he had actually survived his start in life, and it was no surprise that he and the gnomes had joined forces, so to speak. The old lady, who had somehow kept him alive as a baby and followed him in his life, had taught him how to see and speak with the gnomes, who she had told to look after him. She knew he would work in the crystal caves and would need their help.

Aurora had many other lovely trips that involved these wonderful jolly old men, as she called them. Their laughter was infectious and her trips were always a wonder to be on. She had managed to take Crystal on a couple of the trips that involved the gnomes and they had had great fun, despite the seriousness of the work they were doing. These trips involved mostly men and young boys and once they realised the truth of their situation, they were often happy to have some fun, before they went home to spirit with them.

Aurora and her daughter were always happiest when they worked together, which lasted for some time, although time, as you now know, in spirit is a misnomer. They had together completed over three hundred trips, but Aurora, herself, had lost count of the number of different trips she had carried out, to all sorts of places. Sometimes they involved the faeries, sometimes the gnomes, and then the special ones with the mermaids.

Aurora particularly loved all the water trips. In fact, she often thought that if she had to pick a favourite trip, or type of trip, these would always be her favourite, as she would always get to meet her beloved dolphins, who were, somehow, always there to greet her. Aurora felt that, somehow, she could *mind to mind* converse with them and could almost tell what they were thinking.

Aurora's next move would involve an unexpected turn of events for her. One that she was not prepared for in her current cycle of this, her eternal life, especially as she was so happy in what she did.

Love is the Most Powerful, Vibrational Energy Force in the Universe

Aurora is Summoned to Appear Before the Council

The last time she had been summoned, had been for one of her many talks that she had given, and these requests were never to the Golden Temple. She always knew what she was going to do beforehand, as that talk in the great Meeting Hall was always based on the work she had done, especially if it had been a difficult or an unusual task. I wonder, she thought, what was this request to the *high ones* in the Golden Temple about? She could not think of anything she had done and strangely for her, no answer was forthcoming into her mind, not even from Daniel, and that did concern her.

This time, Aurora, as she had been summoned to the main Golden Temple, knew in herself that this was going to be a very different and special meeting of minds. What she did not know was the subject matter and could not think of what it could possibly be. She wondered, why had she had not been forewarned? As Daniel had not appeared to her to help her in any way, she was now very concerned. What was wrong? She duly arrived at the Golden Temple and as before, the two magnificent tall angels, who were always here at the main entrance, as if on guard, opened the doors for her to enter.

She was told to now make her way to the high chamber where she would be met. So, Aurora proceeded to the appointed area as instructed and at that point, at last, Daniel now appeared before her, telling her to be seated at the long table and the *high priests* would join her shortly. He also said to her 'At this point, I can tell you nothing Aurora, as I also have not been told the reason for your calling at this time.'

Aurora did not have long to wait. As soon as Daniel faded, six of the *high priests* instantly appeared before her and thanked her for coming. Strangely Grace was also with them. 'I am sure you are anxious to hear why you have been sent for, so we will not keep you in suspense any longer. You have been very successful in all that we have asked you to do for spirit. As always, you have far exceeded our expectations of you in every way, so we have decided that it is time you were given the chance...no, the opportunity, to move on in your eternal life. We would like to talk to you about a new Earthly life that we would like you to be a *major* part of.

'There is coming a time when one of the new Pharaohs in Egypt (which is and was the country you called 'Khem', when you were last there on your previous life on Earth), is shortly to be born to this kingdom. In his life, when he marries, his wife will bear a daughter and it is our wish, that the daughter be you, if you will agree to this. I know, sorry, *we* know that you will wish to learn just who the other spirits are, that are to be involved in this new life. More of what your path will include in this new life will be discussed with you, after you have met with them. As always you will have choices in that life, but there are certain things that will be expected of you, while on your path in that life.'

A little of the life path was discussed with Aurora and the next meeting, Aurora was told, would happen after she had returned from the second of two trips she was shortly to make. Aurora was then allowed to return home, to think about all that she had just been told.

Crystal, her daughter, who for a long time now had been a fully grown *being of light*, greeted her as she arrived home, with a big hug and asked her what the special meeting was all about.

'I am about to prepare for a new life on Earth, shortly. I have to meet soon with the others involved with this life, but first I have two trips to make, who for, as yet I do not know. I know that the time of my return is not yet, as the spirit who is to be my father in that life, has not yet departed spirit to take up his new life. I know I will meet him before he goes, but apart from that, as yet, I can tell you nothing. I wish I could see your dad, as I do not seem to be able to get hold of him and I would like to talk to him about this proposed new life.'

'I wonder if I will be involved in your next life, Mum, that would be very nice. I suppose I shall just have to wait and see if I get called. I know that Rebecca and I are about to go and collect another child who does not want to come home. She has fallen into a deep hole in the woods where she was playing with some other children, and the rescuers are having to dig to get her body out, as it is very narrow. We know all that because

232

she believed in the faeries and two from the woods are now with her, trying to console her and your friend, the Queen faery, is coming with me.'

'I will still be here for you when you get back, so please, do not worry about me.'

So Crystal went off on her trip to get the child, knowing, that again, she would have to shrink herself at first to child size, to get the child's confidence. This was a regular occurrence for her in the work she now did. Aurora now went outside to sit in her garden to think, at the same time she thought about her 'other' father, that very special man from that other planet. Although she had spoken to him many times since she had returned to spirit, she thought it was now quite a while since she had last spoken to him and she wondered just where he was. Suddenly before her, stood that very special man, the man she had sought to speak with and he took her in his arms in a way he had never before done and just held her close.

'What? How? When did you…? How did I not know you were here in spirit, dear man, how did I not know? Oh, it is so nice to see you, but what happened, why are you here?'

'I have been back here, in spirit, for quite a while. I got too old for all that travelling and then my heart started to give out, so I just walked through our portal door, a door similar to the one that was once on Earth in Atlantis. Because I belong to a different soul group and type to you, I have had to wait till you were ready and wished to see me, only then could I come to you. As you can now see, our spirit bodies are slightly different, just as we were slightly different when we met before on Earth.

'Where I could survive on Earth, you could not survive on my home planet, the gravity was far too strong for you and the air that the people of that planet breathe, it also has a difference. Here, where we are now, if you wish I can be with you, but only if and when you wish it. We can still do *mind to mind* as before, but it's a while since we did that, as I, in my last days, was not in total control of what I did. As I had not heard from you for such a long period, I was not sure if you still wished to see me.'

'Oh it is so good to see you again, why would I ever not want, nor wish to see you? You were so special to me on Earth. You were my saviour at a time when I was very low and so you, for a while, kept me going while I was on my own. It was because of you that I never, ever gave up, and it is because of you, my special man who gave me that hope, that I have my man who came into my life and then my beautiful daughter. Oh yes, I have a lot to thank you for. You were always so very, very special.' These two, dear friends talked and talked till suddenly, Crystal was back asking "Who is this, Mummy?'

'Meet, again, my very dear friend. The man I call my second father, who you met as a very young baby and child. This is the wonderful man who helped me, at a very difficult time in my last life on Earth. It was he who gave me the strength and courage to carry on, and in a way, because of that, I was able to have you.'

234

Now all three of them talked and talked, about a time long gone and of the happy memories of that time. Aurora now told him, she was soon to go on another Earth life, that she was waiting for further details about it and assured him she would see him before it was her time to go. Eventually they parted, with a friendship that they both knew would last an eternal lifetime, knowing that if they were ever to share a life experience, something very special would have to happen to one of them, because of their differences.

Aurora now went on the first of the two trips she had been told about, to bring back an old man. A rare old man, whose life had been full of the faeries in his gardens. He had four, very large garden areas, all very colourful, that were full, not only of beautiful flowers, but also of his beloved faeries. He had never, ever had any other special person in his life and hence, no children. He said, 'With these wonderful little people in my life, how could I possibly ever need or want anybody else?' It took Aurora many days on Earth to persuade him to come, but between her and the Queen faery that had travelled with her, they finally succeeded and brought him home.

The second trip followed almost immediately after her return, having now secured the man with his family. Although at first, he was not keen to go with them, as they had parted in anger. This second trip was for a young child, a boy who had been hounded by very bad people, all because he did not conform to their beliefs. He was slightly disfigured and he talked about and loved his faery friends, as he called them.

Aurora thought, 'It's amazing, nobody ever wants to leave the faeries and who can blame them? They are wonderful little people' and her open thought transmitted out to the general mind thought.

(Now she received a message back in her mind, saying 'Now you know, why what you do is so special. These little people are so very special, so very important to all plant life, for without them, there would be no beautiful plants, the food chain would suffer in every way and so all of life would suffer. There are very special people who also look after the bees and the insects that pollinate all the plants, to ensure life goes on, but people forget these important things. It's as if they were of no consequence, but every tiny microbe has a very valuable place in the life chain on Earth. The love that these little people, these faeries, put into the work that they do, that also keeps all these other things going.')

Aurora pondered on that thought she had received, as she travelled for the little boy she was now going to collect. When she arrived at her destination, she was greeted by a group of faeries and nymphs who were all around the little boy. It was as if they were protecting him from those who were looking for him, as the boy and all those who were searching for him, were unaware that he was now dead. The little boy was trying so very hard to get back into his body, but he could not understand why it just would not allow him back in. His neck was broken, as was one of his legs, which was now at a very strange angle, and he could not figure out why that was so.

Aurora spoke very gently to him, so as not to frighten him, and the faeries were trying to get him to look at her, as he was so intent on what he was trying to do. Suddenly, he saw her and asked her who she was. Then he told her he did not want to go with these bad people who had chased him, he had climbed a tree to hide from them and fallen, but he knew he had to get away from here or they would torture him.

Aurora, still very gently, again spoke to him and told him why she was there for him. She told him that she loved him dearly and admired him for what he was trying to do, and that if he came with her and the Queen faery she had with her, he would be fine. She gently explained to him, that he no longer needed that old body, as he had a nice knew one. One that was not broken like his old one was. They chatted, as she explained everything to him, until he was, at last, happy to go with her. She picked him up and with the Queen faery still beside her, but now sitting on her arm as she held the boy, they gently travelled home.

Whereas the man had had an understanding family waiting for him and went more or less straight to them, the little boy was all alone and had been since he was a very young child. His parents had abandoned him, as the group of people they lived with had made their life intolerable, all because of his disabilities, and so he had been, for a long time, living on whatever he could find. Thanks to the faeries who had befriended him and who he had been clearly able to see, he had plenty of good food, because they let him see the roots and plants they knew that he could eat safely.

It was quite a task for Aurora to find his family and Crystal had helped her in this task. She had to do this herself for some of those she had collected, so she also knew what was involved in trying to find his family relations.

Job complete at last, Aurora now thought she could relax for a while, but she was again quickly summoned by the *high elders* in the great Golden Temple, to talk about her new life on Earth that was planned for her.

To her surprise, she discovered that her beloved man, her rock, as she had told him every day that was what he was, was now in this new life she was soon to embark upon, to be her father. He was also at this meeting and he told her that she would be worshipped in her life, not only by him in his life, but also by all the people of his kingdom, who she would eventually rule over as queen.

She would also bare two children in her life, two *spirit beings* who she also now met. Crystal, sadly, was not included in any of this and it was explained to Aurora why this was so. On completion of this meeting, Aurora and her man were now given leave, to have some special time together, before he would leave to prepare to start his new Earthly life.

On Earth, it was some two thousand years that had passed since his last Earthly life, but of course, when he was reborn he would be totally unaware of his last life. It was now up to his *higher self*, his angel and his long time *spirit guide*, who all went with him, although he knew he would never actually see any of them in that

238

life. Their joint task was to keep him on the path that had now been laid out for him.

Aurora was saddened to see her man go, but she was pleased that, in a funny way, they would still be together as she now had to follow his new path very closely. In Earth years, the King would be thirty before he would marry and a further two years before he would have any children. Aurora knew she would be the second of his two children born to his wife. His first child, a son, would die in battle and this is how Aurora, who would become a princess when she was *reborn,* would then become queen, although Aurora was not aware of a hiccup that would happen in the Queen's life.

Aurora's task was also now, to watch over the lady who she had also met, who, now born a princess herself, but in a different country, would become the queen through marriage and would eventually give birth to her. She was there at the birth of her mother-to-be, mainly to ensure it went smoothly for her. There was, sadly now, no longer any of the birthing pyramid rooms she remembered from her last days on Earth. The world had changed very dramatically from when she was last living there. It appeared to her now to be a very cruel place, a place where nobody trusted anybody.

Anger and aggression was rife everywhere and children were cruelly treated. The women now seemed to be totally controlled by the men and were no longer allowed to go out on their own anywhere. It made her very concerned about her new life she was about to embark on, yet she knew she had to go and to make a difference. Show them that women could also be tough and strong. She knew she would be a good warrior queen, as that was what she was destined to become, and she would ensure that somehow, she would be that queen, although she also knew she would still carry *love* in her heart. She would make a change and she would look after her country. So now the queen was safely born and she would watch her every day, carefully, and ensure that no harm came to her.

Aurora was given one last task to do, before she could keep a close eye on that lady who was to be her mother. She had been asked, by those same *higher spirits* with whom she had discussed her new Earthly life, if she would give a talk to others who were about to embark on the work she would now relinquish, as she prepared for her new Earthly life. This she said, she would gladly do, as it had given her a wonderful feeling to have been asked to do that type of work for spirit. Work that she had carried out so magnificently.

She told those that she spoke to, of the great joy it had been, and the *privilege* she felt had been given to her, to work with these amazing little people. These wonderful little *spirit people*, who all had such a wonderful happy disposition, and this, despite what had happened to many of them in what, at times, could be very dangerous work for them, if they were not swift enough to move. Show them the *love* and *care,* she said, to both the little people, and to all those who they went to collect.

You have been carefully chosen, she told them, to do what is probably the most amazing job in spirit. Enjoy the experience of it and these little people will always make you welcome. I sincerely hope I get the opportunity to work with them all again.

An amazing thing happened to Aurora as she completed her talk. Something very rarely seen even in spirit. The Queen faery and some of the others from that very special garden, came to this great theatre, which in itself was a very rare occurrence, to thank Aurora, and to tell her she was somebody very, very special. That no matter where she went in the future, or what she did, the faeries from the Faery Kingdom, would always look out for her. They would always know her and watch her, to keep her safe, now and always. Such was the incredible *love* these little people had for her, through the *love* and affection she had shown to them.

They were then joined by two of the amazing sea creatures, as they now became visible for all to see. This, an even more special visit, as these magnificent creatures had only on very, very rare occasions ever been allowed to do this. You could feel the change in this Meeting Hall, as most who were present did not even know of their existence. But it was known by the *high ones* that they had wished to add their thanks to Aurora, as never before had they been treated so warmly, and with such great enthusiasm in what she, Aurora, did with them, as they had lovingly worked together for the greater good of all concerned. They also told Aurora, that they had been given a very special message from Aurora's other special friends, the two dolphins. They said to tell her that whenever she was at, or near the sea, where they could get close to her, that they would always show themselves and speak to her and ensure she was always safe in the sea.

241

That message finally brought Aurora as near to tears as she could now get, as a *being of light*. The *love* she felt being passed to her in this great hall, from so many directions, everybody felt and they all knew they were witnessing something very special for somebody very special. Now the six great *beings of light* that had organised this meeting, also now, each in turn, held Aurora in their arms and wished her well in the new challenge that now awaited her.

So to great rejoicing, Aurora left this great theatre, another one of these very remarkable buildings in spirit, that totally gleamed and shone. A building that she had spoken in, not just now, but many times before. She had to go now and prepare for her rebirth to her new life, which would again be on Earth, knowing exactly what she still had to do before that event could happen.

Aurora carefully watched over the one who had been chosen to be her mother, from her birth, and as she now grew on Earth, to become a beautiful proud woman. She saw her marriage, as she now became the new Queen. Soon after her marriage, as Aurora knew was planned, she became pregnant and gave birth to a son. Aurora knew it was now getting very close to her time to be reborn. She knew that in Earth time, over two years would pass before the Queen would become pregnant again and so she watched her every move very carefully, totally aware of everything the Queen did. Almost exactly as they had discussed when they had been all together, prior to this new journey they were all going on.

At last the time came for the Queen to again become pregnant and as the two seeds met, so Aurora tried to make the connection to them at that same instant. But Aurora knew something was not quite correct, she could not make the connection. Within weeks, that foetus was ejected as the Queen had a miscarriage. Aurora, almost at the same instant that she saw the spirit, as it disconnected, was immediately summoned by the six spirit masters and then told what had been allowed to happen and why. Aurora was assured all was well and it would all happen now, just exactly as had been discussed. Not long after, the Queen again fell pregnant and this time all did go as planned and Aurora made the connection.

It was Aurora's main work now, to ensure that the baby, to whom she was now permanently connected, was now growing perfectly inside the Queen's womb, and would develop true and strong and perfect in every way, as had been directed. She watched over her new, soon to be, Earthly body, ensuring every bone that grew was perfect, every organ that grew was perfect, the eyes that had to be clear and perfect, the nose, mouth and teeth that would develop after she was born would also be perfect. She had to ensure that her hearing would be strong and clear, as she knew in her life, that many times her success and the lives of others would depend on her hearing ability.

As a warrior queen to be, she was determined that she would become the strong successful queen that she was meant to be. She grew true and strong and even though still in the womb, as she flexed herself to ensure everything was working as it should be, this gave her mother to be, little peace. Nothing was being left to chance, this was a very important life she was about to embark upon and she knew many others would depend on her strength and abilities.

Very shortly before the due day, and although still totally connected to the baby, she said her goodbyes to all her soul group, a group that had changed considerably as some had gone on to other lives on the Earth plain. Others had arrived back home to spirit, as in spirit it is a constantly changing scene, as *spirit beings* come and go, just as they do on Earth as a human. She said a very special goodbye to Crystal, her daughter who told her she would watch over her. Then there was her other very special friend, that very special man from a different place. They had conversed often, after Aurora had discovered he was back in spirit. He was sad to see her go, but said to her 'We will meet again, I promise you that, Aurora. I will see you again, so in the meantime, be successful in your brave new challenge and remember that, although we are different you and me, I also *love* you and my *love* will stay with you forever.'

Crystal's parting words had also been a great comfort to her. She told her she knew she would be here to welcome her home at the end of her very busy new life, the life that she was now about to embark upon.

Alone now, she went to where she needed to be at the time and place of her rebirth, where others, including Grace, her guide, who had always been close by her side, were waiting to assist her and ensure all went well in her birth, as she departed for the Earth plain again.

The Queen had a very unexpected short labour, as her baby had quickly exited her, into the Nile waters, in a clean clear area specially chosen by her, as her place to give birth. Now the new life of the baby now born, a princess, started with her father giving a great celebration at her birth. Soon he would teach her all she would ever need to know, to be the successful warrior queen she had set out to be.

We will take our leave of her now, to begin her new life. A life that does not concern us at this time. We will now journey forward in time, and pick up our spirit friend, after several other lives have also been lived, and she now comes to the close of the one we are allowed to know about.

So the spirit that we all know as Aurora, will have a new name, but we were not privy to the name given to her in the life that she has just embarked upon. It is not relevant to our amazing story, but we will wish her well in that life. We shall thank her now, for that amazing glimpse into the life in spirit that she has just left, and for all the wonderful and truly amazing things that she has shown us. The amazing creatures that through her, we have been allowed to meet. Creatures that have, I know, truly amazed me, and I am sure that applies also to you. I also know that now, many of you will also have questions. Many, many questions, but wait a while longer, because you know that we are not complete yet. You have more to learn from her, as we get the chance to look in on another phase in her eternal life.

You will remember from the start, that we had travelled back in time to approximately a time around the year we know and understand as 5000 B.C. just as her life on Earth then, was about to end. You will also remember that as Aurora set out on her new life on Earth that we have just left her to have, time had moved on to about 2500 B.C. This will give you an idea about *spirit time,* which as we now know, does not exist as we know it.

So, we are now about to travel forward again in time. So sit back again and relax, as the time clock starts to roll, as it picks up speed going forward once more.

'Love' - A Warm
Affection

(As Quoted in the
Collins Dictionary I
Have Here.)

A Warm Affection

A warm affection. I think from what we have just learned, *love* is a great deal more than just 'a warm affection'. I feel these words do not even come close to that which we have just learned about *love*. It is the whole essence of life in spirit. Everything revolves around *love* in spirit. It's not a way of life, IT IS LIFE in spirit as a *being of light*. That I feel, is how it should also be, here on this amazing plain that we call the Earth plain. *Love* should be everything, but sadly, on Earth at this moment in time, it is not. But this complete story about the spirit lives of an amazing *being of light,* is all about, and given with, that amazing gift of *love* and as you read, you will find just how *strong* that *love* in spirit really is.

So now, as we continue our story, and our clock, that has been set rolling forward again, to a time that is much nearer to our own. From 2500 B.C. where we left Aurora as she was reborn to a new life, so we pick it up 2400 B.C., 2000, 1500, 1000 and 500 B.C. Jesus is now among us and it is A.D. time, 100 A.D., 500, 1000, 1300, 1400, 1500, 1550. Stopping here and the story of our spirit's Earthly life, from a period in time of around late 15th to early 16th Century, comes into view and to a place in England. To a county we call Kent and to a place that is called Ightham Mote.

Now I, having been educated in Scotland, where I lived for the first twenty one years of my life, have to admit to knowing Kent as a county (having been to a few towns there in my younger years), but however, to being totally ignorant of this place that is called Ightham Mote. So I set about finding it. It turns out it is near Seven Oaks in Kent, a place I have heard of and I now believe actually only has six oaks, as one was, I believe, blown down a few years ago. I do not yet know if it has been replaced yet, I hope it has, as 'Six Oaks' just does not have the same ring to it; seven is a much better number.

The building itself and the Mote still exist to this day and are now owned by the National Trust. It was built over 700 years ago, with very strong Tudor connections. Fortunately, Oliver Cromwell, so Aurora tells me, failed in his instruction to have it raised to the ground. Which beggars the question why did he (as the story goes, if it is true), buy it for the so called 'five pounds' he is supposed to have paid for it. At that time, I understand it was actually owned by the Selby family. All this, I am told by our spirit, that is still as we know her, Aurora. But her name in the Earthly life you are about to meet her in, we will learn shortly. She also informs me that the spelling of Ightham Mote has changed many times over the years. She originally gave it to me as IGHAM Mote, but we are in the correct place. The man who started it, by building the original part, was known as Mr. Ightham.

We meet our spirit friend, who at this time was called by the servants 'The Lady of the Manor', as she lies ill in her bed. Her name is Lady Anne, who she informs me was actually known as 'Bounteous Lady Anne', and she has been, for some time, confined to her bed, through this illness. Those who would seek to help her seem totally unable to do so and her strength now deteriorates every day. Her mind, although still fully active, is wandering, as it often does for those so ill in bed, as she thinks back on her short, but busy life.

(Our spirit friend informs me, that many records were destroyed, with no ability at that time for people to actually write things down accurately, and as a result most things were passed through word of mouth, and through this have also sadly been 'misrepresented.' Sadly, there is very little truthfully known about our Lady Anne. She was, however, of a very kind nature and very helpful to many less well off than herself, doing what she could to help those that had a difficult life. A major problem of the time, as she said, was that very few had the ability to form a written word, so as you know, when anything is passed down by word of mouth, you know how much that can change, as each person relates their version of what they believe they have just been told.

I would also state here, that although this life was around the time of Cromwell, she will not be specific as to the exact time. She said, she does not wish me to go down the route of actually trying to find exactly what happened to her, because, as I have told you before, some memories can cause a *spirit being* pain. I am also told that she was not a Selby, but she did have more than one surname, which suggests she was married more than once. She has also informed me that although this building has no 'priest holes' as they were known in various buildings, one of the ladies of the house, when that particular Lady lived there, was a Catholic; but that point was kept very quiet so as no harm would befall that Lady.

She also informs me that there are many things in the accounts that are not completely correct, for the reasons you have just read, but she is not going to change them, it would have no relevance to this story.

I understand and respect her for that and it is not my intention to cause hurt, as I know that can happen. Digging up old and painful memories for those in spirit, as we have mentioned before, can and does hurt a spirit in ways we could not, from our understanding, feel, and that is not the intention of this story. *Love* is the strength of all of this story and that is what counts. With this in mind, what we are writing will be factual regarding her own life details, as she herself dictates to me.)

So let us now join our Lady Anne, as she lays on her bed in the last few days and hours of her life at this time.

Love Really is All You Need

Lady Anne

As her mind wanders, she remembers her children fondly. She has had three children, two sons and a daughter. Her daughter she remembers, yes, she sadly died at a very young age. A tear now comes to her eye as she remembers that very painful time in her life. My sons, ah! Yes, I have two boys, always up to mischief, but good boys really. It gives me so much pleasure to see and hear from them. Both big strong lads and now with places of their own, yet they do visit me often.

A smile appears on her face as she recalls her younger son was here earlier today, or was it yesterday? No, it was this morning. She tries to get up but her strength fails her and she falls back on the bed. She thinks to herself 'OH! If only I could get to the window and see outside, see my beautiful gardens with all the beautiful flowers. I wish my husband was still here, he would have ensured I could see out. He is quite, no, *very* attentive to my needs when he is around, which sadly, is not very often. Why, oh why, did my first husband, my first real love have to try and prove his point and get himself killed? That stupid duel, a pointless deadly duel, and his life totally wasted. Why, oh why, was he so stupid? Even now he would still have been young enough to be in good health. Oh, the silly, stupid, stupid man.

Ah! What's that noise I hear? What's that terrible commotion that I hear down stairs? What's it all about? It sounds like soldiers again. They must not yet have found who they are looking for. Why can't they just leave well alone? Instead of upsetting the people here, trying to seek him out. She laughs inwardly as she knows that they will not find him. They have searched this place many times, but they have never found one here yet, and they *never* will. They don't even know the proper places to look. Even if they did find somebody that had been hidden here, as some in the past have been after they have left, and then they tortured them, they will not get the answer as they don't know the way in, we have always made sure of that. That blindfold was a brilliant idea and none of them ever knew they were even in this house.

Oh! So many different people have been saved here and hopefully many more, even when I am gone. I know my days are numbered, as I sadly seem to get weaker everyday, but I know they will carry on the good work when I am gone. All these soldiers, I know most of them really only come here for the drink, as they know they will always receive one. One day they will learn that the man who rules them, is really only a bully.

Another night passed more peacefully this time, and again she surprised everyone by being bright and smiling, saying 'I would like to see my gardens and my beautiful flowers one last time. Will you see if they can do that for me please?' So the men that would be needed to carry her down the stairs were assembled, and then she was carefully placed in a special chair so she would be safe, and downstairs they all went. Well wrapped up, she was taken on a very pleasant trip around her beautiful gardens, the gardens that had been her pride and joy as she had done so much to make them what they now were.

There was great excitement in the house this day, as they all thought, at last she is getting better. All her staff were very excited about this unexpected trip outside for her, they did not wish to lose this special lady who had been so good to them all. They wandered slowly around her colourful gardens, as many of the flowers were in bloom. They stopped at one point for light refreshments, on her instructions, and then returned her to her room late in the afternoon where, from exhaustion, she soon fell soundly asleep.

The following morning, sadly saw a great change in her, and they were all glad that they had at least been able to grant her that one last wish. The physician was again called, as she seemed so very feeble and not very lucid now. Her lady, who was responsible for her, grew anxious, as her breathing was now getting very, very laboured.

She now lapses more into a dreamlike state, and as such, she sees those that are coming to collect her, for her last journey on Earth, her daughter among them. 'Not yet Mama, not yet', her daughter tells her, and a smile appears on her face as her daughter cuddles her and tells her, 'We are preparing the way for you Mama, but no, it is not yet time, you need to stay just a little longer.' The lady in the room watching over her smiles, as she sees her charge now relax, as her face takes on a more peaceful look. The physician who has been looking after her since she first fell ill, knocks and enters the room. He is surprised to see she is actually still with them and tells the lady, 'I thought she would have gone before I returned today. I am surprised to see she is still with us.'

He questions the lady who now sits with her constantly, and asks as to how she has been, and what has happened since he was last here, very early this morning. She informs him about all that has happened, even that they had had a quite lucid conversation, just a short while ago, before she drifted off again. That surprised him. She also informed him that the soldiers had been here again this morning, looking for some person, but they left empty handed again. 'There is definitely no one here at this sad time. Why don't they leave her in peace', she says.

He smiled. 'She was a very crafty and wise lady', he said. 'She would allow no one in this house ever to suffer misfortune while in her care. I have seen the way she dealt with the soldiers, her hospitality for them. Well, I sincerely wish there were more people like her in this world, it would be a better place.'

'She is well known for her care and affection throughout the area and many people have brought her flowers and their good wishes for her recovery', the lady informed him.

'Sadly, she will not recover from this' he said, 'I know of nobody who has ever made a recovery from this illness. It is only a matter of time. Today, tomorrow, I am not sure, but it will not be very long now.'

'I know it sounds strange to say it, and I know you will understand when I say, that sometimes, it's as if she can see others around her. Her face lights up and then she smiles. Sometimes her hands, her arms, open and rise up as if she is welcoming them. It is nice to see that; she looks so peaceful and so very happy at these times, and her face lights up when she smiles.'

'Ah! Yes, I have heard of that before, when others have seen the same thing, as they watch the dying during an illness. I am sorry to say, I do not know why this is, because when you die you die. This is all I know and understand, and yet, truthfully I have seen it for myself. I know the priests all talk of an everlasting life, but I do not understand how that can be possible. I also know that, strangely, if you talk about such things in certain circles, it means instant death, as you well know, and of course, that is why they seek out those poor people. Why that is, I know not, because people should be allowed to believe what they wish, as they are doing no harm to anybody.'

'I understand that it was not always so, and that people long ago were allowed their own thoughts, but sadly, those that rule us seem to enjoy dictating everything these days. It is very sad. Yes, very sad that those who rule should be allowed to dictate everything, it just doesn't seem right somehow. I must admit I don't go to church as often now, because of the domineering attitude they spout out.'

'I agree with you, but in my profession I have to be very, very careful who I talk to or I might find myself in grave danger. Despite my profession.'

'Would you wish for a drink before you depart, as I can call for one for you, if you so wish?'

'Yes, that would be nice. It's nice to be able to talk freely to somebody who is open and understands, and not always having to check what I am saying. There are not many places left that you can do that.'

'The good Lady herself, would wish it no other way for either yourself, or indeed, for any other visitor to this house. All are always made most welcome. Even the majority of the soldiers when they come, receive a drink and reasonable hospitality. I often think they come here just for that, as their inspection here, by most, is usually very lax, unless it is one man in particular, he usually gets 'short shift' when he comes here. Even his own men do not like him and nothing would surprise me more, to discover he winds up dead one day soon.'

'Ah! I know who you speak of. No, he isn't a very nice person, he will get his just desserts one day soon, I am sure. I know I have taken an oath, but I would find it very hard to keep if he became a patient of mine.'

The drinks arrived and they chatted for some time, unaware that the Lady herself was not sleeping and could hear everything being said. Ah! She thought to herself, I knew he had a fancy for my companion. Good luck to them I say, good luck to them both.

Eventually he left to go to his next appointment and just after he left, smiling to herself, she pretended to awake and asked for some water. I could truly write an amazing story, if I told all I knew, she thought. The things I hear and am often told, it's nice to know I am trusted so.

The day and night wore on, as she drifted in and out of consciousness, still seeing and speaking to those only she could see, except unbeknown to her it was *mind to mind* only, as she spoke to them. As the new day dawned and wore on, she became more and more feeble. The physician came and went twice during the day and said he would return this evening, as he did not think she would last much longer.

Now she could see even more people who were almost gathering together for her, as she drifted in and out, in and out, but always with a very happy smile on her face. Her two sons had now arrived in her room, almost as if they had been called for, yet no special message had been sent to them. They sat with her, watching her every move, as her breathing became more and more laboured and almost scratchy. 'How much longer do you think she will last?' The elder son asked the lady who was also still sitting with them. 'I hate to see her labouring so much, is there nothing you can do for her?'

'Sadly no, I know of nothing that I can do, but I know it will not be long now till she passes.' As she stopped speaking, they heard the death rattle as her breath now ceased and she was gone from them. The physician, who strangely had re-entered just at that exact moment as she left her body, now checked her over and assured them yes, she was gone. Her time to return to spirit had come.

Although her family in spirit had come for her, she told them she wished to stay at present with her body. She made no attempt to try to re-enter her body, she already knew it was no longer of any use to her. It was solely her wish to see that all her wishes were carried out, exactly as she requested. Her daughter had stayed beside her, although the others had returned to spirit. They both watched with interest what they now did to her body that she no longer needed, and indeed, was no longer of any further use to her. She watched, as they carefully washed and prepared her body for burial.

She, or rather her old physical body, now lay prepared on the bed, dressed in the clothes she had asked to be buried in, and all her servants and many of her friends, came to her bedside and paid their last respects. They mourned the loss of a very special lady, who always had a kind word to say to all. What she had, she shared whenever possible, and her staff knew they had now lost a very special and totally irreplaceable friend.

Three days after her passing, they held her funeral and she was buried according to her wishes. There must have been over 200 people at her service, many kind words were said about her and many tears were shed that day. They had lost a special lady, this Lady of the Manor, and Ightham Mote was all the poorer for her passing, at what was still such a young age. Her two sons remained at the graveside long after all others, including her husband, had departed with their own thoughts and dreams.

So, now knowing within herself that her basic wishes had all been carried out, she could do nothing else, but leave them to carry out her bequests regarding her estate. All that was left was for Lady Anne, with her daughter beside her, to take one last look around her estate, and then they took their leave of this beautiful amazing place they call 'Ightham Mote' and return home to spirit and the family she knew now awaited her. One last look, a smile on her face, and she took her daughters hand as they sped through the veil to the light. Once there, her daughter left her, saying 'See you soon, Mum, just relax, you're safe. See you on the other side of the light', and she was gone.

The LOVE That Never Dies but is Forever in Our HEARTS

Lady Anne Arrives Home

Our *spirit being,* Lady Anne, is now fully into the white light all around her, giving her a feeling of calm, and a peace that she had never felt in her life. Every day in her life that she had just lived, had always been, even as a child, full of some form of activity that she had had to perform. She could not think of a time where she had just relaxed, in the way that she now felt, here in the power of this amazing white light. As she thought for a moment about that life she had just left, to her amazement, before her eyes, she now suddenly started to see the life she had just left, now replay around her.

Starting with her birth, a birth that appeared to have been a very long and hard labour for her mother, as she had tried to exit her mother's womb. Still, she had safely arrived, with great relief from her mother and great cheering and celebration from all concerned with that birth. Her father was so delighted he now had the daughter he sought, that he now allowed all his employees, and there were many, a whole day off work in celebration of his daughter's birth. At first she had a nursery to herself, but as she grew and was able to walk, she was soon to join all the other children in the house, including the other two children, both boys, her mother had had before her.

They had been a fairly well to do family and money had been freely available to keep them all. Her childhood had been a good, but fairly uneventful one, except she never appeared to have any time on her own, even her bed she shared with her brothers, certainly at first. They were all well fed and she was certainly, always very beautifully dressed. Their mother, after the painful birth of Anne, had had no other children, and had spent her time joyfully looking after and caring for all her family.

Her father was a wealthy land owner, a careful man, and very unusual for the time, he had always respected his workers and valued their worth in what they did for him and his family. All the children of his workers had joined his own three children every morning, so that they *all* could learn to read and write. He felt that these were essentials for all children, if they were to have any chance of a future in life. She thought it was interesting, as she watched this part replay, and saw how much her father was respected by all, for his kindness. She, herself, as she grew, was very much influenced by her father, and had always tried to follow his lead in what she did. Hence the nickname she was to be given in the future, 'The Bounteous Lady Anne', as she did her best to ensure the smooth running of her own homes, for she had more than one in her life.

She continued to watch her life as it wound on. She saw herself in her first marriage and smiled to herself at that very happy part of her life. She watched her children being born and the trials that each birth had given her.

She was deeply saddened at the tragic death of her daughter at barely two years of age, and yet, she remembered she had somehow just seen her now a fully grown woman.

What magic was this, she thought, that I am seeing all this so clearly? Now her life progress stopped, as she now sadly watched her daughter's burial and she thought more about what she had just seen. Her daughter's burial, and yet, she had just been with her, so alive and bubbling with energy. *How* was this possible? *How* could she have seen her so... and *how* was she even now watching this life review? Maybe what the priests had said when she was young, was true. You did return to God's house. 'Is that where I am?' she thought.

Then slowly, as she let that thought go, her review started up again. Then came another very sad part of her life, the time of her then husband's needless death. Through the stupid dual that he had allowed himself to take part in, all because he would allow no one to dishonour her name. She would much rather have had him alive, no matter what some other fool had thought of her. She knew what he had said was not true.

She had not actually seen the dual, either then, nor did she see it now. As she had not been present when the event had happened, it would not, and could not, be a part of her life review. Now, she sadly watched his funeral and saw the great number of people who had attended with her, as indeed many had accompanied her in that service that day. The review stopped again as her thoughts dwelled on that very sad time in her life.

Why had he been so foolish, why could he not have just let it go? Nobody would have thought any worse of him. They all knew the idiot who had challenged him. He did not get off scot-free thankfully, and his life now was not a good one, because of his injuries. Also, the doctor had barely helped him, as he had seen the arrogance of the man and wanted him to learn just how foolish he had been. His suffering was a daily reminder. He had actually wanted Anne to be his wife, but that was never going to happen, whatever the outcome of the dual was.

Again the review restarted and slowly carried on as her thoughts kept its progress slow. She watched her two boys growing, and her own life as it twisted and turned. Then she saw the man who would become her second husband. She may have had three children, but because she looked after herself well she was still an exceedingly attractive lady with a good figure and only in her late twenties.

The next part of the review passed quickly. It was a happier period as she was courted again by this new man in her life. He was good to her and happily the boys liked him and felt comfortable with him. He took the time to teach them what they needed to know about life.

Now she started to see herself as she prepared for her second wedding, a much more lavish affair than the first one. He took her on one of his ships, to places abroad for their honeymoon. At first she felt strange on the ship, until she got used to the movement as it travelled over the water. One day, to the amazement of all on board, two dolphins appeared and they stayed with the ship all the time they were at sea. When Lady Anne, as she was now, through her marriage, was at the side of the ship these two dolphins squeaked and squeaked at her in great enjoyment. Every time they saw her they appeared to show off in front of her, jumping in and out of the water for her and racing ahead of the ship.

The Captain had commented that he had never witnessed anything like this in all his years at sea. As the ship docked when they all came home again, these two dolphins gave one last display for her and then just disappeared. Why was that time so important to me? She wondered.

She now watched the rest of her life, now spent as Lady Anne of Ightham Mote. Such a dramatic change in her life, as she was now the Lady of this great house. The staff soon learned, just how great a lady she was, and because she always treated them with respect, they returned that in spades. They could never do enough for her. She took a great interest in the very large garden, that suddenly took on a great new look. Her husband was amazed at the transformation, both inside and outside. Now he enjoyed being at home, which sadly, was not as much as he would have liked.

He arrived home one day to find his wife, sadly, very ill in bed, and as she watched this part of the review, it saddened her to see the pain in his eyes, as he was told they knew of no cure for her. Their life together, all far too short. More especially, because of the great enjoyment she had brought into his life, he had a reason to live like never before. She watched as the illness took a great hold on her, and then her last days, as she saw herself now seeing the family members from the past, including her daughter, that now assembled by her bedside. What is this amazing sight I am seeing again? There is my daughter again, how can this be? She thought, how can this be?

Suddenly, the light around her changed and became even brighter now, and from within the light a wonderful rich voice spoke to her saying, 'You have now reviewed your life. Have you completed all you had to do in your life on Earth. Do you need to return, or do you now wish to stay here?'

It took Lady Anne a few seconds to realise just what had been said to her, it was so unexpected. At last she replied, 'I am done, please can I stay here with my daughter and my family.'

'Let all rejoice and let *love* abound, as our dear one returns home again.'

Slowly, the light again changed and Lady Anne felt as if this light now totally consumed her, and as it did, she felt more complete and much more at ease within herself. 'What is this strange feeling I have within me?' As she watched, the light yet again started to change, and before her now, stood her family. But also, in front of them all, stood this very beautiful lady whose colours shone so bright and clear. She now spoke to her saying, 'I am Grace, I am your *spirit guide* and it has been my great pleasure to be your guide from the very beginning. Welcome home, my precious girl, welcome home. In you, I am so very, very proud.' For just a moment in time, they held each other and Lady Anne thought a moment to herself, and then saying to her 'I know you, I remember you. Thank you for being here.'

Grace replied, saying 'We will talk much, but first, say hello to all your family, and first, here is your precious daughter, who I know you are anxious to speak with, as you cannot believe she is all grown-up now.'

Lady Anne now took her daughter in her arms, wondering at this precious moment in time, how all this could be. What miracle had allowed this to happen? 'Oh, my darling daughter, I cannot put into words just what this moment means to me, to hold you so close, something I thought I would never be able to do. When you left us at such a young age, a large part of my heart went with you. It took me a long, long time to get over the loss of you in my life, but look at you now, so beautiful. So very, very beautiful.'

'Thank you, Mummy, thank you. I have watched you a great deal as your life progressed. I have seen your high moments and your low ones, and my heart went out to you when Daddy so needlessly died. As you can see, he is here with us now, waiting patiently to hold you, as he too has watched and looked out for you. He was happy when you took your new husband, for he knew he would look after you, as he did.'

'Thank you, my beautiful girl, although you are quite the young lady now and I am very proud of you. Let me speak with your dad now, please, as I have much I wish to say to him.'

'Do not be angry with him Mummy, because I know you are.'

So our Lady now turned to her first husband with a serious look on her face. 'We meet again and I don't know whether to be angry with you or sad. Why did you have to leave us like that? Why? You did not have to fight.'

'My dear Anne, my precious wife, please. I ask you, please just listen to me and what I have to say to you before you get angry. Nothing ever happens by accident, and I know what you are thinking. That was no accident. No it wasn't; however, it was meant to happen. It was *my time* and if I had not died in that sword fight I would have died at that precise moment for some other reason. Everything happens exactly as it should, when it should, and there is nothing anybody can do to change that fact.

'My life, as did our daughter's life, went exactly as was written, prior to our even being born to that life. We knew, as you will…I was going to say learn but that is wrong. As you will rediscover shortly, that what I am telling you is the truth. It took me a while to actually come to terms with this fact myself, as I did not want to either leave you or indeed lose you. I know you married again. Let me say that was also planned, or should I say written, as everything is written in the 'Akashic Record' and what is in there cannot ever be changed. If you want to review a previous life then you can do that by visiting that record building.

'Very few ever do that, for really, there is very little reason to re-visit a previous life, although I know a long, long time ago you actually did that. I know what you are thinking and yes, you did, but deal with that later, as

270

there are many here who wish to welcome you home. First, let me take you in my arms and just hold you, please.'

So our Lady Anne held her husband close and whispered something we are not privy to. (They are entitled to their own private moments.) Lady Anne now went on to meet with all the other people there to greet her, including her own parents and grandparents. Grace helped her with many she could not remember. There was one lady, however, who was anxious, if not a little nervous, to meet with her, and Lady Anne had noticed her as she hung back. Everybody else had to be dealt with, before she would even try to come forward, but when she did, she had a very bright smile on her face that just lit up at the sight of the lady now before her.

As the lady came forward, Lady Anne felt somehow, an instant bond between them, yet at present, she did not know how that could possibly be. 'I feel I should know you well, but please excuse me for the moment as, for some reason, I cannot yet place you. Yet I know, no I *feel* you are very important to me. Who are you? Why do I know, deep within me, that I know you? What is our connection? Help me, please.'

'So soon after your return from the life you have just had, to know that you *feel* something between us already, is reward enough at this stage for me, but you always were a truly remarkable lady.'

'You do have me at a disadvantage here, yet I know, no, I definitely *feel* you are so very important to me, from a time long gone. Why is this, who are you, please?'

Grace now replied, saying 'Here is part of the very special bond between the three of us. She was at first, my daughter when I last walked the Earth, and the last time we three were properly together like this, she had been your daughter. She has followed everything you have done, right from then until now, although she has had two very short lives on Earth in that time. She made a promise to you then, and she wishes to keep that promise now, as she has at the end of each life you have had, by always being here to welcome you home again and that she has a *love* for you that has never been equalled. You taught her soul, way back then, about *love* and she has never forgotten that, nor has she ever forgotten *you* and all you have done for her. A strong eternal bond such as this is rare.'

'Please, tell me who you were, or perhaps more to the point, what I called you as my daughter and how that bond, even now, is so very strong?'

'You knew me. In fact you called me Crystal when I was your daughter in our first connection. Sadly, although you never knew this, between the first life I ever had, which was as Grace's daughter and my short life as your daughter, I had three other lives. Lives that for me to remember them, bring great pain to me. *Cruelty* was their mainstay and all that I knew then. I had been back for a while receiving great counselling after these lives because I was so badly damaged. I was persuaded, by the *higher ones*, to become your daughter

272

for that short life. This was part of my healing from these lives that I had lived and left me *marked*.

'The ones from the *dark side*, yes they had marked me very seriously on my last return. I was in a very sad state, full of anger through the way I had been treated, both by my father and by his evil friends. This anger and aggression that I was carrying, allowed them to get through to me here. The time that I died was at the time when the *dark side* was sweeping Earth. At first I refused to accept any help, I was so angry inside myself, but eventually, through the counselling I had constantly been receiving, I started to return to the light, and then I was able to return to my family soul group, of which you are a part of.

'The *high ones* knew you needed a soul to be your daughter and they told me that they felt the *love* your soul always carried would help me. The *love* that you showed me as your child, as back then as your child, I did have serious health problems. This was also part of my healing, and you were very strong for me and yes, the *love* you gave me, as indeed, everybody that you touch, either in life on Earth, or as a *being of light* in spirit, nobody ever forgets.

'But that *love* you gave me, and taught me to have and show, meant that when I returned at the end of that short life, I was no longer able to be marked by the *dark side*. Through your strength for me, you had made me strong. You, through that *love,* had turned me round. *You* really are something very, *very special*. A very remarkable being in every way, and thanks to you and the continuing *love* that you gave me when we returned here, that 'mark' has been totally removed in every way and through that *love*, I can ensure it will never again, *ever* happen to me. That is also why I was thought quite highly of on my return and allowed to work as I did. But there are more than just me you affected in that wonderful way, as you will soon learn.

'There are also some very special creatures that want me, no sorry, have asked me, to take you back to see them, when you are ready. You have much to do before that and if you will please let me, I will help you. I can never hope to repay you for the amazing grounding and patient learning you gave to me when I needed it most, this will be my way of trying, in a small way, to repay you for your *love* and kindness. You really are very special.'

'My dear Crystal, *please*. You have absolutely nothing that you ever need to repay me for. Please do not ever feel you owe me anything. To have been *allowed* to be your mother and to bare you as the fruit of my womb, that itself was a priceless gift for me.'

Grace now told Lady Anne that the reason why Crystal had only two very short lives, between the period when she was her very sick daughter and now, was because her spirit was still in healing, mainly strengthening, from being so very badly marked. 'Thanks to that experience with you at that time, her healing was based on a very firm foundation. I know you have seen and met Rebecca, the angel who is always with Crystal and I am sure you have seen just how much brighter she shines. Rebecca is a very high and special angel who was given to her as a special gift, for what she had been through.

'That third life, because of what was happening on Earth, had gone very wrong. When she finally returned to the light, after much counselling, she was sent for by the *high ones* and told everything, and then given her special gift. Another thing you will notice is that whenever Crystal is around, Rebecca is always visible, no matter where she is, no matter what she is doing, you will always see Rebecca. Sometimes she is very small, but *always* visible. That was another promise made to Crystal. Now Lady Anne, I think it is time we met another *special being* who also plays a very special part in *all* your lives. I'll let Crystal take you to where you will now meet this being.'

So Crystal and Lady Anne went off hand in hand, talking as they walked, as they had much to talk about. '*Mind to mind*', of course.

There Are No Barriers When Love is Involved

Lady Anne Returns to the Golden Temple

'It seems very strange to me, to be calling you Lady Anne, as you were not known by me as that, apart from me calling you Mummy or Mum, and somehow that now does not seem right either.'

'So what did you call me, or what was I called then, what was my name?'

'Oh, you had a lovely name, but I think I will tell you after you have been into this building we are approaching now and you have done what you need to do there.'

'This is the Golden Temple. Yes, I remember well this place, it's so amazing inside and outside.' So as they approached the entrance, the two angels, as always, opened the doors and bade them enter, saying 'You are expected.'

Crystal now took her leave of Lady Anne, telling her she would be outside waiting for her in the gardens when she was finished here. Suddenly this magnificent angel appeared before her, saying 'I am Daniel. I am your guardian angel and have always been with you, wherever you went and whatever you did. It has been my pleasure to share your life, your eternal life with you.'

'How and WHY do I feel so at ease with you? You are so much larger than me, yet I feel safe with you, how is this?'

'That is how it should always be when we are together, or you can see me, as I actually never leave your side, *ever*.' Lady Anne and Daniel now talked as if they were the only two people there in that massive, great hall. But we know they are not the only people there. It's just that, at this moment, they need no other being as they converse, nor do they hear others, as all communication is *mind to mind*. They discussed the life that has just been and indeed many other subjects, including the second part of the white light, where Lady Anne and her *higher self* had re-joined again, as always happens when one returns to spirit. They discussed that re-joining in full, and other linked subjects, until they eventually got round to Crystal.

'Why Daniel, was I never aware of Crystal's serious past when we were last together? Surely that, Daniel, because of our connection, was important?'

'No my dear, trust me, it was not. It was better you were not aware of her circumstances. Then she had a better chance to heal naturally. Because of the way it was known you would treat her, *love* has always been so very natural to you, even in the life just lived. *Love* shone out from you like a big golden beacon, and people just felt it when they were around you. Let me tell you, you have left a lasting legacy, not only for your daughter Crystal, but one that is, even now, working its magic on those you left behind from this last life. All because of the way you treated people. Crystal, as was hoped for in that life, felt that *love* from you from the moment she was born to you, and it just flowed constantly from you. They were correct, as always, they knew you had it in you, it is such a large part of you.

'Now we have done all we need to do at present in here and I know there are others who are all very anxious to see you again, so why don't we call Crystal in and get her to take you to all the places she wishes to. You will be busy for quite a while, that I promise you.'

So Crystal, in the blink of an eye, was beside them in the Golden Temple with a great big grin on her face. She was so very, very happy to have her mum back. Her very special mum, that no mum in the future, whatever it holds, would ever replace that special bond they have.

'Can I still call you Mum, please? Because I've given it some thought since we spoke, and to me you will always be my mum, whenever we are together.'

'If that is what you want to call me and you are happy, then so am I. It is a wonderful compliment that you give me. So where are we now going?'

'To the Hall of Colours first, for refreshment. It's very important that you do this. When we meet all those we are going to meet, you will be shining like a new star. So take my hand and let's go.' In the blink of an eye they were both now at the entrance to the shimmering building that is the Hall of Colours. Lady Anne now remembered this building, this magnificent place where anything could, and can happen. All good.

'Oh I've missed this place, I remember it so clearly now. People back where I have just come from, they would not believe me when I tried to get them to have more colour in their lives, which was something I did manage to keep, my love of colour. My houses were always full of flowers and with the beautiful colours they had, they made the place so much nicer to be in. All my gardens were always so beautiful, I think I might miss them. I love my gardens.'

'You will not have a chance to miss them when you see what I have in store for you, you are going to love it. So come on now, let's work our way through these colours.'

'Crystal, you said I had a lovely name and you were going to tell me it when we met after the meeting with Daniel. What is it please?'

'You were called Aurora, when you were my Mummy and it suited you, as your colours were always so bright, just like they are becoming now.'

'Aurora. Aurora. Ah yes, that *is* a nice name.'

'It suited you then, because of the way you were so full of *love* and the colours that shone from your aura, as they will again when we are done here.'

'I think I might just go back to that name, I really like it, and much as it was nice to be Lady Anne, Aurora sounds so nice and friendly. Yes, that is what I shall do, that's if you are OK with it. Are you?'

'Of course I am Mum. Oh, it's so nice to have my Mum back beside me, so very nice and now with her proper name, YES. I know this might sound silly to you, but, oh it's so nice. I really missed you. I have really, really missed you, Mum. I know there is no such thing as time here, but yes, I have missed you, your presence and your being. *My special mum,* nobody can take your place ever.'

'Thank you Crystal. Forgive me please, I feel as if I have a tear in my eye, which I know is not possible. You know that I have another daughter, don't you, who I know will be anxious to be with me, because although she is now all grown up, she was barely two when she had to return here.'

'Yes, of course I know her, Mum, and if you look at the rose pink colour over there, you will see her awaiting us. I asked her to meet us there. We are very good friends, you will see. We have been doing lots of things together. She could not remember her name when she got here, but as she was carrying a pink rose in her hand, I called her Rose. I was the one asked to be there to meet her when she came over and she was, and still is, as beautiful as a pink rose. She also has a lovely disposition, just like you and we laugh all the time.'

'I put that pink rose in her hand before they closed the box.'

Rose picked up in her mind what her mum had said to Crystal, saying 'Thank you Mummy, it is still a beautiful rose that I can still hold whenever I want to.'

Now our three girls, all safe in each-others company, enjoyed a great, big hug, wrapped up in each other's arms as never before, with a tiny Rebecca floating above, just as she always is. 'Can I join in please?' A little voice in their ears said.

'Oh! Grace, I'm sorry, of course you can', and so now it was four girls in a big hug and *love* was what held them all together. So now, all four walked through the Hall of Colours, with each taking refreshment and all laughing and dancing as they went. That tiny ball of light that is Rebecca, always visible beside Crystal.

'Come Mummy. Before we take you to meet all these others, who I know are excited to see you, let us take you somewhere you might just recognise. In the middle, Mummy please, let's all hold hands, it's only a short walk', and so the four that were clearly visible together, started to walk from the Healing Halls. Let us remind you, that although there were four visible, there would still be four other *beings of light,* that would be close beside them and the little ball of light, clearly visible above, never encroaching, but never leaving Crystal's side. Who would they be? Ah, let me remind you, that each one of us has an angel and a *spirit guide*.

Very soon they arrived at a beautiful pink, shimmering alabaster house, complete with a beautiful garden full of all different types of flowers, all in bloom.

They stopped outside to view the sight that greeted them and Crystal said, 'Oh, I am so glad they were able to keep their promise.'

'What promise was that?' Lady Anne, sorry, Aurora asked.

'Do you recognise this place, Mum?' Crystal asked.

Aurora thought for a moment, 'Is this still our house, Crystal, is it still ours?'

'Of course it is Mum. It will never belong to anybody else and some special friends have done the garden, as they promised me they would, for your return.'

'Who are they, I must go and thank them. It is so beautiful, it must have taken them a long time to get it looking like this.'

'Let us go, Mum, and you can think who it might have been as we walk.'

So Aurora thought about who could have done her garden so nice for her. 'Why are we going back to the Healing Halls?'

'We are not going to the halls, Mummy, but you are close. Have you not thought yet who could do that for you? Who does all these things?'

As they opened the great gates into the special gardens, Aurora remembered, and as she remembered, suddenly all the gardens came into full bloom, the trees bore fruit and the colours all shone bright, just as the water in the cherub fountain began to flow. Everything was just as it had been long, long ago, except it was just a second ago. There is no time.

Now the gardens were full of faeries and the Queen faery greeted Aurora, saying 'We are glad you love your garden, all the best faeries worked their magic on it, just for you our *special friend*.'

'Somehow, I know you all also helped me in my other gardens that I have just left behind me, they were always so full of lovely bright flowers. Thank you, thank you, it is so nice to see you all again. Such happy wonderful memories, they are all flooding back to me now. Thank you.'

'We are all so pleased to welcome you back and we hope we can still work with you as before.'

Aurora answered, saying she was sure that would happen. All *mind to mind,* but they all chatted together, as friends do, for ages. Then Crystal said to Aurora that there were a couple of others they must go and see, but they needed Daniel's help to accomplish that task.

No sooner was Daniel requested and he was there beside them, asking what was requested of him. Crystal now spoke only to him, *mind to mind,* asking him if he could take them all to see some special people that had requested to see Aurora on her return. This meant two separate destinations, but yes he would do that for them, especially as he knew it would make Aurora happy to meet with them again. He asked when and the reply was, NOW PLEASE.

'Sorry to disappoint you Crystal, but there are two things LADY ANNE,' and he stressed Lady Anne as he said it, 'has to do before we can do what you ask of me. She has been asked to go to the hall of the *high ones* and that is where I must take her now, then her husband wishes to spend a little time with her, before he goes to do some work he has been asked to do. I am sure you would not begrudge him that time.'

So Lady Anne, now aware of what Daniel had said to Crystal, went with him to the meeting with the *high ones*, greeted as always by the high angels that always guard, or appear to guard, the building.

We are not privy to the reason for this meeting. It was a very private one between her and the ones she met. We know that she did discuss her name change back to Aurora and it was agreed, and that when she was ready, she would resume the work she had always done, while here in this wonderful place that is the land of spirit. She was told that, 'Although they all have different rolls, you can please yourself. Nobody coerces you into doing anything in particular, but hopefully, we all do things that will help to turn around these situations that are not as anyone would wish them to be, on the other side of life, on Earth.

'We know that there are many, many difficulties. There are many happenings that are not very good for their world on Earth, but we do endeavour to help wherever we can, but as you know, everybody was given, by the *supreme being,* free will, so we *CANNOT* interfere.

'It was hoped that free will would be used to further the benefit of mankind, but unfortunately, as you know, there are many who use that free will on the wrong side, by exploiting their fellow men by either not doing things they should or by doing things they should not. But if more and more people recognised the fact, of how important their prayers and their thoughts are. They come to our world as an energy and that energy can, if gathered up, be used to endeavour to help make certain things easier and better. It is not us interfering, or it's not the spirit world interfering, we are following what has been asked. Now that is a very, very strong thing to know and we would wish that more and more people understood it. That their prayers or thoughts are always gathered up and the more there are, the stronger the energy that comes forward to help for certain things, in the world they live in.'

The meeting had been a long one and would have taken over two days of Earth time, had time been involved, but as you know, time here does not exist. Daniel, as always, was close by her side.

Aurora, now free to meet her husband, by *mind to mind* communication, asked him to meet her in the special gardens by the 'Cherub Fountain'. In the blink of an eye they were together again and in each other's arms, as they had been, as often as they could in the short lifetime they had that last time together on Earth.

The bond between them had been forged a long, long time ago when the Earth had been a very different place, and was now strengthened even more, as their *love* for each other shone brightly for all to see. They remained in the gardens, relaxed in each other's company, oblivious to all that went on around them, just enjoying the pleasure of each other. Crystal, however, was one subject they did again discuss. Aurora, still very sad that she had not known her daughter's previous plight, but very glad now, that she had indeed helped her to overcome that severe difficulty.

How long they stayed there, and whatever else they said to each other or did, is of no concern to us. They are entitled to their privacy, as we all are. A day, a week, a month, time does not matter where they are. Eventually, perhaps sadly, two angels, one of them being Daniel, reminded them they both had other matters that now needed their attention.

True Love is an Eternal Bond

Happy Memories

Our couple now parted, happy in the *love* they felt for each other. Daniel told Aurora, that Crystal had requested he take her, and her two daughters, to a couple of special places that they knew she would love. They were places of very happy memories for her. Aurora replied, saying that she would be delighted to visit these memorable places and asked him where they were. To that question there was no reply, just a great big smile on his face.

So, Daniel *'mind to mind'* contacted the two daughters, telling them they were ready to embark on Crystal's request to visit these two special places. An immediate response from them both was 'YES PLEASE' and then Daniel, laughing, knew he had been set up by the two sisters and Grace, as only Aurora did not know where she was being taken.

'Relax Mum, you will really love where we are going.'

'Take my hand and hold tight everybody', Daniel said, as nine *spirit beings* set off on their journey, with Daniel leading the way.

Nine *spirit beings?* I hear you ask. Well, yes. Aurora with her two daughters, also with their own angels, and their all-important *spirit guides,* as they are always together.

In the blink of an eye, they were all at a lovely lagoon back on Earth, where the water was a beautiful turquoise colour and all was calm and clear.

'I know this place, Daniel. I've been here before, a long, long time ago, and yet, it feels like... Oh! I don't know, this is all so amazing, so wonderful, thank you Crystal.'

'Yes, Aurora, you have been here. Just sit quiet a moment and try to see if you can recall anything about this place. Watch and listen, to see what you can, or hear something, other than the motion of the water.'

Crystal was all smiles, she knew what to expect, but neither Aurora nor Rose, at this moment, were aware of what was about to happen, as they all sat on the rocks looking out to sea. Although all communication is *mind to mind,* Rose called out first, saying 'What is that disturbing the water? It looks like two people swimming far from shore.'

'Where are you looking, Rose?'

'See where I am pointing, Mum, way out in the water. Oh! Look, they are swimming closer to us. They look as if they are coming over to us. Are they?'

Suddenly, Aurora saw and recognised who was coming to see them and she remembered them clearly now. But wait, what is behind them? Further out, but coming faster than them, she wondered. But as yet, she could not make out the shapes in the water. Then beside them, two mermaids flipped out of the water beside Aurora and just hugged her. Rose looked on in shock, as she had never seen, nor heard of, such creatures as these. But she now saw how happy her mum was, so she knew that all was well, whoever they were. Now she saw what at first she thought were sharks and for a brief second, fear gripped her.

'Relax Rose', said Daniel, 'they cannot harm you. They are not sharks, they are two dolphins who know your mum and just want to talk to her.'

'Rose, Rose my dear, meet my two mermaid friends. Are they not the most beautiful creatures ever? Oh and there also are my two dolphins! My wonderful dolphins. How can this be Daniel? How can this be, that they are here for me?'

'Remember, in spirit, Aurora, everything is possible and they have never forgotten you. Think back to when you were on that ship, when your second husband took you to sea. What did you see there that the Captain remarked about?'

'I do remember, yes. I saw two dolphins and the Captain said he could not believe what he saw. They talked to me and they stayed by the ship's side all the time we were at sea. It was amazing to watch them.'

'They told you a very long time ago, in Earth time, they would always watch over you when you were at sea, and they kept that promise, as they always will. Can you remember I told you once about soul groups? Soul groups that animals have, as they do not have an individual soul.'

'Yes I do remember, we were talking about dogs then, especially the dog we once had.'

'That is correct. Well dolphins also have a combined soul, as it were, the same as dogs and all animals, and so through that, they remembered their promise to you.'

'This is so amazing, Daniel. So amazing and thank you Crystal, for I also know you had a hand in all this. I have two very amazing daughters, they are so very special, thank you all for this. Thank you, my friends, you are two beautiful creatures in every way, thank you.' They all talked for quite a while, until Daniel said it was time to move on, as they also have another place to go. The dolphins squeaked and squeaked, as they did not want Aurora to go. The two mermaids prepared to leave, but not before they said, 'We hope we can work with you again Aurora, as we did before, it was always such fun.'

'I hope so, my special girls, I hope so. I feel we will, and I would like to see my dolphins with you again.'

So Aurora was now starting to learn just how much life in spirit carried on as before, noting that perhaps, she now thought, it was the Earthly lives and their experiences that were always different. We'll see, she thought, we'll see.

Daniel now got them all together again and hand in hand they shot off again at great speed, to their next destination.

Suddenly, they arrived at the top of a great mountain that was covered in deep snow on the top. They stopped at the top and Daniel told them 'We are now going to go right down deep into the centre of this mountain. You all know you can travel through this ground, just as you can travel through any wall, or indeed, anything. You all also know, that you can always see, whatever the conditions. Are we all holding hands tightly? We will go slowly so we stay together. Ready? Let's go.'

Slowly, they now went deep down into the mountain, passing through two or three small caves on the way. They soon arrived at a massive, clear quartz, crystal cave that appeared to give off its own light. Only Daniel, and of course Aurora from a long time ago, had been here before, and she was now trying hard to remember why she knew that she had been here before. They all looked amazed at the sight that greeted them. This cave that now gleamed and shone out so brilliantly at them. Suddenly, it clicked into place. *She knew*, she just knew who was here.

True enough, who should walk into the cave? But two of the cave dwellers, the gnomes that she had met and worked with so long ago. Both of them, seeing who had now joined them, ran to Aurora's side and each hugged a leg as she bent down to cuddle them both.

Then slowly the cave began to fill with dozens of the lovely little men, and in their deep resonance voices, they began to sing her name. The deep sound of their voices, just singing Aurora over and over, was such a wonderful sound, a sound that only these little men could produce. You could almost see the tears in Aurora's eyes.

Rose, now totally amazed at this site and sound that was now happening before her, could not believe her eyes. Crystal just smiled, as she watched her mum and the immense pleasure it was giving her to see them again. 'Crystal, how can I ever thank you for organising this wonderful trip for me. How did you know all this and remember it, for although I know time does not exist for us, I also know just how long in Earth terms it has been.'

'I have been able, thanks to you and your help long ago, to do the trips that you used to do, and so, through this, I met all these wonderful creatures, that we have again seen here in this beautiful cave. I have got to know them well, we have often talked of you, simply because they all still love you. Think of the reception the faeries gave you when we visited the special gardens. Then, there were the mermaids and the dolphins. They were so excited to know they were going to be able to see their special princess again, because that is how they all think of you.'

'I am speechless and totally in awe of all this that has happened to me since I returned. Thank you all.'

'Have I not always told you how special you are, Aurora?'

'Yes, Daniel, you have, but you are always nice to me. I just thought how lucky I was to have such a special angel, but this, this is simply so incredible and so amazing. How these very special creatures, these wonderful little men, have all remembered me, yet to me, I was just doing my work with their special help.'

'Mummy, I told you when we first got back together again, just how special you really are. *Believe* it, there are very few like you who have that very special gift of *love* that you naturally have, and it is thanks to that gift that I am now as I am.'

They knew that their visitors had to leave them, but that cave had never before seen such great joy and happiness as it had just witnessed. For the gnomes it would always hold a very special significance. Nobody would ever be allowed to take any of the crystal out of this cave, *ever.* This place was now a very sacred place that the gnomes would, and do still, revere through all time. Only when the world goes back to as it was at the time of Atlantis, when it was at its best, is it possible that this cave just might be seen again. In the meantime, the entrance is securely sealed and not visible to the naked eye.

Our little group now again joined hands, said their goodbyes to the gnomes, who told them to please return some time soon, and in the blink of an eye they were back at the top of the mountain and somehow all the snow was gone.

'Thank you, girls. Thank you for that incredible trip and these happy memories again. Thank you to Daniel and all our guides and helpers, for helping us on this trip, but now I know that the *high ones* are starting to call me, so we must go back now.' As soon as Aurora said that, they were all now back at Aurora's house. On arrival, she found her husband there resting, having been working with a couple of young soldiers who had just returned to spirit. She now said to him, 'I am being called to the *high ones* to a meeting in the Temple now, can you wait for me please? As I do sincerely wish to spend more time just being with you.'

He replied, 'I will always have time for you, whenever you want to be with me, I will always be here.'

'See you soon, my love' and she was gone.

In Spirit, Love is All Around

The High Ones Speak

Aurora now wondered why she had been requested to meet with the *high ones* again, in the Golden Temple, usually that meant great changes for those in spirit. I wonder what I am about to do now? She thought to herself. Again she noted that Daniel, who was always there to guide her, had not made his presence felt. No point in worrying, I'll just have to deal with whatever it is they wish of me.

As always, the two great angels who stood guard, opened the great doors and said 'You are expected, take a seat in the Rose Gold Hall.' Now that is different she thought. I have to go straight to the Rose Gold Hall this time, and still no Daniel. Strange.

She arrived in the Rose Gold Hall and sat down, as instructed, in front of a long table that also had six seats positioned on the other side. Now, gentle music played as she waited, and again she thought, this is different, what's going on here? Now a voice in her head spoke *mind to mind,* saying, 'Patience, Aurora, relax and enjoy the music. Yes, we know that is what you again wish to be called and we have agreed, be patient.'

So Aurora sat and relaxed and enjoyed the music that was playing gently in the background, and now wondering what was about to happen. Now, quite suddenly and unexpectedly, Grace joined her, also bringing a chair so she could sit beside her. 'What is going on?' Aurora asked. 'This is concerning me a lot. Why is it just you here and Daniel is not? Have I done something wrong? Why won't Daniel also show himself for me?

'Relax my dear. Although I do not know specifically what they are going to say to you, I do know you will enjoy what they are going to say. They have always thought very highly of you. Daniel will not show himself at present. Although he does know everything, he is not allowed to say anything to you and he knows you will ask him. That would put him in a very difficult position.'

'Thank you for putting me at ease, or should I say trying to, as I am still a little apprehensive. I am sorry Daniel, I know you are here, forgive me for being impatient.'

'Time I think, for you now to get your self-confidence back, Aurora. You know how everybody feels about you. You also know how everybody has greeted you and I assure you, this will be the same. They are absolutely delighted in you and were amazed at the success of the trip you have just had with Crystal and Rose. I know you think Daniel was the guide, but in truth, I know Crystal could have done it on her own, but we also know how you feel about having Daniel always clearly with you.'

As they chatted away, like the two old friends that they really are, they were joined by six of the *high ones,* who arrived with happy faces and jointly said 'Welcome back Aurora, welcome back. We are absolutely delighted in you and how you deal with everything that you are handed. Nothing seems to phase you, either on Earth or here.'

'I'm not so sure about that.'

'Be assured Aurora, *we are.* You have been closely watched, as you went through that last life, as it was a life that we knew would be a very difficult one for you, because of the *love* you always carry in your very being. Again it shone brightly through, even to the soldiers. One in particular, who sadly, has a connection to the *dark side.* We know he tried so very hard to connect with you in the wrong way, but your strength and your natural *love,* prevented that from happening. Your work that you taught all who worked with you, is, we are pleased to say, carrying on just as you asked them to.'

'That pleases me to hear. I could only ask them. I could not dictate. The choice had to be theirs.'

'They had a brilliant teacher and you taught them well. Now you have returned again to us, we would like to know, if you would like to return to the type of work you did before? It is thanks to your daughter, if you will excuse the phrase, 'jumping the gun' by taking you to the places you have just been, you have already met some of your co-workers and you already know they all want you back. So, how do you feel about that?'

300

'I would be delighted to work with them all again, but first, please can I have a period with my husband? Please, as our life together was so very short? I would also, when I do start work, like to be more involved with children, please.'

'Both these wishes are granted for you Aurora, and it gives us much pleasure to know that you will take up your work position again, but only when you are ready. You have been greatly missed by all.'

Further discussion followed, regarding the life she had just left. Aurora talked about the feeling on Earth at present and the unrest that was always underlying everything that happened every day. She also told them that, sadly at present, there was very little *love* around, although she did try so hard to spread as much *love* as she could.

'You have done a good job on that front, Aurora, in more ways than you know.'

She now talked about how religion seemed, in a bad way, to rule everything. From the way people thought and acted, even in the simple everyday things in life. It was as if they were frightened of the men in the pulpit, as they dictated their every move. 'Surely', she said to them 'life was never meant to be like that.'

'Indeed it is not, as you well know Aurora. However, as you also know, they have all been given freedom of choice. Sadly very few are ever allowed to know that, because of these men in the pulpit. They are very aware they would lose 'their powers' over these people, if they knew the truth. It will come out some time in the future, but not yet, the time is not yet right for that to happen on Earth. You will see my dear, it will happen. However, Aurora, it is time now, although as you know time here is a misnomer. It is time you, as you so wished, went to see your husband. You will find him in the beautiful gardens outside the Healing Halls. Go and surprise him.'

Aurora then left, with Grace by her side and Daniel just above her. They respectfully withdrew as they neared the gardens and left her to surprise her husband. Grace, saying to her with a twinkle in her eye, 'See you soon, precious girl, have fun', and then she was gone.

The smile that appeared on his face as she approached him said it all, enough to tell everybody just how he felt about this amazing woman that was, or should I say, *is* his wife. How, he thought, did I ever get to be so lucky? That this beautiful woman, even after all is said and done, especially that senseless stupid dual, still loves me. Me who is barely good enough to wash her feet. Oh, but I do love her, and he held her tight as she came up to him, saying to him, 'I love you silly boy, you know that I love you.'

They went straight to their house, that beautiful pink Alabaster house that they had both had so long ago, where her husband now took her in his arms again saying, 'It is far too long since we did this my dear, far too long.' For a while, there was just the two of them and we are all old enough to know, detail is not needed. Just know their chakras still fitted perfectly, as they knew they would.

Eventually, after a time, who knows how long, time does not exist here, they started to talk in a more general manner and he said to her, 'Aurora, can you think back to a happy time when there were just three of us together here in this wonderful place? Happy, with not a single care to worry about.'

For a millisecond, Aurora thought and answered, 'You are talking about you, me and of course, our daughter Crystal, aren't you?'

'Yes my dear, we were so perfect then, the three of us.'

'Yes, and yet, little did we actually know about her then and what she had been through. I am glad I was able to have her as my daughter and show her *love*, a real true and positive happy *love*. She has done us proud, since then my dear, and it is a pleasure and an honour to say she is the fruit of our loins, our beautiful daughter.'

'But then Aurora, we do have now another daughter, who in her own way is also very special. To see them now, both working together as they do, it is as if they were twins and yet they are not. But you can see and feel the bond between them both, a bond that is the *love* you taught them both to have.'

'All life, in whatever form is special. But yes, you are correct, *we do* have another daughter and I would never want her to feel that she was not as special to us as Crystal is.'

'I think she knows that, Aurora. No, I know she does. Just see how happy they both are when they are together, and I have watched them since Crystal brought her home to me.'

'I keep forgetting that you have seen a lot more of them together than I have. It is nice to know that, in their hearts, they have had a good grounding that is based on *love* and understanding from us both.'

'My dear Aurora, you are my very special girl. The girl who I *love* with all my heart, who touches everybody who is privileged to meet her with her *love*, her generosity, and leaves them always with a smile on their lips, always feeling so much better for having met you. Our daughters see the way you are with people, so it's no surprise to me they are as they are.'

'It has been nice to be able, for us that is, to just sit and chat as we have about our family. Sadly, on Earth we never seemed to be able to do that. Something was always getting in the way. But let us not forget we have two sons who are still living their Earthly life experience. I know we will see them soon, here with us again, although I also know in Earth terms it is quite a few years away yet, as they both have much to do.'

Husband and wife, together in a way they had wished they could have, but you cannot change a single thing from the way it was. To the way you, perhaps, would have preferred it. We do not know how long this situation continued. For us that is not important. What we do know now, is that a general call has gone out for as many helpers as possible. A major storm and earthquake, that has caused a very bad land slip, is occurring. As a result, a very large loss of life for many on Earth, means that a great many souls will be returning. There are also many that will be stuck where they are and will be very frightened, as they do not understand what is happening and they will need urgent help to bring them home.

Aurora and her husband, together with their girls, have banded together with many others, to go and help those in most need; frightened children, parents, some with their babies, and so many now in need of careful and patient assistance. This was the start now, of Aurora back doing what she loved doing, helping in a way that came so naturally to her. She found a mother and a baby that had just been born, seconds before the storm struck. A very hard one for anybody to deal with, but for Aurora with her level of understanding and *love,* they were soon with her and back to a desperate loving family that were preparing a place for them already.

Safely delivered, she did another trip for yet another young child that was stuck up a tree, knowing something was wrong, as she could not get back in her body. Soon collected up and brought back, but this time finding a family was not easy. That said, it was soon accomplished to everybody's satisfaction.

So now Aurora was back in the swing of life in spirit again, as she started working, doing exactly as she had asked for. A trip with the mermaids was also on the cards, as a ship had gone down during the storm, with all hands. To her delight, as she worked with the mermaids, her beloved dolphins joined her. Another successful trip with everybody safely collected and all now safe and secure and back home.

So we will now start to take our leave from Aurora, as she once again settles back down into her new life in spirit, to continue with all the wonderful and amazing things that she does. Our beautiful spirit, Aurora, has shown us that life truly is never ending. What we now do with that knowledge is up to every one of us, as we have learned, we do have a choice, or should I say choices.

As Aurora returned from the trip to the ocean floor, she had settled down to await the return of her husband. She knew he was still working with some of the soldiers he had been helping. His work, as she well knew, was also a difficult task, as rarely did they ever expect anything but more fighting.

Daniel disturbed her peace saying, 'Another very successful trip with some very happy and relaxed men, who I know are full of admiration for you, Aurora, and for what you have just done for them. Their families, all so very thankful to you for bringing them safely home, because they remember how they felt at first when they returned. I know you think it is only because that is the job you have chosen to do, but very few have the knowledge and understanding that you have.

'I am sure that you remember well, how little thought is ever given by those on Earth about a life after their death. Because of those in the pulpit and their talk of hell and damnation, most fear death in every way. This is now a task that many of the people, who try to do what you do in bringing these poor people back, are finding difficult.'

'It is what I have chosen to do, Daniel.'

'My dear Aurora, my very precious, special princess. The ease with which you go about this now difficult task, truly is THE WONDER OF YOU. Let no one ever doubt that you are a very priceless, very precious and very special GIFT FROM GOD and when you smile the whole universe, for me, just lights up.'

'Daniel, I am always amazed by what you say to me. I am nothing special, but the way you *love* me, my angel, as you do, that truly is also the wonder of you, the way you make me feel every time you see me and speak with me. Thank you, Daniel.'

With great love from
Aurora.

Love Gives Strength to
All Relationships

Thank You Aurora

Let us now sincerely thank Aurora for this glimpse into these parts of her everlasting life and hope that you have taken pleasure from what you have read. Every page is given with her *love* and she wishes each and every one of you happiness and great joy in whatever you do. Take heart from what she has said and know above everything else, that you truly are *loved*.

I personally thank Aurora, for allowing me to be the one who has been able to bring all this forward to you. I do feel very humbled and honoured to have been given the privilege to write this book on her behalf.

I know that there will be many who will question what has been written and said. That's OK, that's their choice. But perhaps, just perhaps it has made either them, or you, think. I sincerely hope it has shone a little light into your life and that the light gets brighter everyday.

However, this is not unique, for there are others that could certainly link with the spirit world, and help to bring understanding to a vast number of people. Everyone has an ability, if only they would open up to it and recognise it. I hope that these words would make those that have enjoyed what they have read, see that it can become more of a way to follow their lives, than just an interesting read. Perhaps, just perhaps, it will help you to find your own true pathway.

Just remember this please, that 'nothing is done in our Earthly world' unless it comes into the imagination first. But what is even more important is this. You cannot imagine anything that is not there, it is an impossibility.

Now that might sound strange to you, but that, I am assured, is a true fact. There are people who imagine all sorts of things and they think 'It is just pure imagination' and they brush it away, but it isn't. For some of them it is actually a link with the spirit world. With others, it is that they have got the right side of their brain tuned in to the world of spirit and the world where there are happenings that cannot be explained away completely.

Still, there are, in parts of the world very indigenous, people who are very remote and haven't been brought into the happenings and technology of the world we live in now. They are very, very aware and they can form things in their mind that make things happen. They are very, very spiritual, because they have not yet, thankfully, been tainted by the modern way that there is on the planet now. So in effect, whatever you get into your mind has been put there by the forces of those that you are thinking about

If you ever wish to comment or even to ask a question you can get me on spiritoflite@gmail.com I will do my best to answer you.

Alan.

For those who may wish to know a little about me I am now retired. I have just passed my 75th birthday and hoping for a few more yet. I am basically an engineer, but have had a varied career throughout my working life. Married with six grandchildren, the youngest being only seven, I was born in London as the Battle of Britain started. Mum went back to Scotland, where I was educated and remained until I was twenty one.

A qualified 'magnatherapist' and also a Reiki healer, I work mainly with the body's own natural energies. Magnets give off an energy that is the nearest energy there is to the body's own natural energy. A simple exercise to check that energy, if you think it does not exist is this. Hold your two hands apart by about six inches. Keep them there for a few minutes and then very gently, barely moving them, just believe there is a soft sponge between your hands. That gentle to and fro action of you barely moving your hands, you will feel that sponge and yet there is nothing there that you see. That is your own body energy.

Happily married, although my wife has been ill for several years, we now live in the beautiful Cotswolds.

Love and Light
Alan.

Just remember 'wanting achieves nothing'.

Remember to quieten your mind and quieten your emotions, for as little as ten minutes every day and you will be surprised at what you can actually achieve.

Fact one. Only the dead can still their brain completely, because they no longer need it.

Fact two. The brain and the mind are two entirely different things. The mind can never die.